HITLER'S ESCAPE PLAN

Hitler glanced up at a large map of the world hanging on the wall of the conference room.

"Can one of your U-Boats reach Argentina without refueling?"

The question was so totally unexpected that Bergman had to pause for a few moments while he collected his thoughts. "Yes, it could be done," he ventured cautiously. "The new *Type XXI* boats could make the entire passage without surfacing."

The Fuehrer's eyes softened and he actually smiled.

Other Pinnacle Books by Edwyn Gray:

No Survivors
Action Atlantic
Tokyo Torpedo

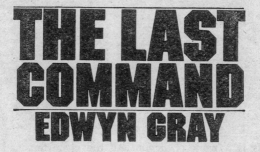

THE LAST COMMAND

EDWYN GRAY

PINNACLE BOOKS • LOS ANGELES

THE LAST COMMAND

Copyright © 1977 by Edwyn Gray

All rights reserved, including the right to reproduce this book or portions thereof in any form.

A Pinnacle Books edition, published by special arrangement with Futura Publications, Ltd. First published in Great Britain.
First printing, June 1978

ISBN: 0-523-40183-3

Cover illustration by Ed Valigursky

Printed in the United States of America

PINNACLE BOOKS, INC.
One Century Plaza
2029 Century Park East
Los Angeles, California 90067

To my son Mark

AUTHOR'S NOTE

The central characters in this story are wholly fictitious as indeed are most of the incidents. However, this is a book about Germany's U-boats at war and for reasons of historical accuracy many of the subsidiary characters are real people. Some fought and died for their country. Others survived the conflict and are, happily, still alive today. I wish to make it clear, therefore, that the words and actions ascribed to these real-life officers and men of the Kriegsmarine are entirely the product of my own imagination and do not necessarily reflect either their characters or their political views.

These men were dedicated professional seamen and true patriots. I have a great admiration for their skills and a profound respect for their integrity. I hope they will understand and excuse my wilder flights of fancy. Any attempt to recount the story of the U-boats at war would be the poorer for their exclusion, even though they only play fictitious roles in this narrative of Korvettenkapitan Bergman's career as a U-boat commander.

EDWYN GRAY

The Last Command

CHAPTER ONE

The circle of red-painted buoys had been moored into position with meticulous precision. And bobbing gently on the surface of the cold grey water they stood out like bright spots of fresh blood on an ancient shroud.

The misty half-light of the February afternoon had drained every element of colour from the dismal scene. Sea, land, and sky had all merged together to form a single, featureless monotone that faded indistinctly into the bleak mudflats of the *Stollhammer Watt* guarding the right flank of Jade Bay and the seaward approach to Wilhelmshaven. Even the gulls swooping low over the huddle of small boats anchored inside the buoyed area mirrored the drabness of the atmosphere, and their normally shrill cries echoed mournfully like a muted lament for the dead.

With the temperature hovering around zero and a chill north wind sweeping down from the Kattegat it was the sort of day when sensible landsmen remained indoors around a blazing fire.

Bergman shivered, hunched himself deeper into the upturned collar of his Kriegsmarine greatcoat, and wondered why the hell he was bothering to supervise the job in person. He knew nothing about salvage operations—he left that to the experts. But submarine salvage could be a tricky matter and, as the local flotilla commander, the Korvettenkapitan considered it his duty to be on the spot, so that his specialised knowledge was available to the experts if they needed it. Bergman accepted that the demands of duty took precedence over his own personal comforts.

After more than four years of gruelling combat service with Germany's U-boat flotillas there was little he did not know about underwater warfare or the vessels that lived and fought in the dark demi-world beneath the surface. But commanding a U-boat on operational patrols had very little to do with the task of raising a dead submarine to the surface, after it had lain rusting on the bottom of Jade Bay for nearly two years.

Bergman had viewed the entire operation with distaste from the moment Kommodore Lutz made the original suggestion. And his feeling of revulsion deepened as every hour brought the salvage team nearer to ultimate success. He felt like a grave robber despoiling and desecrating an ancient tomb. The bodies of thirty-seven U-boat men lay silent and undisturbed in the steel-hulled coffin that had become their final resting place for the past twenty-two months. And, while he was no sentimentalist, there seemed something macabre and unwholesome about disturbing the sanctity of their grave.

A stream of silver air bubbles rose to the surface on

the port beam and Bergman moved to the bridge wing of the salvage tug to watch the diver emerge. There was a brief scurry of water. And then, gleaming dull red in the feeble rays of the winter sun, the bulbous copper helmet broke surface. Schroeder leaned over the bulwarks and while the diver clung to the ladder hanging down the side of the tug he unscrewed the armoured glass eyepiece with a quick twist of finger and thumb and removed it.

Oberleutnant Zetterling's head was masked by a woollen balaclava helmet to ward off the cold, and he grinned cheerfully through the oval opening that framed his face.

"All lines and lifting chains checked," he reported. "Everything seems secure. If the No. 2 team have fixed the pontoons and connected up the hoses I reckon we're all set to start lifting."

Bergman hurried down the companionway to join Scraffe and the rest of the underwater team. Schroeder and another man hauled Zetterling up on to the deck and sat him on a low wooden bench while Willi Kelso twisted the helmet through a half-turn.

"Christ! That's better," Zetterling commented as the helmet was lifted clear. He glanced up at Bergman. "Are you ready to go ahead with the final lift, sir?"

"Can we get her up by sundown?"

Zetterling picked his nose thoughtfully. It was a luxury denied him when he was encased in his diving suit. He looked across at the watery disc of the sun sliding towards the western horizon. He shook his head.

"Not a chance. It's a slow haul—we'd need all of three hours. And if those bloody air pipes ice up it could be double that."

Bergman nodded and Zetterling sensed an expression of relief in the casual shrug of the Korvet-tenkapitan's shoulders.

"Very well," he told the diver. "Secure all gear for the night. We'll start lifting first thing tomorrow." He turned away and hesitated as he reached the foot of the bridge ladder. "Will you report to my sea cabin as soon as you have changed, Herr Oberleutnant?"

The cabin lights went out automatically as the door opened. It was a routine precaution and Bergman waited for them to come on again when the door closed. The Kriegsmarine's black-out regulations were irritatingly stringent but with RAF patrols constantly sweeping the skies over Germany's main naval bases, a few seconds of inconvenience was preferable to the snarling roar of an enemy aircraft and the whistling crash of exploding bombs.

He looked up as Karl Zetterling entered the cabin. The Oberleutnant was of medium height with the square-built body of the practical man. His hair was black and curly and his dark eyes stared like those of a watchful eagle from under heavy hooded lids. Bergman thought he looked a few years older than himself—probably in his early thirties. And he had the indefinable assurance of a man accustomed to giving rather than taking orders. In fact he was the sort of character who could cause more than a little trouble to his senior officers if he chose to be awkward.

Bergman's eternal coffee pot was simmering in its usual position on the electric ring—a relic of his career in combat U-boats—and reaching forward, he poured out two mugs of a black poisonous looking brew. Then nodding the Oberleutnant to sit down he leaned back against the bulkhead planking of his deck cabin and looked straight into Zetterling's eyes. He put his question with complete frankness. Bergman was not a man to mince words.

"Can't you make something go wrong, Herr Oberleutnant?"

Zetterling grasped the enamel mug in both hands, leaned his elbows on the table, and gulped a mouthful of steaming coffee. The Korvettenkapitan had puzzled him from the moment they had first met, just three months previously in December 1943. For some reason he could sense that Bergman did not really want the salvage operation to succeed. And it was an unpleasant feeling for a diver to have, when working sixty feet down in muddy tidal waters, on a freezing winter's day.

In any case the Oberleutnant had more than enough personal problems without the added worry of falling down on his job. He wondered what Bergman was getting at, and parried the question with equal directness.

"What do you mean, sir?"

"You know very well what I mean, Zetterling. Do we *have* to raise *UB-59*? Why the hell can't she stay where she is?"

So that's the way it is, Zetterling thought to himself as he swallowed a mouthful of scalding coffee. I wonder why? He shrugged.

"I don't have your advantages, sir," he said carefully. "I've been sent down here to do a job whether I want to do it or not. And I can't buck my orders. With respect, sir, I'm responsible to Kommodore Lutz."

Bergman made no comment. Lifting the blackened pot from the hot plate he poured himself some more coffee. He sipped it in silence for a few moments and then changed the subject abruptly.

5

"I was looking through your personal file last night, Oberleutnant."

Zetterling's eyes narrowed but he kept quiet and waited.

"You're a good officer," the Korvettenkapitan continued without any change in the tone of his voice. "The Navy needs men like you. It is a pity, however, that you do not choose your friends more wisely."

Zetterling knew what Bergman was getting at. It was easy to guess what was docketed in his papers. The Gestapo would have passed their information to the Kriegsmarine's Intelligence Branch and they would ensure that the right people knew about it. He wondered, suddenly, just how much Bergman really *did* know.

"They weren't friends," he said defensively. "They were employees of the salvage firm I used to run in Hamburg before the war. I can't be blamed for what my employees got up to."

"I'm sure you can't," Bergman agreed. "But I wonder why the Navy enlisted a man who fought for the International Brigade in Spain in 1938?"

"Because I'm the best bloody deep-sea diver in Germany!"

Bergman nodded. "Quite so, Herr Oberleutnant. And that is exactly why I need you to foul up this salvage operation tomorrow. You're the expert. No one will hold you to blame if things go wrong."

"And that's precisely the reason I won't, sir. I can't afford to lose my reputation for no good reason."

Zetterling was not telling the whole truth. He had several other reasons why he wanted the operation to succeed. But something about Bergman's strange request intrigued him and he wanted to know more. Why, for instance, had the Korvettenkapitan been relegated to command a relatively unimportant reserve flotilla. He was probably Germany's best-known U-boat ace, the holder of the Knights' Cross of the Iron Cross, twice a recipient of the Fuehrer's personal commendation, and the man who had sunk more enemy tonnage than any other U-boat skipper alive. Yet here he was supervising the salvage of an obsolete submarine that was fit for little but the scrap heap.

Perhaps Bergman liked to be his own boss as well—he'd heard plenty of rumours about the Korvettenkapitan's various brushes with the Navy's top brass. Or perhaps he had too many enemies in the Party. Whatever it might be it was an odd situation and Zetterling scented a trap.

"I have equally good reasons," Bergman said mildly. "I would not ask you otherwise."

Zetterling put the empty coffee mug down on to the scrubbed top of the wooden table. He looked straight into Bergman's eyes as he weighed his next move. His private knowledge of the Korvettenkapitan was more than sufficient to make him cautious. And yet, despite his reputation and the four gold rings on his sleeve, there was some indefinable air about the former U-boat ace that inspired confidence. He decided to take a chance.

"If you are prepared to forget rank and talk man to man I'll tell you my reasons. Will you do the same?"

Bergman answered the question with a smile. Taking off his gold-peaked cap, he threw it carelessly down on the table.

"Go ahead—man to man."

Zetterling reached into his pocket, pulled out a packet of cigarettes, and paused while he lit one. He threw the blackened matchstick into the ashtray.

"I'm only in the Navy on sufferance," he admitted.

"With my record I'm lucky not to be in a forced labour camp—or worse." He shrugged. "Not that I admit the charges you've got listed in your file. But if the Gestapo say I'm guilty that's enough in itself. I'm only in the Navy because I'm the most successful salvage expert in the Third Reich. And the Kriegsmarine can't afford to forgo my skill. But the first time I fall down on a job, the Gestapo are going to be on my tail. They're going to use the chance to undermine my reputation and get me kicked out of the Navy. And if I *am* . . ." He shrugged and left the sentence unfinished.

Bergman nodded sympathetically.

"You certainly seem to have a more than adequate reason," he conceded. "I'm afraid that mine is very flimsy by comparison. In my view once a ship has been sunk she should not be disturbed without good cause. A sunken ship is a tomb of honourable and honoured men. And it should remain that way for ever."

Zetterling contrived to look sympathetic but underneath, he knew the Korvettenkapitan was lying in his teeth. As if a man who had twice won a personal commendation from the Fuehrer would give a damn about thirty-seven dead German sailors—or live ones either for that matter. But Bergman had made it sound plausible. And, he congratulated himself, his own blatant lie had sounded equally convincing.

The two men stared at each other across the narrow cabin like dogs sparring for battle. Each knew the other was lying yet neither was prepared to reveal his own true position. It was Zetterling who broke the hiatus.

"I can understand your feelings, sir. It is a natural reaction for anyone who has commanded a ship. But my position is a matter of life or death. If I go wrong on this job the Gestapo will have me under arrest inside twenty-four hours—just long enough for me to become a civilian again so that I come within their power." His smile was open and frank. "As you know, sir, while I am wearing Kriegsmarine uniform they have no authority over me."

Bergman nodded grimly. He didn't need Zetterling to remind him. He had fought a successful battle with the Gestapo himself on that very issue two years previously.* And the bitter memories associated with the episode still burned deep in his heart. He had promised to square accounts with Gruppenfuehrer Görst on his return from his Far East mission; but official duties had prevented him from meeting up with the Gestapo chief and the promise remained unfulfilled.

He swallowed the remains of his coffee while he bought time to think.

"I appreciate your position, Karl." Bergman chose his words carefully. "But I doubt if a solitary mistake would give the Gestapo the opportunity they want. And remember that although you are responsible to Lutz, I am in a position to cover up for you—to share the blame. To be honest, I think you are being over-anxious."

Zetterling's smile hid the thoughts passing through his mind. At least he had the consolation of knowing that the Korvettenkapitan was lying as well. Only a fool would be taken in by all that mumbo-jumbo about desecrating graves. But whatever his real reasons might be, the fact remained that Bergman wanted to sabotage the *UB-59* salvage operation. And that, thought Zetterling, was *very* interesting.

* See *Action Atlantic.*

9

"I'd prefer not to take the gamble," he said equably. "The Gestapo may have much more incriminating information in their archives than the evidence they've passed on to the Navy. I can't take a chance on it going wrong."

Bergman sipped his coffee thoughtfully. He decided it was time to change tactics. He knew no more of Zetterling's history than appeared on the Kriegsmarine files. But if the reports were correct . . .

"Do you intend staying on in the Salvage Section until the war's over, Karl?"

Zetterling shook his head. "No—I want to learn something new. Without boasting, I reckon I know all there is to know about diving. I've asked for a transfer to the K-unit at Lubeck."

Bergman knew little about the K-unit's activities. It was a top secret venture and it was virtually impossible to pierce the security screen. He was aware that it had started out as a training scheme in underwater demolition, along the lines of the Italian and British frogmen teams. And since his return from Japan with the prototype Kaiten weapon* he'd heard rumours that the Kriegsmarine was developing its own midget submarines based closely on the kaiten design. But, as he was the first to admit, it *was* only rumour. Bergman's interest, however, lay with ocean-going submarines and not idiotic sardine cans with an operational range of forty miles or less. And, despite his Kaiten experience, he had kept well clear of Admiral Heye and the K-flotilla.

Zetterling's suspicions were, in fact, ill-founded, and Bergman had only taken over command of the 32nd (Reserve) Flotilla to avoid an appointment to the Lubeck experimental base. Allied air attacks had slowed

* See *The Tokyo Torpedo.*

10

production of standard U-boats and for the moment no new submarines were coming off the slipways. And to ensure that he was not available should Admiral Heye ask for his services, the Korvettenkapitan had taken the precaution of wangling his present appointment in the backwater of the Reserve Flotillas.

"What's the attraction of the K-units?" he asked casually.

"Underwater demolition, sir. They've produced a new type of diving suit that doesn't need air pipes or a life-line. The diver is completely free-swimming and takes his oxygen from tanks he carries on his back."

"You think this new technique will come in handy when you go back to civilian salvage after the war?"

"Partly . . ." Zetterling shrugged and contrived to leave the admission dangling in mid-air as if reluctant to admit his true motives.

Bergman sensed the half-truth in Zetterling's reply and he changed the subject again with the easy facility of a trained lawyer.

"Do you know why they're trying to salvage the UB-59?"

Zetterling shook his head. "No—why?"

"Because the Kriegsmarine is so short of U-boats they've got to recover any submarine lost in home waters so that it can be refitted and put into service again. There are over thirty U-boats lying on the bottom around the coast. And if the UB-59 operation is successful they intend to salvage every single one of them to replace war losses."

"And you don't want that to happen?"

It was a neat reversal of the tables and Bergman found himself facing a question he was reluctant to answer. He hesitated for a moment.

"If you put it that way, Karl, no, I don't."

"Why?"

From a simple check to mate in one move. Bergman had the feeling that Zetterling probably played a good game of chess. Clasping his hands together, he rested them on the table, and carefully avoided meeting the Oberleutnant's eyes.

"*UB*-59 has killed thirty-seven men already. Why give her the chance to kill another crew. Once a submarine has been sunk she should stay sunk. Call it an old sailor's superstition if you like but it's as simple as that."

Zetterling shook his head.

"Sorry, sir, but it's still not enough to persuade me. If you give me a direct order in writing I'll do what you want. Otherwise we start lifting tomorrow."

Bergman nodded wearily. He shrugged, stood up, and reached for his cap. Now that the precedences of rank were restored he felt on surer ground.

"What is your programme tomorrow, Herr Oberleutnant?" he asked in a sharp tone of voice, their previous conversation dismissed.

"All the holes are patched and we've sealed the inner hull. The next job is to pump her full of air to blow out the water, so that she regains neutral buoyancy. Then we start lifting with the pontoons."

"She's still flooded at this stage, then?"

"Yes, sir. At least, so far as we can tell. We can only get into one section of the hull—a submarine isn't exactly built for men in diving suits."

A thought suddenly crossed Bergman's mind. He tried to dismiss it but it returned instantly. He looked up.

"I propose to dive with you tomorrow when you go down for the final inspection of the hull."

"I know I'm in charge of the diving team, sir. But do I have a choice?"

"No, Herr Oberleutnant, you don't. It's an order." Bergman tried to read Zetterling's reaction from his eyes but the salvage expert's expression gave nothing away. "Have a suit ready for me first thing in the morning. And allocate someone to brief me on elementary diving techniques."

Zetterling nodded. Standing up from the table he moved across to the cabin door and paused with his hand resting on the knob.

"When we're below the surface, sir, my position as salvage leader takes precedence over rank. You appreciate you will be under my orders."

Bergman nodded. "I fully understand the situation, Herr Oberleutnant. I shall not interfere—I merely wish to see things for myself."

"Naturally I'll keep a personal eye on you and see you don't come to any harm. But, with respect, sir," Zetterling's eyes went suddenly hard, "I won't guarantee your safety if you start any funny business while you're down there."

The Korvettenkapitan looked up sharply at the barely concealed threat. Then he broke the tension with an easy laugh and reached for the coffee pot again.

"I'm glad you added 'with respect', Herr Oberleutnant," he said softly.

It was still dark when Bergman joined Zetterling and the rest of the diving team in the narrow well-deck amidships. Heavy blackout screens hung down from the lip of the shelter deck above and the only light came from a cluster of shaded blue lamps swinging from the overhead bulkhead. The busy scene was reminiscent of a U-boat control room during a night attack and Bergman felt slightly reassured by the familiar memory.

For once in his life his breakfast had remained uneaten. And he had even contented himself with a single cup of coffee. The thought of getting caught short when he was ten fathoms down on the muddy floor of Jade Bay did not appeal to him and, always a stickler for appearances, he preferred to go hungry. The empty sensation in the pit of his stomach added to his general tension and the Korvettenkapitan had to remind himself that it was hunger and not fear he could feel gnawing at his guts.

The air temperature had dropped suddenly in the final hour before dawn and hoar frost glistened whitely on the exposed upperworks of the salvage tug as he crossed the bridge from his cabin abaft the chartroom. He wore the regulation roll-neck sweater and thick thigh-length woollen stockings but even so, the chill morning air bit sharply and he could not repress a shiver.

"Nothing to worry about, sir," Willi Kelso said comfortingly. "You'll soon get used to it."

Bergman realised that Kelso had mistaken the cause of his involuntary shudder. Perhaps he was a little scared. Who wouldn't be? But if he *was* he saw no reason for admitting it.

"If you'll sit on this, sir, we'll start getting you into the suit."

The Petty Officer pushed a small wooden stool across the deck planking with his foot and wedged it firmly against the bulwarks as he spoke. Bergman did as he was told and waited while Scraffe and his assistant lifted the diving suit out of its locker.

It was made from a single piece of heavy rubberised twill and, so far as Bergman could see, the only way inside it was through the uninviting hole of the neckpiece. There were no buttons, zippers, or other fasteners. In fact, Bergman concluded, it looked as if it had been designed by a man who spent his life building ships in bottles. The problem of getting inside seemed similarly insoluble.

Kelso knelt down beside the stool and carefully explained what had to be done:

"Stick your feet through the hole, sir . . . that's it. Now slide down and we'll pull it over your hips. Fine! Now push yourself right down inside."

The clinging rubberised material restricted Bergman's movements and he had to kick his feet down into the legs of the suit like a man swimming in a narrow canvas tunnel filled with treacle. The physical exertion beaded his face with sweat and he was breathing hard as he sat back on the stool with the suit pulled up around his waist while Kelso smeared his wrists with olive oil to prevent chafing.

"Arms next, sir," Kelso prompted and Bergman nodded.

Scraffe's muscles bulged as he strained the rubberised dress out to its full stretch and, while he held it taut, the Korvettenkapitan ducked inside like a squirrel climbing into its tree hole. His hands found the armholes of the massive sleeves and he thrust down into them. The rubber watertight cuffs were unyielding and Bergman had to punch his fists through the narrow circlets. The tight constriction of the cuffs clamped his wrists like tourniquets and he felt a tingling sensation in his forearms as the blood supply was cut off.

Flexing his wrist muscles experimentally he got the blood moving again and then, like a tortoise emerging

15

from its shell, he thrust his head through the opening of the neck. The fresh salt air smelled sweet and pure after the stench inside the suit and Bergman breathed it deep into his lungs with obvious enjoyment.

"Boots next, sir. Hope you don't suffer with corns." He chuckled deep down inside his barrel chest as he dropped them on to the deck with a thud that made Bergman jerk his stockinged feet away in alarm. Looking down he could see two rounded dents in the bruised planking where the boots had landed.

They weighed over 14 pounds apiece with soles cut from solid lead an inch thick, heavy leather uppers, and massive brass toecaps. Kelso gripped his left ankle and pushed it down inside one of the boots. Then, having adjusted it to a surprisingly comfortable fit, he buckled the three security straps firmly into position before moving on to the other foot.

Bergman could feel the weight straining his ankles and he wondered how the hell he was supposed to move. He soon found out. Kelso grabbed his arm and helped him up from the stool and the Korvettenkapitan felt as if he was standing embedded in solid concrete. He was about to make an appropriate comment when Scraffe suddenly stepped forward without warning and stood on the brass toecaps while he drew the heel lanyard taut.

"Have to have a tight fit, sir," Kelso explained as he bent down and tightened the buckles two more holes. "We don't want 'em dragged off your feet if you get caught up on something on the bottom." He waited while Scraffe secured the lanyard carefully around the Korvettenkapitan's ankles as an extra safety precaution and then, going across to the locker, returned with the belt, which he buckled firmly around Bergman's waist. It was a heavy leather affair from which hung a canvas pouch containing the diver's working tools, a small slate, a brass battery lamp, and a metal scabbard in which nestled a sharp-bladed knife.

Bergman settled back on to the stool again while Kelso lowered the copper corselette over his shoulders. The bronze dog-collar was designed to fit over the rubber neck-cuff of the diving suit and, to make a watertight seal, the tailoring allowed no latitude for irrelevant protuberances such as the diver's nose or ears. Scraffe did his best to protect the Korvettenkapitan from the worst of the buffeting but grazed skin was inevitable as Kelso jammed the collar over Bergman's head and forced the corselette into position.

"You don't look as though you're enjoying it very much."

Bergman looked up as Zetterling hobbled across the deck in his weighted boots like a man struggling through quicksands. He managed a wry grin.

"It could be worse I suppose—although it's difficult to see how. I didn't realize it took so long to put on this fancy-dress."

"Would you believe it if I told you we can get a fully-trained diver completely kitted out and into the water inside four minutes?"

"No I wouldn't," Bergman told him truthfully. Kelso was doing something with a spanner at the back of his neck. "What the hell's going on now?" he asked petulantly.

"Willi is tightening the flanges to force the neck cuff into the corselette—it's got to be watertight or you'll find the suit filling with water as soon as you submerge. It doesn't take long to drown," he added unsympathetically. Kelso muttered an obscenity as

17

the wrench slipped. "And mind his bloody ears with that spanner, Willi!"

Kelso grinned and threw the spanner into his toolbox.

"That's fixed the nuts, sir. Hope I didn't damage you too much. Ready for the helmet?"

Bergman nodded and Scraffe emerged from the deckhouse carrying a bulbous copper diving helmet with the reverence of an archbishop presenting the State Crown to the monarch at a coronation ceremony. He passed it gravely to Kelso who raised it above the Korvettenkapitan's head and then lowered it down carefully. Bergman instinctively ducked his chin into the bronze collar of the diving suit as the twenty-pound dome came down, and there was a metallic clang as it ground against the bronze dog-collar. Willi locked it into position with a sharp clockwise twist that meshed the greased screw-threads securely tight.

Despite the cold on deck, Bergman was already feeling hot and clammy inside the suffocating closeness of the rubberlined suit. The revolting smell was not improved by the acrid tang of his own sweat and his mouth tasted like the bottom of a birdcage. He peered out through the circular opening of the front eyepiece waiting for his next instructions. Odd noises echoed and clattered inside the domed helmet, the sounds intensified by the hollow acoustics of the copper sphere, and Zetterling bent his lips close to the opening so that Bergman could hear him.

"Willi is fastening the air-hose to the rear of the helmet. You should be able to feel the hose passing down behind your left shoulder, under the armpit, and then up to the helmet again where it will be lashed and secured." Bergman nodded that he understood. "Now you'll find a spring-loaded non-return valve in the spigot connection—and there's a similar one on the right-hand side of the helmet."

Taking Bergman's hand Zetterling guided the Korvettenkapitan's fingers to the outlet valve so that he knew where to locate it. "Excess air and nitrogen escape from this valve," he explained, "and there's a small milled wheel which you can operate with your thumb to control the rate of exhaust. If you close it up nothing will escape, your suit will inflate with air, and you'll float to the surface like a dead fish—okay?"

Bergman nodded. He would have preferred a more cheerful analogy but it was comforting to know that in at least one respect he was master of his own destiny. He hated relying on other people and his chief fear of diving lay in his complete dependence on the men operating the air pumps on the tug.

"The other connection contains the telephone system," Zetterling continued. "It's linked direct to the surface but we can arrange talk-through if you want to speak to me when we're on the bottom." He leaned closer and dropped his voice. "But remember—everything you say has to pass through the exchange operator on deck and he's got big ears. So be careful. If you want to say something to me without the message being overheard write it on that slate you've got slung from your belt."

Zetterling leaned back slightly and resumed his normal voice. "If the phone goes on the blink and you want to come up in a hurry just give the lifeline two sharp jerks. And if that doesn't work either you'll have to shut off the exhaust valve and float up. Have you got all that?"

"Yes—it sounds simple enough. But I'd like to get

started. I feel bloody stupid sitting here all dressed up with nowhere to go."

"Okay, it's your funeral. Kelso will help you across to the ladder. When you're over the side they'll fit the last two weights and test the air line."

Bergman felt like a senile old man being helped around a hospital ward as Willi and Scraffe supported his arms and guided him to the opening in the bulwarks leading to the ladder. The sheer physical effort of lifting the leaden-soled diving boots made his ankles scream with pain and he walked with the dragging gait of a Frankenstein monster. He wondered how the hell he was going to manage once he was submerged and deprived of Kelso's assistance.

On reaching the side of the tug Scraffe made him turn round so that he was facing inboard with his back to the sea before guiding him on to the rusty ladder. Bergman climbed down awkwardly—halting cautiously at every step while his left foot searched blindly for the next rung. Kelso leaned over the bulwarks checking his progress and as the cold black water swirled around the Korvettenkapitan's hips he shouted for him to stop.

Bergman clung tightly to the barnacled ladder and waited for the Petty Officer to fit the final weights into position. The lead circlets, each weighing a solid 35 pounds, were shackled to the corselette—one on the chest and one on the back—and the Korvettenkapitan's shoulders sagged under the additional burden. He waited while Kelso looped a safety lanyard through the eyes of the weights and fastened it with a slip knot around the base of the helmet.

"If you get into trouble, sir, just slip the knot and let the weights drop off. And make sure you regulate the buoyancy of your suit with the exhaust valve."

Bergman felt there were too many ominous references to getting into trouble. The dive in itself was nerve-wracking enough without the added worry of what *could* go wrong.

Something sighed gently behind his head and then hissed sharply. A sickly rubbery smell filled the inside of the helmet and Bergman realised that the air pump had clattered into wheezing life. Well, it wouldn't be long now. And as if reluctant to lose his last tenuous link with the flesh and blood world outside his watertight sarcophagus he peered anxiously through the small circular porthole at the front of the helmet. But even this final gateway was about to be closed irrevocably and, before he had time to change his mind, Kelso pushed the brass-rimmed window of half-inch armoured glass into the threaded socket, screwed it firmly into the face of the helmet, and cut off his last remaining contact with reality.

Bergman could appreciate the feelings of the unfortunate nun of Monza as she watched the final brick being cemented into place. The thick glass window had the same effect and, almost immediately, an unreasoning claustrophobic panic churned in his guts.

Taking a grip on his nerves the U-boat ace fought back the initial surge of panic, drew the air deep into his lungs with studied concentration, and regained his self-control.

"All ready to descend, sir!" The disembodied crackling of Kelso's voice through the telephone set the adrenaline flowing again. "Fifteen minutes only. I'll tell you when it's time to come up."

Bergman chinned the telephone switch.

"All received, Petty Officer. I'll call you up if I need any help." He pushed the telephone switch into the "off" position and groped his way down the ladder.

The daylight faded slowly as he slid beneath the surface and he breathed a silent prayer as the sea drew a green veil over the glass window of his helmet.

The buoyancy of the water made the weights seem lighter and he found it easier to move than he had anticipated. But, even so, movement was still very restricted and every action seemed sluggish and awkward. Reaching the end of the ladder he released his grasp and waited expectantly to sink slowly to the bottom.

But nothing happened. And to his consternation Bergman found himself hanging in the water with his head still level with the keel of the salvage vessel he had just left. What the devil had he done wrong? He chinned the telephone switch down.

"On deck—over!"

"Receiving—over." Kelso's voice sounded quietly reassuring.

"How the hell do I go down—I seem to be floating at an even depth. Over."

"Nothing to worry about, sir. Turn the outlet valve on the right-hand side of the helmet. Let some of the excess air out so that you lose buoyancy. Over."

Bergman reached for the milled knob that Zetterling had shown him earlier and twisted it tentatively. A stream of bubbles gushed upwards towards the surface and, almost immediately, he felt himself slowly sinking.

Kelso saw the bubbles rise to the surface. His voice sounded urgent as it crackled into the helmet.

"Not too fast, sir. Close off the valve. We don't want you squeezed.*

---

*"Squeezing" is diving jargon for a lethal phenomena brought about by the pressure of the sea. This pressure can literally squeeze the diver up through his suit until his body is no more

Bergman closed the valve without further prompting and as he sank down towards the sea bottom he grabbed hold of the shot-line to prevent the surge of the tidal currents drifting him too far away from the wrecked U-boat that lay somewhere in the dark mysterious depths below.

The sudden pain struck without warning.

A burning needle lanced both ear-drums simultaneously and Bergman's face contorted like a man under torture. His grip on the shot-line tightened instinctively and he clung to it in desperation as he shook his head inside the helmet and struggled to escape the blinding pain. His involuntary groan filtered up through the still opened telephone line and Kelso, poised and watchful on deck, hurried to assist him.

"Take it easy, sir. Don't panic. Swallow hard a couple of times and waggle your jaw about. It's only a pressure pain. Once you've adjusted the pressure inside your ears you'll be okay again."

Bergman forced himself to swallow. Then he moved his jaw from side to side and swallowed again. Something clicked inside his skull and the pain immediately disappeared as he equalised the pressure on his ear-drums. The tears of pain running down his cheeks, quickly dried against the warmth of his skin.

"Thanks, Willi. I'm okay now. Continuing dive. Over."

"You're doing fine, sir. When you get to the bottom just stay put where you are. The Oberleutnant is already on his way down. He'll be able to locate you from the shot-line. Over and out."

---

than a pulpy mess of crushed flesh and blood inside the helmet. A Royal Navy diver suffered this frightful death in Alexandria harbour in 1944 while salvaging the Fleet Oiler *Brambleleaf*.

Bergman lumbered slowly down the line. He was rapidly adjusting to his new environment and his initial nervousness dissolved into interest as he peered out through the tiny circular glass window.

It suddenly struck him as strange, that after spending six years in the U-boat service prowling nearly every ocean in the world inside the stout security of a steel-walled hull, he had never before seen the underwater kingdom in which he operated.

And now, like a knight without armour, protected only by the vulnerable rubber diving suit and the thin copper sphere of his helmet, he was descending into that kingdom for the first time. What terrors, he wondered, did it have in store for him. And what revenge would the denizens of the deep take for the hundreds of men he had mercilessly killed beneath the surface of the sea, who now lay rotting on the ocean bottom?

It was perhaps fortunate that the Korvettenkapitan did not count a strong imagination as one of his principal attributes.

CHAPTER TWO

Bergman's first reaction was one of disappointment and anticlimax as his weighted boots sank into the muddy ooze ten fathoms down beneath the surface of Jade Bay. He had no clear idea what he expected to find on the bottom of the sea but, subconsciously, he had anticipated an exciting new world of darting fish and luxuriant marine vegetation.

In practice, however, all he could see through the thick glass window of his helmet was a few feet of dark murky water behind which lay a black void of impenetrable gloom. There was something slightly frightening about the silent stillness of the depths, and suddenly, he felt very alone and vulnerable.

The comforting hiss of the cold rubbery air pumping into the helmet restored his spirits and, forcing his legs forward against the clinging resistance of the water, he moved one foot gingerly in front of the other like a baby taking its first experimental steps across the nursery floor.

"I'm putting the Oberleutnant on talk-through." Kelso's voice broke into his thoughts as it crackled down the telephone. There was a sharp click and Bergman heard Zetterling's oddly distorted tones.

"Stay exactly where you are, Korvettenkapitan. Don't move away from the shot-line. If we lose you it'll be like looking for a needle in a haystack. I'm only about two cables behind you."

Bergman waited obediently and wondered how the Oberleutnant had guessed he had started exploring his new environment—experience with novice divers presumably. He was not given long to consider the problem. Within moments, Zetterling appeared out of the murk like a weird copper-headed monster from a cheap science-fiction film. His stooped body moved with strangely ponderous steps and a stream of tiny silver bubbles rose from the outlet valve as he regulated the pressure inside his diving suit.

He greeted Bergman with a half-raised arm and brought the glass window of his helmet close up against the Korvettenkapitan's eyepiece, so that they were staring at each other like two imprisoned goldfish swimming helplessly in separate bowls. Pointing his hand to the left he indicated which way they were to move and Bergman nodded his head inside the copper dome.

Although they covered little more than ten yards, their movements were laboriously slow, and Bergman found himself sweating with exertion by the time they reached the vague green shadow of rusted steel that marked their target. Zetterling wrote something on his slate and held it close to his companion's helmet.

Bergman lurched forward eagerly and, misjudging his step, half fell against the weed-encrusted hull plates of the sunken submarine. Zetterling steadied him quickly and waved an admonitory finger of warning. He heard the click of the telephone behind his ear.

"Take it carefully, sir. No use hurrying in this game—not if you want to stay alive. If you fall and snag your airpipe you'll suffocate. And if something sharp rips your diving-dress you'll drown." He waited while Bergman regained his balance. "The submarine is lying on an even keel and we can get into the control room through the conning-tower hatch."

Bergman chinned his transmission switch.

"Surely we can't get inside the U-boat in these suits?"

"Yes we can. The hatch is oval in shape. If you twist your body slightly as you go down, you'll find you can just squeeze through. Now close your outlet valve, get some air in the suit, and you'll float up to the level of the bridge platform on top of the conning-tower. I'll go first—you follow."

The bubbles rising from Zetterling's helmet died away as he shut off the exhaust valve, and with the slow grace of a ballet dancer, he floated gently upwards until he had vanished into the murk. Bergman waited for him to get clear and then carefully turned the milled knob of his own valve. The air continued gushing into the suit but with no means of escape it gradually inflated the heavy watertight dress until the resulting increase in buoyancy overcame the gravitational pull of the lead-soled boots and the body weights.

Bergman's feet sucked clear of the mud and he

found himself rising slowly upwards—his ascent increasing in speed with each fresh pulse of air. With arms flailing to protect his body he brushed against the bulbous ballast tanks of the sunken U-boat, saw them curving back into the narrow deck, watched the steel stanchions drift down past his eyes, and then sensed rather than saw the sheer steel wall of the conning-tower falling away.

It was almost like a dream. The relentless pulse of air hissing into his helmet had an hypnotic effect, and the buoyancy of the inflated diving suit made him feel as if he was lying in some vast, luxuriously soft bed.

His dream was rudely interrupted as something gripped his ankles with the tightness of a vice. And the telephone shattered his euphoria with clipped urgent tones.

"Open the exhaust valve or you'll float straight up to the surface—you're rising too fast, sir!"

Bergman pushed against the resistance of the water as he reached his hand towards the helmet. He groped along the smooth copper surface until his fingers found the valve and he gave the knurled knob a quick twist. The bubbling sound of air escaping through the outlet caused a momentary panic at the thought of losing all his air and suffocating. But it passed quickly. The distended suit slowly deflated to normal shape and the sudden eruption of silver bubbles made a shoal of inquisitive fish dart nervously away. The weight of his lead-soled boots carried him down gently until they grated against the deck plates of the conning-tower platform.

Taking a deep breath he adjusted the outlet valve and looked around. He was now on familiar ground and his expert eye quickly assessed the scene, noting the opened hatch, and the gashed hull plating, where the steamer's bows had sliced into the submarine and sent her plummeting to the bottom.

"You know the way, Korvettenkapitan," Zetterling pointed out over the telephone. "You go down the ladder first, I'll follow and make sure you don't get your lines tangled. Once you get inside move a couple of steps towards the periscope and wait there until I join you."

"Have you been inside before?" Bergman asked.

"No—but you can help me find what I want."

The Korvettenkapitan walked carefully across the weed covered bridge until he was standing directly over the gaping black void of the conning-tower hatch. He wondered what Zetterling was after. Perhaps he was looking for some piece of secret equipment. Bergman dismissed the idea almost as soon as it entered his mind—UB-59 was an old pre-war boat. She certainly wouldn't have anything of value in her.

As he lowered his feet through the hatchway and felt for the rungs of the steel ladder leading down into the bowels of the sunken U-boat, another far more sinister thought entered his mind. Perhaps Zetterling had sent him down first deliberately. It would be a simple matter to close the hatch cover and leave him trapped inside. And with his total lack of diving experience it would be easy to make it look like an unfortunate accident. Bergman hesitated, swallowed hard, and forced himself to climb down the narrow ladder. He hoped that his assessment of Zetterling's character was right. If not he knew he had little chance of ever reaching the surface again.

But the gamble had to be taken if he was to find out why the Oberleutnant was so determined on bringing UB-59 to the surface. Bergman had long since discounted the excuse that Zetterling's reputation was at stake. No—it had to be something else. Something so important that the salvage of a U-boat that could be refitted and put into combat service again was of little consequence. With Zetterling's history it was unlikely he would do anything calculated to help Germany's war effort without a good and sufficient reason.

He gripped the ladder tightly as his foot missed a rung and sank into something soft and yielding. Clinging firmly with his hands he felt blindly for a foothold. The sensation transmitted back to his brain was that of standing on an octopus and for a moment he had a vivid picture of a giant squid lying in wait at the bottom of the ladder.

Bergman's lack of imagination—which had enabled him to embark on this foolhardy venture in the first place—helped him to dismiss the fear almost as soon as it flashed across his mind. The giant octopus waiting to trap an unwary diver was only the stuff of schoolboy adventure books—in the cold, inhospitable waters of the North Sea the octopus was a puny helpless creature rarely more than a foot in diameter.

The alternative, however, was even more horrifying and Bergman had to steel his nerves to go down further. His foot found the next rung and the soft jelly-like substance shivered gently against his leg. The restricted vision of the diving helmet made it impossible to look down to see what he was standing on. Judging that he had almost reached the deck, he pushed his hands away from the ladder and allowed himself to float gently downwards. The deck plating was covered with a thick carpet of marine weed and as his boots slipped on the green slime Bergman grasped at a steel support pillar to keep his balance.

The interior of the flooded control room was pitch dark. And unhooking the battery lamp from his belt the Korvettenkapitan shone the beam in the direction of the conning-tower ladder to discover what had entangled his legs. As the bright pencil of light picked out the details, Bergman felt the sour taste of bile rise into his mouth.

He had seen death many times before. The sight of a drowning man was no new experience. But this was something for which he was totally unprepared. Every instinct urged him to climb out of the luckless *UB-59* as fast as he could and return to the surface. But by a tremendous effort of willpower he fought back his natural reactions and took a grip on himself.

Bergman recalled his words to Zetterling when they had first discussed the salvage operation in his sea cabin aboard the tug. Desecrating a tomb seemed a fine rounded phrase at the time and he had given no thought to the revolting reality of what he was saying. Thirty-seven men had died inside the U-boat when she had gone down under the bows of the steamer *Oldenberg*. In the abstract and as a statistic it meant little—a minor loss of life measured against the scale of the war now waging. But the reality was different. It was all very well to talk of U-boat crews entombed in their iron coffins. It was a different matter to look upon the results with one's own eyes.

Only the tarnished gold lace spanning the cuff of the sleeve identified the corpse as that of an officer. A spreading film of algae had transformed the once blue Kriegsmarine jacket to the colour of soft green moss and the material was strained obscenely tight around the bloated body of its wearer. Swollen and grotesque, the outlines blurred into a shapeless mass of pale flesh, the body clung tightly to the hatch ladder,

31

trapped by the hungry sea in the final embrace of death. It was barely recognisable as human. And where voracious fish had nibbled at the exposed skin shreds of flesh floated lazily like white fronds of seaweed, from the bones of the hand still grasping the fifth rung of the ladder.

Bergman looked away and retched violently. Turning the spit-cock on the front of the helmet, he admitted a small squirt of sea water, swilled it around his mouth, and spat out the sour tasting bile. The nausea receded and he began to recover. The sharp click of the telephone switch echoed through the helmet like a pistol shot.

"Are you okay, sir?"

"Yes, I'm fine," Bergman lied. "I'm on the floor of the control room. Watch out as you come down. There's a body tangled up with the ladder."

"Nasty," Zetterling chuckled callously. "I wonder if it's the one I want . . . stand by, I'll be with you in a couple of moments."

What the hell does Zetterling want with a body, Bergman thought angrily. He was about to put the question when he remembered the Oberleutnant's warning. Say nothing over the telephone that Kelso or the others can overhear on deck. What mysterious secret was hidden in the flooded hull of *UB-59*? Whatever it might be Zetterling seemed intent on unearthing it.

Three frightened fish darted across the front of his eyepiece and he sensed rather than saw the bulky shape of the Oberleutnant dropping gently into the control room past the pathetic object entangled with the ladder. Zetterling's lamp blazed suddenly in the darkness and the beam circled and settled on the bloated body of the dead officer. He scribbled something on his slate and then shone the lamp on the black surface for Bergman to read.

LEUTNANT - NO GOOD

Bergman lifted his thumb to indicate that he had read the cryptic message. The fact that he did not understand it seemed irrelevant for the moment. This was scarcely the time for a lengthy session of laboriously scrawled questions and answers.

Zetterling rubbed out the first message and chalked another. He held it up to his chest so that the Korvettenkapitan could see it.

DIVING STATION SENIOR TORPEDOMAN?

Bergman shook his head to indicate the message was not understood. The murky gloom of the flooded control room made it impossible to see inside the helmet and his negative gesture was lost on Zetterling who tapped the slate impatiently for an answer. Bergman pulled his own slate from the belt around his waist and scribbled:

NOT UNDERSTOOD

The painstaking catechism resembled a ridiculous parlour game being played between two robots. But Bergman could sense that Zetterling's questions were deadly serious and he was curious to see where they led.

The Oberleutnant returned to his slate, added two words, and held it up again.

WHERE IS DIVING STATION SENIOR TORPEDOMAN?

So *that* was what he wanted to know. But what the hell for? There was only one way of finding out and Bergman quickly wiped his slate clean before writing his reply.

33

BOW END

The telegraphic style of cross-examination was becoming easier with practice and Bergman had no difficulty in understanding Zetterling's laconic answer.

SHOW ME

Turning slightly to his left the Korvettenkapitan moved towards the forward watertight door of the control room and, despite the ponderous bulk of his diving-dress, squeezed carefully past the massive brass column of the navigation periscope. Something soft and grey drifted slowly in front of the glass window in his helmet. It was floating, face down, with its arms hanging limp. Steeled to the horrors of the underwater tomb he pushed the body to one side and, groping forward, reached the heavy counterweighted hatch-cover. It was shut and clipped—an indication that *UB-59*'s crew had had time to close the watertight doors before the submarine started on its final, fatal plunge.

Holding his lamp to the inspection window he tried to see into the next compartment. The beam, obscured by the muddy water and weakened by the thick glass, reached barely six feet into the steel cavern. But there was sufficient light to see that the water level inside was only three or four feet above the deck. The occupants trapped inside had not drowned like their more fortunate comrades in the control room—their end had come more agonisingly and more slowly. Huddled on tables and ledges clear of the water their bodies were not bloated and swollen with sea water. Their deaths had been different.

Bergman knew they had died from suffocation; either from chlorine gas generated by the chemical action of sea-water coming into contact with the acid in the U-boat's batteries, or from carbon-monoxide poisoning as they exhausted the oxygen from the trapped air inside the sealed compartment. Two of the men had broken open freshener cartridges, in a vain attempt to buy a few more hours of life. But even these had finally run out. And with them—life itself.

It was a fate all U-boatmen feared. And Bergman wondered how long they had survived inside the cruel steel trap. Twelve hours—perhaps as much as twenty. And to what purpose? They must have known rescue was virtually impossible for the Kriegsmarine did not equip its U-boats with the escape apparatus carried on British submarines, and once sunk, their chance of survival was minimal. Yet, faced by certain death, they had sought to prolong their lonely agony by breaking open the oxygen cartridges to gain a few more minutes of futile life.

Zetterling banged him on the shoulder and he moved to one side so that the salvage expert could weigh up the situation. The Oberleutnant peered through the glass inspection port in the watertight door, moved his torch to examine the interior of the half-flooded compartment, and then stepped back. He scribbled on his slate and held it up.

IS HE HERE?

Bergman's shrug was cloaked by the diving-suit. Even if the man Zetterling was seeking was inside the bow section it would be madness to try and get inside. The pocket of air trapped between the water level and the curved arch of the overhead bulkhead, must be compressed under tremendous pressure. And once the watertight door was opened, the trapped air would blast out with a force that could hurl them backward against the jagged instruments of the diving panel. It would be like pulling the valve out of an inflated tyre—only a thousand times more power-ful. He wrote on the slate.

PROBABLY. BUT TOO DANGEROUS.

Zetterling motioned him to one side with a languid gesture intended to express impatience. Reaching towards the door he began unfastening the butterfly nuts that held it clamped in place.

One . . . two . . . three . . .

Impeded by his diving-suit Bergman lumbered for-ward awkwardly and tried to push the Oberleutnant away from the vital door. Once released, the force of escaping air would slam the heavy steel hatch back with the strength of a sledgehammer, and he suspect-ed that for once in his life, Zetterling's eagerness to get inside the mysterious compartment had overcome his normal caution and commonsense.

The Oberleutnant's lips flared in a snarl behind the glass face-piece of his helmet. He pushed Bergman away angrily and the slow-motion of their movements gave the underwater struggle the appearance of a grotesque ritual dance. The Korvettenkapitan lunged forward again but Zetterling's underwater experience enabled him to parry the clumsy attack, thrust Bergman aside, and renew his assault on the last re-maining locking-nut.

The nut had already spun three-quarters of the way up the coarsely threaded stud when the Korvetten-kapitan made another effort to prevent disaster. Scrawling an urgent warning on his slate he pushed it in front of the Oberleutnant's helmet.

AIR PRESSURE. STOP!!

Zetterling's reply was to punch the slate from his hands and smash it against the steel bulkhead where it snapped into a dozen jagged pieces. He shouted something but the angry sounds were swallowed by his copper helmet and he busied himself with the recalcitrant nut again.

Bergman's chin dipped down on the telephone switch. "On deck! Do you hear me? Do you hear me? Over."

"Kelso here, sir. I hear you loud and . . ."

The crackling buzz of static stopped abruptly and for a brief puzzled moment Bergman thought he had turned off the switch accidently. He chinned the switch up and down but there was no answering click in the loudspeaker. From out of the corner of his eye he caught a sudden silver flash of movement and, turning the great copper-domed helmet to the left, he stared in mute horror as Zetterling's sharp-bladed knife sliced down. Something thin and black floated in front of the glass window and sweat tricked down his face as he recognised it as his own telephone cable.

Zetterling had cut the line! And moving like a giant slow-moving water snail the Oberleutnant was reaching towards him with the knife.

I won't guarantee your safety if you try anything funny.

Zetterling's warning suddenly flashed into his mind with terrifying clarity. So *that* was what he meant. Bergman backed away as the knife slashed at his chest and he heard a dull clanging sound as the tip of the pointed blade struck his chest weight and was deflected harmlessly to one side.

The Oberleutnant lunged again and Bergman swayed to avoid the savage thrust. It was impossible to parry the attack with his arms for even the smallest cut in the twill diving-suit would quickly let the water inside. And as he retreated from the menace of

Zetterling's knife he fumbled awkwardly to drag his own weapon from its leather sheath.

With the knife grasped securely in his right hand the odds became more even. But, matched against the Oberleutnant's underwater experience, Bergman was still at a disadvantage and he was forced to give ground inch by inch. Slithering and sliding on the silted floor of the sunken U-boat the two men manoeuvred for position. And stirred by the massive diving-boots the mud added to the blackness of the water until it was almost impossible to see anything. Zetterling appeared and disappeared in and out of the murk as he slashed wildly at Bergman's air-pipe and the Korvettenkapitan knew that the fight could only end one way.

An exploding roar suddenly threw the two men apart. A silver thunderbolt spiralled across the compartment like an underwater typhoon and disappeared upwards to vanish through the open hatchway leading to the conning-tower. The shockwave hurled Bergman off his feet and he fell back helplessly—the water cushioning his fall and turning it into a slow nightmarish descent during which he was aware of Zetterling looming over him, the rasping hiss of air still pumping into his helmet, and his total impotence to withstand the forces of gravity. Lying on his back half stunned Bergman was still sufficiently alert to realise what had happened—the butterfly nut on the door had stripped its thread. And the surge of compressed air escaping from the bow compartment had blasted him backwards as effectively as an exploding bomb.

The control room was pitch black again now that the swirling silver vortex had vanished through the hatch, and sensing a movement above his helmet,

Bergman tilted his head back awkwardly to stare up through the glass. He saw a hand reaching towards him. *Zetterling's hand!*

The Korvettenkapitan had no idea what the Oberleutnant intended to do. But in the circumstances he had little doubt that their life and death struggle was about to be renewed. Summoning his last reserves of energy he raised his knife to ward off the expected blow.

Suddenly his fear of Zetterling was overwhelmed by an even greater terror—*the sea was flooding into his diving-suit!*

Reaching downwards with his free hand Bergman felt his hip and moved his fingers down his thigh searching for the telltale slit in the rubberised material. He located the hole just below the knee—a jagged tear where a piece of sharp metal had sliced through the heavy canvas twill when the rush of compressed air had thrown him off his feet.

Instinctively he tried to hold the two sides of torn twill together in an effort to seal off the flow of water seeping into the suit. It was a futile gesture and Bergman knew it. But untrained and inexperienced in the techniques of diving he had no idea how to remedy the desperate situation in which he now found himself. If Zetterling hadn't severed the telephone cable he could have asked Kelso for instructions. But with even this tenuous link to the surface gone, he realised he was as cut off and helpless as the other thirty-seven men who now lay dead inside *UB-59*'s stricken hull.

Clinging to the torn material with one hand the Korvettenkapitan tried to ward Zetterling away with the other as the Oberleutnant sank level with his helmet. He saw his opponent's hand reach towards the right-hand side of the copper dome and, realising he could resist no longer, he waited fatalistically for inevitable death. Even if Zetterling's murderous designs failed, he knew that the cold black sea flooding slowly into his diving-dress would soon achieve the same object. The salt water was already lapping gently against his lips. And for a brief moment Bergman considered whether to open his mouth and end it all there and then ...

Zetterling located the outlet valve on the side of Bergman's helmet and shut it off with a quick anticlockwise twist. His emergency action brought immediate relief. With no means of escape, the build-up of air pressure effectively prevented the water-level from rising further and the Korvettenkapitan realised suddenly that for the moment at least, he was safe. He wondered why he hadn't thought of the solution himself. And as the original shock gradually passed he heard a quickening rasp of air wheezing into his helmet as Zetterling used his telephone to instruct the deck party to increase the speed of the pumps.

His head cleared rapidly as he drew the oxygen deep into his lungs and, with the increase in air pressure, he could feel the water being slowly forced out through the elongated slit in the left leg of his diving-dress. Within a minute the water level had stabilised around his hips and the air-pump resumed its previous routine five-second rate.

It was not in Bergman's make-up to worry about the whys and wherefores of a situation. All he knew was that Zetterling's quick-thinking reaction in an emergency had saved his life. And even though it was the same man who had, minutes earlier tried to kill him, the Korvettenkapitan was content to wait until later for the explanations. Right now all that mattered was to get out of the flooded control room and back to the surface.

Strong hands gripped his arms from behind and, scrambling his boots on the weed encrusted surface of the deck to obtain purchase, he strained to help Zetterling drag him upright. He swayed awkwardly and felt the Oberleutnant pull at the slipknot securing the two body weights to the corselette. As the heavy lumps of lead dropped way, his lightened body began to rise upwards and Zetterling grabbed him firmly around the waist, pinned him bodily against the ladder, and held him there.

The Oberleutnant's glass eyepiece pushed to within half an inch of his own and he saw Zetterling's lips mouth the words: *Hold on*. Reaching behind his back Bergman found the sides of the ladder, gripped the rungs firmly, and did as he was told.

Although he knew little about diving techniques the Korvettenkapitän was sufficiently familiar with the laws of hydrostatics to realise that, even without the lead body-weights, his waterlogged suit would have insufficient buoyancy to lift him to the surface unaided. And unable to inflate the diving-dress so that he could float upwards out of the trap there seemed little hope of ever escaping from the sunken U-boat. Certainly in his present exhausted condition there could be no question of climbing the conning-tower ladder. He had not given up hope as yet, but with almost detached interest, he wondered how the hell Zetterling proposed to save him.

The Oberleutnant sank slowly down out of sight and, moments later, he felt something being tied around his leg a few inches above the gash in his diving-suit. It was almost like a tourniquet being fastened and Bergman winced with pain as the leather

41

strap cut deeply into his flesh. It was a primitive way to make the diving-suit watertight again—almost like using adhesive tape to seal a punctured tyre—but it was better than nothing.

Zetterling drifted up in front of his eyepiece and held the slate up for Bergman to read.

I WILL LIFT YOU THROUGH HATCH

Having delivered his message the Oberleutnant disappeared up through the murky water leaving Bergman alone with his thoughts. And the Korvettenkapitan certainly had plenty of things to reflect upon—not least the fact that Zetterling could have quite easily left him there to die. Yet for some unknown reason he wasn't going to. And Bergman wondered why.

When Zetterling finally reappeared he was holding two lengths of rope which he had presumably found inside the conning-tower. He tied them tightly, harness fashion, under Bergman's armpits to form a hoisting line. Then having carefully checked that the knots were secure he scribbled the next set of instructions on his slate.

COUNT TWENTY AND LET GO LADDER

Shining his torch into the Korvettenkapitan's helmet he waited for the nod of acknowledgement before wiping the slate clean for a further message.

OPEN OUTLET VALVE WHEN CLEAR OF HATCH

Zetterling was playing a dangerous game and he knew it. But it was a chance that had to be taken. Without lifting-tackle Bergman's weight would be too great to hoist through the oval shaped hatch of the conning-tower and he needed some other form of assistance. By closing the Korvettenkapitan's exhaust valve very slightly he could increase the amount of air inside the suit to improve its buoyancy without creating sufficient pressure to burst the temporary repair.

It called for a fine calculation of the forces involved. And if he misjudged the valve adjustment the build-up in air pressure would snap the leather tourniquet, sea water would flood in through the torn canvas, and his companion would be dead within seconds. But there was no other way.

Bergman, too, appreciated the risk. And, like Zetterling, he decided he preferred to take the chance of a quick death from drowning than the slow suffocation that would be his inevitable fate if he was not released from the sunken U-boat. He began counting slowly as Zetterling adjusted the exhaust valve and then floated upwards through the black water towards the invisible hatchway.

The Oberleutnant was sweating like a pig as he eased himself out through the narrow hatch and on to *UB-59's* bridge. He, too, was counting off the seconds and he drew the rope over the horizontal bar of the periscope standard to obtain the necessary leverage before leaning back to take the strain. The hoisting-line pulled taut and still counting, he waited.

Eighteen . . . nineteen . . . twenty.

His bare hands ached with the cold but winding the rope around them and ignoring the pain he began to pull. He felt a slight resistance—then a dead weight. Bergman was either counting more slowly or his scheme to inflate the diving-suit had failed and the Korvettenkapitän was already dead.

Suddenly the resistance eased and the rope began sliding over the fulcrum of the bar. Despite the slight buoyancy of Bergman's inflated suit there was still a little negative weight to contend with but, fortu-

43

nately, not enough to be beyond the limits of his strength.

The hoisting-line inched upwards and he could sense that the Korvettenkapitan was doing his best to help by pushing down on the rungs of the ladder with his feet. He hauled on the rope again and the yellow beam of his battery lamp reflected back from the enormous copper dome as Bergman's helmet emerged through the hatch. He eased his pull on the rope and waited for the Korvettenkapitan to twist round and wriggle through the narrow opening.

Bergman's grotesquely inflated body squirmed through the hatch like an insect struggling out of its chrysalis shell. It was easier without the additional bulk of the two body weights and a few moments later the Korvettenkapitan was clinging to the periscope standard—using it as an anchor as the air-filled suit tried to float upwards.

Zetterling groped his way across the narrow bridge and reached forward to reopen the valve. A stream of silver bubbles rose up from the helmet as the pressurised air escaped and the diving-suit gradually deflated back to its normal dimensions. He breathed a silent sigh of relief. It had been touch and go but at least that bloody strap had held. And although it would be easier to get Bergman to the surface with a buoyant suit the risk of bursting the weakenened rubberised canvas outweighed the advantages.

Both men dropped wearily against the rails of the conning-tower as they gathered their strength for the final phase of their ordeal. Bergman was totally exhausted. All he wanted to do was to shoot to the surface as fast as his equipment would take him. But Zetterling, with the caution of experience, knew it had to be otherwise.

They were still ten fathoms—sixty feet—down. And a rapid rise to the surface would create nitrogen bubbles in the blood. It was the thing all divers feared. Decompression sickness. The dreaded "Bends". And even from sixty feet it could be fatal.

Zetterling pushed himself away from the rails, shortened the rope which was still tied around Bergman's chest, and secured it around his own waist so that they were linked together like two mountain climbers. He wrote his final instructions on the slate.

DO NOT CLOSE OUTLET VALVE. WE STOP TEN MINUTES EVERY TWENTY FEET

The Korvettenkapitan nodded. He was none too clear about the hazards of a rapid ascent but, like most sailors, he had heard of the "Bends" and he was willing to accept Zetterling's expert guidance on such matters. It took considerable moral courage to follow the Oberleutnant's advice for the water was already beginning to creep up past the tourniquet strap around his leg and he could feel it rising slowly inside the diving-suit. Obviously the additional air pressure necessary to lift him up through the hatch, had stretched the leather strap and it was no longer working efficiently as a watertight seal.

He decided against worrying Zetterling with any further problems. If the Oberleutnant realised that Bergman's suit was flooding he would probably risk a quick ascent and the Korvettenkapitan knew there was only one decompression chamber on the salvage tug. He knew too that the diving team would place him inside in precedence to Zetterling. It seemed pointless to risk two lives. And uneasily aware of the water level now creeping up to his waist Bergman decided to give the Oberleutnant no indication of his critically dangerous situation.

45

Zetterling closed off the outlet valve, inflated his suit, and started to rise gently upwards, dragging the Korvettenkapitan behind him at the end of the tow-rope. His hands, cut to the bone by the thin hoisting rope, reached for the shot-line and he counted the knots that marked off each fathom of its length.

At forty feet he opened his outlet valve and hung motionless in the water so that his body could adjust to the decrease in pressure. Bergman swung gently beneath him on the end of the rope and the Korvettenkapitan gave a cheerful thumb's-up signal to indicate all was well.

In fact all was not well. But Bergman had no intention of telling Zetterling the truth. The water inside his suit was now lapping his chest and he glanced at his watch to check on the time it had taken to rise that far. The answer was scarcely reassuring. If his calculations were correct he should drown roughly one minute before they reached the surface. At least Zetterling had done his best. If anyone was to blame it could only be himself for being fool enough to go diving when he knew nothing of the hazards involved . . .

By the time the Oberleutnant began on the next stage of the ascent the water inside Bergman's suit had reached his shoulders. And at twenty feet, when Zetterling halted for the final period of decompression, it was lapping his throat. Tilting his head back Bergman could see the fleeting shadows of sunlight playing on the surface of the sea directly overhead. And, to the right, he could just make out the dark shape of the salvage tug's rounded bilge keel.

So near. And yet so far.

He spat violently as he tasted the cold salt water in his mouth. Lifting himself upwards he strained his chin clear of the slowly rising water and gulped the rubbery air into his lungs.

An animal instinct for survival urged him to close the exhaust valve so that the air pressure would build up and hold the rising waters at bay. But even as he reached upwards towards the milled knob he knew that if he did so, he could well upset Zetterling's carefully considered rescue plan. Drawing on his last reserves of will-power Bergman forced his hands back down to his sides and waited. The sea was lapping greedily at his lips and, keeping his mouth tightly clamped, he breathed through his nose.

The air-pump wheezed with the chesty rasp of a chronic asthmatic and the terrible pressure building up inside his copper-domed prison made his ears ache and his head throb. He wanted to scream aloud with the pain but dared not open his mouth.

The rope tightened across his chest and he knew that somewhere above his head Zetterling was moving again. The final stage of decompression had been completed and he felt the sharp tug of the line under his armpits as the Oberleutnant towed him slowly towards the surface.

Only twenty feet to go . . .

The water level inside the copper helmet reached Bergman's nose and he had to breathe carefully to prevent the sea from being sucked into his nostrils. Forcing his arm up he looked at his watch. They should break surface in exactly one minute and twenty seconds.

As the salt water lapped over his nose the Korvettenkapitan stopped breathing.

They were going to be precisely twenty seconds too late.

CHAPTER THREE

Kelso's massive hands pressed down slowly, moved evenly towards Bergman's elbows, drew the limp arms upwards, and then let them drop gently back on the deck. He repeated the respiration cycle exactly twelve times every minute. And he had already been working for nearly half an hour.

Bergman was lying face down on the deck with his head turned to one side. His mouth was open and his tongue had been pulled forward into strict accordance with the Holger Nielsen method of artificial respiration. Willi Kelso was squatting on one knee beside the Korvettenkapitan's head and his body lifted sharply with each compression phase of back-pressure.

"Keep at it, Willi," Zetterling urged. "He was only under the water for a minute or so. And he's a tough bastard."

"How long do we keep pumping?"

"The book says four hours—but I've heard of survivors recovering after as much as eight. Scraffe can take over when you get tired."

It had begun to snow and as the cold white mantle quickly blanketed the exposed deck of the salvage tug, Bergman was reminded of his first winter of the war. There were no outward or visible signs that his brain had started working again and the Korvettenkapitan's eyes remained tightly shut. But he was aware of Kelso's strong hands kneading his ribs even though he was unable to respond to the life-giving pressure.

As the snow chilled his fingertips, it triggered the memory cells of his numbed brain. And as he relapsed into a langorous stupor he started to recall the inconsequential events that had brought him fleeting moments of happiness in the past. The glorious winter of 1939 and those breathtaking ski runs down the glistening white slopes of the Grunnenberg mountain during his last home leave in Bavaria. And the short happy months between his first appointment to command of a combat U-boat and that fateful mission to the Gulf of Mexico.*

The bewildering kaleidoscope of memories faded as he saw the sad face of Rahel Yousoff. His fists tensed into tight balls of physical pain as he recalled his visit to Kiel and her refusal to meet him.

Bergman's mind reeled in a jumble of half-forgotten incidents as it shied away from the memory of the girl he had once loved. Searing flashes of yellow light split the blackness of the unconscious void, as he relived the night attack on Convoy HR-15.† And he stirred angrily at the memory of the atrocity he had been unable to prevent, when von Eckholdt had

* See *No Survivors.*
† See *Action Atlantic!*

gunned down the innocent survivors in the lifeboat . . .

"He's showing signs of life," Kelso said excitedly. "I felt him move."

"Let Scraffe take over—he's fresh."

"No, sir. Not now—not now I'm winning." Kelso's hands squeezed down hard, circled to Bergman's elbows, raised his arms, and pumped another mouthful of air into the waterlogged lungs.

Gruppenfuehrer Görst's face gloated down as Bergman's eyes flickered. He winced in anticipation of a boot thudding into his ribs. What the hell was the Gestapo chief doing on board the salvage tug? Rahel's tortured scream echoed across the deck and the sound sent the blood coursing through his chilled body. The sudden surge of warmth made him cough violently as the salt water choked his throat and dribbled from his mouth on to the wooden planking.

Görst's evil face faded. And through the reeling mists of unconsciousness Bergman could see the scene inside the Gestapo office as he recalled his last meeting with Rahel. Once again the terrible memories brought a violent reaction. Opening his eyes wide he tried to lift himself up from the deck to throw himself at the Gestapo chief who had been responsible for her sufferings.

The sudden physical movement sparked his chest muscles back to life and he collapsed to the deck with water pouring from his mouth. Fighting for breath, he raised his head from the snow-covered planking. It was not Görst who was staring down at him. It was Oberleutnant Zetterling!

Pushing Kelso away Bergman heaved himself up into a sitting position. He was seized in a violent paroxysm of coughing as the cold morning air rasped

51

his lungs and, when he tried to speak, the muscles of his throat would not respond.

"Get him on to his feet," Zetterling snapped. "Gently, man—gently. Take him up to the sea cabin and make sure he's kept warm. And you stay with him, Willi. I'll be up as soon as I've put some dry clothes on."

He stood back as Kelso and two other members of the salvage team, wrapped the Korvettenkapitan in blankets and carried him up the bridge ladder to the tiny cabin abaft the chartroom. For a moment he was struck by sudden doubt. Perhaps he should have left Bergman to drown inside the flooded control-room of *UB-59*. But he hadn't. And now he knew he had to face the inevitable consequences of his actions when the Korvettenkapitan recovered . . .

Although the muscles of his chest still ached with every breath Bergman had suffered surprisingly few ill-effects from his ordeal in the sunken U-boat. With a complete new outfit of dry clothes and half a bottle of Schnapps warming his belly he felt ready for the fray again. He looked up as he heard the sharp rap of knuckles on the cabin door.

"*Kommen sie!*"

Zetterling ducked through the low hatch, saluted smartly, and came to attention with his cap tucked under his left arm.

"At ease, Oberleutnant."

The order surprised him but he obeyed. He wondered what Bergman had in store for him and he shifted his feet uneasily. A court-martial was certain. And if he was found guilty, Zetterling knew that the death sentence was inevitable.

"Take a seat, Zetterling." Bergman pushed a silver

box across the table and flipped open the lid with his thumbnail. "Cigarette?"

Zetterling took the cigarette with the air of a condemned man being granted his last wish in the death cell. He accepted a light from the match in Bergman's hand and drew the smoke deep into his lungs. The Korvettenkapitan took a cigarette for himself and with slow deliberation struck a fresh match to light it. He let the smoke trickle through his nostrils as he stared at Zetterling through half-closed eyes.

"First of all, Herr Oberleutnant, may I take this opportunity to thank you for saving my life. I gather I owe my rescue entirely to your skill and perseverance."

Zetterling found himself unable to meet the cool blue eyes of the ex-U-boat captain. He looked away and said nothing.

"Tell me, Herr Oberleutnant. Why did you save me?"

Zetterling still avoided the Korvettenkapitan's eyes.

"Because you had guts going down there with me when you'd never done any diving before. I couldn't let a brave man die."

"But why not?" Bergman asked. "A few minutes earlier you'd done your damnedest to murder me." He paused. "Now I wonder why you did that?" There was neither anger nor accusation in the question, merely puzzled innocence.

"You wouldn't believe me," Zetterling began.

"I might."

"It's what we call oxygen madness in the trade—high altitude pilots suffer from a similar thing. If the oxygen in the bloodstream rises above a certain level it affects the brain and has the effect of intoxication. I started getting excited about that watertight door and, somehow or another, it triggered it off. When you tried to stop me I guess I just went berserk."

"And will that be your defence at the court-martial, Oberleutnant?"

Zetterling paused. So the Korvettenkapitan was going to nail him after all. Well, to be fair, he could hardly blame him. The Oberleutnant shrugged.

"I suppose it will be, sir. It happens to be the truth although I don't expect you to believe it."

Bergman gave no indication whether he accepted the explanation or not. He looked at Zetterling for a few moments as if trying to make up his mind. Then, leaning forward, he stubbed the cigarette out in an old tin lid that served as an ashtray.

"Whether I believe you or not rather depends on whether you tell me what all this damned mystery is about," he said quietly.

"What mystery?" Zetterling brazened. "I told you yesterday that I had a job to do. And whether you approve or not *UB-59* has got to be brought to the surface."

"So that you can get your transfer to the *K-Verband*?"

"That's part of it—yes."

"And what's the other part? Why, for instance, were you searching for the body of the Senior Torpedoman? And isn't that the reason you allowed me to dive with you this morning—because you thought I could help you find what you were looking for?"

Zetterling shrugged. He knew he was in an impossible position. He faced a death sentence whichever way it went and perhaps the time had come to reveal the true story about his interest in the sunken U-boat. But just how far could he trust the Korvettenkapitan?

"Have you seen the other diving team exercising off Einser Island, sir?"

Bergman nodded. "Yes—they've been testing equipment or something for the past three days. I thought they were part of your outfit. But what the hell have they got to do with the body of the missing torpedoman?"

"Quite a lot, sir. You see they're part of a special operation's unit of the Gestapo."

Bergman suddenly found himself alert. There was obviously a good deal more involved in this apparently routine salvage operation than met the eye.

"How do you know *that*?" he demanded. "I've been told nothing about a Gestapo operation and I'm the local flotilla commander."

Zetterling grinned. He was beginning to enjoy himself. "No one told me," he said. "They were having trouble with their breathing apparatus and I was called in to give them technical advice. When I saw Gruppenfuehrer Görst I *knew* who they were."

Görst! Bergman felt the adrenaline pumping through his veins as he heard the name. So his old enemy, the Gestapo chief who had hounded him halfway across Europe and who had tried to have him assassinated when he was in Japan,* was in Jade Bay just a few miles away. Görst, the man responsible for Rahel's death—the man he had sworn to kill when the opportunity came.

"How do *you* know Gruppenfuehrer Görst?" he asked Zetterling sharply.

"For the same reason that *you* know him, Herr Korvettenkapitan."

Bergman stood up, walked to the starboard locker, took out a bottle of Schnapps and two glasses, and

* See *The Tokyo Torpedo*.

brought them back to the table. He felt edgy and nervous. Zetterling obviously knew more about him than he had realised. And the salvage of *UB-59* must involve something big—big enough for the Gestapo to take an interest. And big enough for Zetterling to stake his reputation on recovering it.

His hand was completely steady as he poured out the drink and, outwardly, he was as calm and composed as ever. He passed the glass to Zetterling, sat down on the bench, and picked up his own. He looked at the Oberleutnant over the rim.

"You obviously know something about me," he said quietly. "And whether it's good or bad matters very little so far as I am concerned." Bergman swallowed a mouthful of the spirit and paused as it burned its way down his throat. "For personal reasons which I need not reveal at the moment I have sworn to thwart everything that Gruppenfuehrer Görst tries to do. One of these days, when the time is ripe, I intend to kill him. Is that sufficient to make you trust me?"

Zetterling drained his glass and put it back on the table. Reaching out he took another cigarette from the box and lit it. Perhaps it *was* time to tell the truth.

"It's a long story, sir. And you'll be surprised to discover that you already know many of the details. Do you remember being stationed at Kiel before the war?"

Bergman nodded. "I did a training course at the Periscope School in 1938," he admitted. "I was attached to the local flotilla after that."

"And you're the same Konrad Bergman who commanded *UB-44?*"

"Yes—but what the hell has all this got to do with *UB-59?*"

"I'm coming to that, sir. While you were stationed in Kiel you became involved with a young lady—Rahel Yousoff. I believe you wanted to marry her."

A cold finger of fear traced slowly down Bergman's spine. Zetterling's knowledge of his personal life seemed as complete as the dossier which Gruppenfuehrer Görst kept locked up in his office. In fact he could remember the Gestapo agent putting exactly the same questions to him at their last meeting in Lorient. Sensing a trap, and refusing to commit himself further, he merely shrugged.

Zetterling nodded sympathetically. "I know what you're thinking, sir. But you're wrong. You'll understand everything when I've finished telling you the story. But I have to make sure you're the same man as Oberleutnant Bergman of *UB-44*."

"I'm quite ready to admit to that."

"Good. In that case you know all about Rahel. And you'll also know about the Anton Group."

"And if I do . . .?"

Zetterling grinned. "I think it's time someone told you what you nearly got yourself involved in. Didn't you ever stop to consider why Görst was so interested in your affair with Rahel Yousoff—and your possible connections with the Group?"

"No," Bergman said truthfully. "She only mentioned the group to me on a couple of occasions. It seemed harmless enough—just a bunch of students and intellectuals distributing subversive pamphlets and anti-Nazi propaganda."

Zetterling's grin widened. "Rahel must have been smarter than I realised," he admitted. He paused for a moment before delivering his bombshell. "Group Anton was the central directing unit for the entire resistance network in northern Germany. The pamph-

57

lets were only used as a means of screening new recruits for political reliability. In fact very few got beyond that side of things. But when they found someone who could be trusted they were given rather more demanding tasks. Most of the men working for my salvage company were active members of the Group and they specialised in dock sabotage and observation of shipping movements. And, of course, there were others. Well, as you know, the Gestapo finally stepped in. And that was when the Group broke up and dispersed."

"But what has all this got to do with me?" Bergman asked. He was beginning to understand why Rahel had taken such care to conceal the full extent of her anti-Nazi activities from him.

"When the Gestapo closed in, the Group naturally assumed that you were responsible. After all they knew nothing about you and they thought you had been using Rahel to obtain information for Görst and his friends."

"Did *she* believe that?"

"No, she didn't. In fact it was only due to her efforts that you weren't shot by the Group's execution squad. And that's why she wouldn't let you meet her again. I know you thought it was to save you from the Gestapo—and to a certain extent that was true. But the real reason was simply that she did not intend giving the Group any further cause to suspect you of betraying them."

The incidents in Kiel during the winter of 1939 had lain dormant in Bergman's mind for a long time. But Zetterling's words brought them to life again. And as each new fact was revealed, it dovetailed neatly into the pattern of events now stirring in his memory.

"Is that why you tried to kill me this morning—for betraying the Group to the Gestapo?"

"No. I told you the truth—it was genuine oxygen madness." Zetterling drew on his cigarette before continuing. "I know you didn't betray us, sir. And I think I know where your true sympathies lie. We may have different motives but we both want the same thing—the destruction of Nazism and all it stands for."

"Let's not probe my motives, Oberleutnant," Bergman said curtly. "I still want to know what this has got to do with Görst and *UB-59*."

"I've already given you *one* connection—Rahel Yousoff. I'm sure you don't need reminding that Görst was the man responsible for her torture and death." He paused. "And I know all about that little episode in Lorient when you outsmarted the bastard and killed one of his agents."*

"That's a piece of closed history now, Zetterling. What about *UB-59*? Why are you and Görst so interested in her?"

"Well, sir, after Group Anton broke up everyone went their separate ways. Some joined other resistance groups, a few got away from Germany altogether, but most found themselves conscripted into the army or the navy, or the Luftwaffe. Fortunately, no one, not even the Gestapo, knew their identity and they were able to disappear into the ranks of the services undetected and unrecognised."

"Fifth columnists in reverse," Bergman commented.

"That's right. Well, the information they obtained was channelled through a receiving centre in Hamburg and passed on to the right people."

"Like the British?"

"Sometimes, but not always. Quite a lot went to

* For details of this incident see *Action Atlantic!*

59

Russia via their Embassy in Berlin; until Operation Barbarossa put an end to that particular channel. After that it was smuggled to Sweden and passed on from Stockholm."

"What sort of information were you obtaining?" Bergman asked.

Zetterling shrugged. "This and that," he said vaguely as if, even now, he was reluctant to reveal his secrets. "It's safer not to say." He leaned forward to stub out his cigarette in the ashtray.

"One of the Group joined up in January 1940," he continued. "His name was Georg Holst—no point in keeping it a secret now he's dead. Georg was one of the divers I employed at Hamburg before the war, so rather naturally, he joined the Kriegsmarine and ended up in U-boats as an Obertorpedomechaniker. He served in several boats. In fact, and we had a good laugh about it, he even won the Iron Cross, 2nd Class. Well, he finally wound up as Senior Torpedoman on *UB-59*. And that's how he died."

"But if he's dead why is it so important to find his body?" Bergman asked.

"Because Georg was our central liaison agent in the Kriegsmarine. And when he went down in *UB-59* he was carrying a full list of his contacts plus the address of the Group's Hamburg station."

"And you want to get hold of it before the Gestapo does?"

"Too bloody right I do."

Bergman poured himself another glass of Schnapps and pushed the bottle across the table to Zetterling. "I would have said it was a damn stupid thing to do—carrying a list like that. Holst was asking for trouble."

"There was a good reason for it," Zetterling explained. "I won't go into details but, bearing in mind the circumstances, it was a justifiable risk. As I said, Georg was an expert mechanic and he was in charge of *UB-59*'s torpedoes. He'd fixed a G-7(*e*)* so that it would float to the surface, and he put the list in the warhead. The Royal Navy was waiting to pick it up at a prearranged spot to take it back to London, so that British Intelligence had a list of reliable contacts when they sent their own agents over."

"So you only want to raise *UB-59* in order to get at Holst's body—or the torpedo—and destroy that list?"

Zetterling nodded. "That's it. My original idea was to dive down and get inside the U-boat on the quiet. But as you saw for yourself it's an impossible task with our conventional diving kit. So then I put a scheme up to Lutz to have her raised and salvaged. That was where our friend Görst was clever. He sent some of his men to the K-flotilla base at Lubeck, put them through a crash course in free-diving, and borrowed a couple of the new aqualung suits. The Gestapo divers can therefore swim underwater completely independent of the surface and, with a bit of nerve, they can get inside and search through every compartment of the submarine while it's still on the bottom."

"I see—so *UB-59* has got to be brought to the surface today or the Gestapo will beat you to it and get hold of the list first." Bergman allowed himself the luxury of a half-smile. "I suppose in the circumstances I will have to withdraw my objection."

"I take it I have your permission to enter the submarine as soon as it's surfaced and pumped out." He grinned meaningfully. "I ought to make sure every-

* The German Navy's electric torpedo.

61

thing is secure before we start towing her back to Wilhelmshaven."

Bergman knew what he meant. He nodded. "I understand, Oberleutnant. And you will obviously wish to carry out your examination alone. I will let you have written orders to that effect."

He stood up and held out his hand. Zetterling grasped it firmly. The clasped hands symbolised the understanding that had grown out of their original animosity. Neither man voiced his inner thoughts yet each felt he could now trust the other.

"Just one last thing, Oberleutnant."

"Sir?"

"I won't ask you how you come to know so much about Group Anton although it isn't difficult to guess. But you also seem to know a hell of a lot about me. The Navy records have you down as Karl Zetterling. Just who are you *really?*"

Zetterling turned the handle of the door. He hesitated before pulling it open.

"My name is Karl Yousoff. I am Rahel's brother."

Despite the leaden skies and the biting chill of the north wind the first flurries of light snow failed to develop into the blizzard predicted by Weather Station IV. But the air temperature had fallen ten degrees since dawn and a thick rime of hoarfrost glistened on the rails and deck equipment of the tub as she rolled gently in the off-shore swell.

The shrill creak of the power winches drowned the cries of the gulls wheeling overhead and the decks vibrated to the steady thump of the steam donkey-engine working the compressor in the waist. The sea looked as sullen and black as the threatening sky, and Bergman shivered.

Zetterling's plan, based on the salvage techniques developed by the US Navy when they raised the submarine *Squalus* from the bottom of the Atlantic in 1937, looked promising enough on paper. But Bergman did not share the Oberleutnant's optimism.

Divers had already sealed off the U-boat, and high-pressure air, fed into the submarine through wide-bore hoses, was to be used to blow the ballast tanks. The gaping gash left by the impact of *Oldenburg*'s bows was too large to seal and Zetterling was therefore unable to pump the inner hull clear of water. But, by blowing the flooded tanks, he could at least restore neutral buoyancy. And the lifting operation itself would need the help of the eight large pontoons he had assembled for the purpose inside the buoyed area.

Despite their grandiose title the pontoons were no more than hollow steel cylinders 30 feet long and 14 feet in diameter. Flooded with water they had been sunk into the sea a few hours earlier and divers had fastened their chain slings around the U-boat's hull. It was a tricky operation demanding high technical skill and long experience. Zetterling's plan involved having the eight pontoons set at varying depths above the submarine—four grouped over the flooded bow compartments, with two more—the control pontoons—positioned side by side 40 feet above the others. The other two pontoons were shackled to the stern section—the control being positioned 30 feet above the other.

The operation was controlled from the tug and Zetterling's diving team had the task of regulating the flow of compressed air being pumped into the submarine's ballast tanks, while another set of hoses, connected to the compressor in the waist, fed air into the pontoons.

Bergman could feel the tense expectancy of the salvage men as the first strain of the lift was put on. Everything depended on the strength and positioning of the eight-inch hawsers and steel chains slung beneath the submarine's keel. Zetterling's divers had rigged the slings around UB-59's extended diving-planes to prevent them from slipping, and no one could predict whether the massive steel hydroplanes were strong enough to take the strain.

As the air pumps forced the water from the flooded ballast tanks of the submarine, the surface of the sea immediately above the U-boat began bubbling gently. Then the pipes connected to the pontoons came under compression and the water heaved restlessly. Within minutes the entire surface was boiling like a saucepan of milk and enormous air bubbles erupted and burst with the violence of exploding shells. Dead fish and strands of seaweed bobbed wildly in the gathering maelstrom of white water, and the shriek of high-pressure air was overwhelmed by the deafening roar rising up from the sea-bed.

"Controls in sight to starboard!"

"Belay pumps! Stand by to secure lines!"

Bergman's eyes followed the lookout's warning shout and he saw the two control pontoons leap from the boiling cauldron like a pair of playful dolphins chasing the wake of a passing steamer.

"That means she's off the bottom sir," Kelso shouted excitedly in his ear. "The main pontoons should be holding her at a depth of 40 feet."

"What now?"

"First we check the cables to make sure they're still

secure. Then we pump the pontoons clear. If the Oberleutnant's miscalculated, or if *UB-59* has too much buoyancy, she'll shoot to the surface, break the cable slings and pressure hoses, and sink straight to the bottom again."

"Is it likely?" Bergman asked anxiously.

Kelso nodded. "It happened to the Yanks the first time they lifted the *Squalus*. She came straight up like a rocket, smashed the pontoons, pushed more than 30 feet of her bow out of the sea, and then broke free and sank."

Bergman crossed his fingers cautiously. He hoped Kelso had not noticed. Unlike the *Squalus* operation if *UB-59* sank it would be a disaster. It would take weeks to obtain another set of pontoons and Gruppenfuehrer Görst's private salvage team would be able to penetrate the flooded compartments and recover Holst's list at their leisure.

The Oberleutnant was supervising the work from a small motor boat and, as the violence of the sea settled, he ordered his team to secure additional cables to the hull. It was a tedious business and it was more than half-past two before the task was completed. Bergman pulled himself deeper into the collar of his greatcoat and waited impatiently. A rolling bank of black cloud hung ominously over the grey mudflats of the *Stollhammer Watt* and he knew the predicted blizzard could not be long delayed. Once the storm started, all salvage operations would have to be postponed until the weather cleared. And Görst would have won . . .

"Ahoy, *Beowulf*! Permission to board!"

Bergman forced his attention away from the salvage work and hurried to the port side of the bridge.

He was just in time to see a smart 60-foot launch coming alongside. She was wearing no flag of identification and her name had been painted out. But the squat figure of Görst beside the helmsman in the wheelhouse was sufficient to identify her.

"Belay there, Berklestrom!" Bergman shouted to the coxswain as he began lowering a rope ladder over the side. "No one's to be allowed on board!"

Görst had left the wheelhouse and he swayed carefully along the turtle-backed forecastle of the launch as it bobbed in the swell. His trilby hat and black leather coat looked oddly out of place on the open windswept deck, but he seemed unaware of any incongruity in his appearance.

"*Geheime Staatspolizei!*" Görst had to use a loud-hailer although the two vessels were barely ten yards apart. The throat wound—a legacy of a beerhall fight in the early days of the Nazi rise to power—had cut his voice to a whisper and the amplifier accentuated the sibilant hiss of his words. "I demand to come aboard in the name of the Reichsfuehrer!"

"This is a Kriegsmarine vessel!" Bergman shouted down from the bridge. Accustomed to giving commands in the teeth of a mid-Atlantic gale he did not need the assistance of an electronic amplifier. "No unauthorised persons are allowed on board. Stand clear and give me sea room or I'll have you arrested by the Harbour Master for fouling a Navy ship."

Görst's eyesight was as deficient as his voice. Peering up at the bridge of the tug he could just make out the tall figure of an officer but that was all. As a senior Gestapo officer he was unused to such cavalier treatment and he boiled with rage. He jerked the loud-hailer angrily.

"You won't hear the last of this," he wheezed. "What is your name and rank—I shall report your insolence to the flotilla commander."

Bergman grinned. The fact that Görst hadn't recognised him added extra zest to the game.

"I *am* the flotilla commander."

Görst obviously did not believe him. Why should a senior officer be on board a rusty harbour tug. In his own mind he felt sure the man on the bridge was Zetterling. Well, if it was, he'd be laughing the other side of his face soon. The Gruppenfuehrer gestured angrily to the helmsman and Bergman heard the twin MAN diesels throttle up. The launch backed away, turned her bows towards the tug, and came in closer so that her bulwarks grazed the rubber strakes of *Beowulf's* port side.

Bergman hurried down the companionway from the bridge and made his way to the waist where the low bulwarks of the short midship's well-deck made access easier. He arrived in time to see Görst's face peering up over the side. A moment later his hands gripped the edge of the deck as he prepared to hoist himself aboard. The Korvettenkapitan stepped forward, waited while the Gestapo officer secured a firm grip, and then stamped down hard on the clawed fingers.

Görst let out a hoarse scream of pain, lost his hold, and fell back on to the launch. The men in the boat watched in dispassionate silence but no one attempted to pick him up from the deck.

"*Kleine votze!*" Bergman shouted down at him. "If you try to board again I'll have you shot."

As it to emphasize the warning Kelso appeared at the rails with an *Erma* sub-machine gun clasped across his chest. Görst scrambled to his feet, scurried to the safety of the wheelhouse, and used the loud-hailer again.

"You will regret this—I warn you." The amplification unit accentuated the angry tremor in his voice. "I demand to know your rank and name!"

Bergman grinned. It was the moment he had been waiting for.

"Bergman, Herr Gruppenfuehrer," he yelled back. "Korvettenkapitan Bergman. I think we've met before. Now get away from my ship or I'll have you blown out of the water!"

The powerful diesels gunned to maximum revolutions and the launch curved away from the tug in a tumult of white water. Bergman was unable to observe the effect of his words on the Gestapo chief but he glimpsed the white face and the snarled mouth behind the spray-spattered window of the wheelhouse as the policeboat sped away. He smiled at the satisfying memory of Görst's fingers crunching painfully beneath his boot. Next time, with luck, it would be the Gruppenfuehrer's neck!

"Message from Oberleutnant Zetterling, sir."

Bergman turned away from the rails as Ohlendorff saluted.

"Go ahead."

"The Oberleutnant has been down inside the U-boat, sir. He says I am to report that *UB-59* is now on an even keel and that he has dealt with the list."

Bergman nodded gravely. He gave no hint of the hidden message contained in Zetterling's apparently innocent routine report. "Very good, Cox'n. Give the Oberleutnant my compliments and tell him to carry on. I will be in my sea cabin if he needs me."

Kelso was still hovering in the background. He waited until Ohlendorff was out of earshot. Then he turned to the Korvettenkapitan.

"That's odd, sir," he said with a puzzled frown. "I would have sworn she came up on an even keel. I didn't see any sign of a list on her at all."

Bergman allowed himself a half smile. "You don't know much about U-boats, do you, Kelso." The expression on his face was enigmatic. "You can't always *see* the list. Sometimes you have to *find* it."

Kelso scratched his head as the Korvettenkapitan climbed the steps to the bridge and disappeared into his cabin. He's heard some daft things in his time— but that took the biscuit! He shrugged. It was obviously some private joke he didn't understand. But that wasn't unusual. There were a great many things he didn't understand about the flotilla commander. Still, he reminded himself, the old bastard knows how to step on the Gestapo. And he grinned happily at his aptly phrased pun . . .

Bergman closed the door of his sea cabin and walked across to the desk. The buff coloured Form *E-85* (*Transfer of Duties—Application.*) was lying on top in a prominent position. He picked it up and read through Zetterling's formal request for an appointment to the *K-Verband*. Staring out of the porthole he could see the slime covered hull of *UB-59* rolling gently between the pontoons. He turned back to the desk, picked up his pen, and wrote his comments in the appropriate box at the bottom of the form.

Request approved. Transfer strongly recommended.
K. Bergman. Korvettenkapitan.
OC. 32nd (Reserve) Flotilla.

It seemed the least he could do in the circumstances. And a transfer to the Baltic would keep Zetterling safely out of Görst's dangerous clutches for the time being. There was little doubt that the Gestapo would be anxious to balance accounts after the *UB-59* episode.

Bergman was not so much concerned about his own position. He had challenged and out-fought the Gestapo on several previous occasions. And if it came to a show-down with Gruppenfuehrer Görst he felt well able to look after himself.

CHAPTER FOUR

Road Block 37 was situated midway between the blackened carcass of a burned out Tiger tank and two dead transport horses. Neither landmark was noted on the Staff maps at von Kluge's 7th Army HQ. But then neither was Road Block 37.

Korporal Werner lit the stub of his last dog-end and stared down the road from Caen waiting for the next convoy of defeated Panzers to appear over the crest of the hill. It wasn't that GHQ had forgotten them, he reflected bitterly. It was simply that no one even knew they bloody well existed. And so far as Werner was concerned, Road Block 37 would probably still be there long after the last of the rearguard units had passed through in the headlong flight north and east, from the approaching Allied armies. And no one would give a damn!

Just three days earlier, on 17 August, all German resistance in the Falaise gap had collapsed, discipline and command had broken down, and the 7th Army's vaunted Panzer Divisions had turned tail and fled. Werner was quite willing to admit he was prejudiced. As one of the poor bloody infantry he had no love for the Panzer units. But it seemed to him, the entire German army had passed through Road Block 37 during the past twenty-four hours. And now there was only himself, and six men, left to face the entire might of the Allied invasion force.

"What the bloody hell's this lot, Korp?"

Werner felt his guts churn as Schrieber pointed to a column of trucks approaching Road Block 37 from the east. One thing was certain. They couldn't be German troops—not moving westwards against the stream of defeated and demoralised armour fleeing in the opposite direction. He picked up his binoculars and searched for some form of identification. But the high grey sides of the trucks with their tarpaulin covered cargoes were blankly anonymous.

"Who the hell are they?" Schrieber repeated anxiously. He had a young wife waiting for him in Saxony and he was anxious to survive the war. An attack from the rear did not seem likely to increase his chances.

Werner shook his head. "Christ knows! Could be a Yankee column that's outflanked us. Or British glider troops who've landed in our base area."

"But they're German trucks," Eiger pointed out as the leading lorry swept around the bend into full view of the watching soldiers.

"I can see *that*," Werner snapped. "But I don't recognise their unit signs and they're not wearing Wehrmacht uniforms—and that's for sure." He swallowed hard as he made his decision. "Get down and keep 'em covered. I'm going to check them."

Slipping the safety catch of his *MG-34* machine gun, the Korporal climbed out of the sandbagged slit trench, placed himself four-square in the centre of the road, and raised his left hand.

It was not the most sensible thing to do in the circumstances. But after 72 hours without sleep, Werner's judgement was not as incisive as usual. The trucks could have continued through the block without stopping and he could have joined the two dead horses slowly decomposing in the left-hand ditch. Or a sudden blast of machine gun fire from the guards riding shotgun on the roofs of the driving cabs could have cut him down within seconds. But, fortunately for the Korporal, the mysterious convoy slowed obediently and the leading truck came to a docile halt just two feet from the muzzle of his gun.

Werner slipped the catch back to "safe" but kept the machine gun in the firing position as he moved round to the off-side door of the convoy leader. Keeping his thumb poised over the catch he waited tensely as the door swung open. A tall man in an unfamiliar blue uniform and with gold braid on the peak of his cap stepped out on to the running-board and jumped down. The Korporal stiffened to attention almost without realising he had done so. He couldn't make head or tail of the uniform but the man had the authoritative presence of an officer—and a senior one at that.

"You'll have to turn back, sir," he said woodenly. "Direct orders from 7th Army HQ—all roads must be kept clear for the passage of armoured units. No vehicles are permitted to proceed westwards without written authority from GHQ."

The officer did not seem to be listening. He tooked tired, drawn, and dusty. Reaching into his breast pocket he pulled out a sheet of folded paper, opened it, and handed it silently to the Korporal. Werner glanced at the unfamiliar crest heading the sheet and read quickly.

> *Korvettenkapitan Bergman is in charge of a Special Kommando of the German Navy. His task is secret and no person is entitled to question him about it. He is to be given all possible assistance to enable him to carry out his duty.*
>
> *(Signed) Doenitz, Grossadmiral. Commander-in-Chief, Kriegsmarine.*

Werner saluted respectfully and handed the pass back to the Korvettenkapitan. There were at least a dozen questions he wanted to ask but the expression on Bergman's face showed it would be a waste of time. And, in any case, Doenitz himself has signed the Pass. He clicked his heels and waited.

"We've been travelling for twelve hours. Got lost south of Amiens—some stupid bloody traffic controller routed us around the town because of an air raid and we got lost. Where the hell are we?"

Bergman stuck a well-thumbed map under the Korporal's nose and waited impatiently. Werner ran an expert eye over the sheet, located the *Department Seine Inferieure*, and pointed to the junction of two minor roads.

"Right over here, sir. About six kilometres west of Gisors. You were nearly off the bloody map."

The Korvettenkapitan stared down at the small black dot of the hamlet and mentally cursed the traffic controller who had sent the convoy rolling eastwards away from the coast. It must be all of 100 kilometres to Harfleur or Fecamps. And that meant at least another hour's travelling even with clear roads. More probably they'd get tangled up with panzer columns moving northwards, enemy air strikes, and the general chaos and confusion of an army in retreat. In which case it would take all of three hours to reach the sea. He nodded towards the field-telephone in the slit trench at the side of the road.

"Are your communications still open?"

"So far, sir. I've got a direct line to 19th Corps HQ and they're linked to 7th Army GHQ by landline."

Bergman rubbed his chin reflectively. "Well, unless we're unlucky, the enemy won't be able to intercept the call. I daren't use our radio or the whole bloody Allied air force will home in on our signal." He looked at the map again, seeking the answer from his own resources, and obviously reluctant to ask the Army for assistance. Even when their backs were to the wall there was no love lost between the Kriegsmarine and the Wehrmacht. And both equally hated the Luftwaffe.

"What's the current combat situation?" he asked. "Do we still hold Le Havre?"

So *that's* where they're heading, Werner thought to himself. He shook his head and shrugged.

"Not in my Corps area, sir," he explained. "But I'd say it was doubtful. The enemy have broken through around Falaise. If they sweep up towards the coast they'll outflank the town. And from what I've heard we've got no armour left to stop them—they've torn six Panzer regiments to pieces in the last couple of days."

Bergman wasn't particularly interested in the fate of the Panzers—or, for that matter, the Army either. Right now he had a job to do and, if the Army

75

couldn't help, the Kriegsmarine would see it through on its own. But somehow the three special service kommandos, spearheaded by Bartel's *Flotilla 261*, had to reach the coast in time to cut the Allied supply lines. If the invasion force could be starved of supplies and ammunition the Panzers would have time to regroup and strike back.

"Put a call through to Corps and get me a situation report on Le Havre," he told the Korporal. "Tell them to clear all lines for a priority message. Use Prefix ZZ-5."

Werner's respect for the mysterious naval officer rose several points. Prefix ZZ-5! He must be bloody important if he was authorised to use *that* level of priority. The Korporal clicked his heels and hurried down to the slit trench while Bergman paced up and down the narrow road. The stink of the dead horses grew unpleasantly strong as the midday sun aided the process of decomposition, and he turned away sharply. Walking back to the cab of the leading truck, he put his foot on the running-board and looked up at the Oberleutnant.

"Tell the men to fall out for five minutes—they can use those hedges over on the right. But keep the flak defences manned and if any aircraft show up, get the trucks over to those woods on the left."

The Oberleutnant passed the order to the Petty Officer straddling the steel crosspiece of the hood support just behind his back. Taking a cigarette from his pocket he lit it and stared thoughtfully at the glowing tip.

"What happens if we've pulled out of Le Havre already, sir?"

"Then we find somewhere else," Bergman said decisively. "I know Bartel was intending to make for Fecamps and I daresay we'll locate a suitable place."

"But surely we need the launching facilities at Le Havre—how do we manage without lifting gear?"

"I'll find a way, Karl."

"How? Those bloody things weight 5 tons apiece."

"I know," Bergman agreed. "If we can't use cranes or lifting tackle we'll have to call the army in to help. Krieg used 500 soldiers to launch thirty *Negers* at Anzio—and he reckoned he could have done with twice as many.* I thought we could make use of the garrison troops at Le Havre." He shrugged. "There must be *some* way. Tell Giessels to see me—perhaps he can help."

Werner's face glistened with sweat as he clambered out of the slit-trench and hurried across to the convoy to report the results of his telephone call. He clicked his heels obediently.

"Corps HQ says that Le Havre has been evacuated. Can't give any more detail than that. Apparently it's sheer bloody pandemonium trying to sort it all out."

"Have the Allied spearheads crossed the Seine yet?" Bergman asked.

"Not so far as we know, sir. There's been reports of parachute landings in the Pas de Calais, but von Kluge seems to reckon he can mop them up quickly."

Bergman glanced round as Oberbootsmann Giessels came down the line of stationary trucks. He was a bluff blond-haired man in his mid-forties with the ruddy complexion of a lifetime at sea and the hooded careful eyes of a man who has seen everything. He

---

* Hanno Krieg was the commanding officer of the K-force flotilla *MEK 175* which was launched from Pratica di Mare in a counter attack against the Allied landings at Anzio in April 1944.

had been a professional yacht captain before the war and he knew the Channel coast like the back of his hand. It was rumoured that he'd been involved in a smuggling racket as a side-line and Bergman had kept both facts firmly in his mind when he had selected him for Flotilla 271. He was tough but loyal. The sort of man to have around when things got nasty. And his intimate knowledge of the French coast would be invaluable.

"You wanted to see me, sir?" Giessels was accustomed to addressing people as "sir"—it was part of his professional make-up. But the inflection he gave the word made it sound slightly derogatory. Bergman ignored the mannerism.

"You know the coast down to Le Havre?" he asked—making the question more a statement of fact.

"Yes, sir. Very popular area with honeymooners before the war. Plenty of places to hide away at night—beaches that can only be reached from seawards."

"Well *they'll* be no bloody use to us, will they," Bergman snapped. He regained his composure quickly and added quietly, "I need a secluded beach with plenty of cover for the trucks and an easy gradient down from the road. As near to Le Havre as possible and with a minimum tidal movement of eight feet."

"And no mud, sir?"

The Korvettenkapitan nodded with a half smile. It hadn't taken Giessels long to spot what he had in mind. The man might be an ex-jailbird, a con-man in every sense of the word, and a moral reprobate, but he had a quick mind and he thought like a sailor. Bergman decided that Giessels and Zetterling would make a good pair.

Giessels took the map without permission and stared down at it thoughtfully. He ran his finger along the coastline and stopped at a small bay about twenty miles to the north east of Le Havre.

"I remember picking up four crates of rifles just here in '38," he said. "Ran 'em down to Asturias in Northern Spain for the Reds during the Civil War. Made the return run with a couple of wealthy Spaniards trying to get away from the air raids. Nice little trip," he added as an afterthought. "The Spanish guy had no money—all his loot was stuck away in some Swiss bank. And I wanted paying." He smiled at the memory. "His wife had the sort of currency that'll buy anything, anywhere . . ."

"All right, bosun, you can spare me the details. What's the layout of this bay?"

"Le Verdon? Well, it's a private beach belonging to some French baron. Very rarely goes there—likes to be where the sun is hot and the women hotter. You can bet your sweet life he's not there at the moment. The approach road is single track with a concrete surface. Our trucks should make the grade okay and so far as I can remember the trees run all the way down to the winter high-water mark. There's just his villa on the south side—that'll be empty—and a small wooden jetty . . ."

"This jetty," Bergman interrupted. "Any good for our purpose?"

Giessels shook his head. "I don't think so. They only used it for rowing boats and things. Not much more than three feet depth of water."

"And no lifting tackle—winches and things?"

"Absolutely sweet FA. If we're going to shift those *Negers* we'll have to do it with our own bare hands."

Bergman glanced at the map again. Giessels was not encouraging but it seemed the only possible place. *And,* of equal importance, it was at least 20 miles closer to the invasion beaches than Flotilla 261's base at Fecamps. And Bergman wanted to be first!

He showed the map to Werner and pointed vaguely to the coastal area above Le Havre. "What's our best route, Korporal?"

"Turn right at the second cross-roads from here and you'll pick up a *Route National* after about ten miles. Keep on it to Rouen but try to work your way round behind the city—it's bound to be jammed solid with Panzer units. Then take this road," he pointed to a red line on the map, "for Yvetot. After that you're on your own."

Bergman nodded his thanks, closed the map and put it in his pocket, climbing back into his seat in the cab of the leading lorry. He said something to the Oberleutnant and Petty Officer Neitze's whistle shrilled the recall as the driver started the Mercedes diesel engine and waited for the order to move off. As the last of the sailors clambered aboard their vehicles Korporal Werner could restrain his curiosity no longer. Stepping up onto the running-baord he pushed his head through the opened window and whispered hoarsely into Bergman's ear.

"I know I shouldn't ask, sir. But what have you got under those tarpaulins—a new secret weapon?"

The Korvettenkapitan grinned as the gears meshed and the truck jerked forward. "It's a flotilla of U-boats, Korporal. I thought you'd have guessed that by now."

Werner hosted the strap of his machine gun over his shoulder and gave a rueful grin as the line of field-grey trucks lumbered slowly through Road Block 37. It was his own fault. Ask a silly question and you get a silly bloody answer!

Turning away he returned to his isolated outpost,

checked that his platoon were at their stations, and stared westwards. He began to speculate on the possibility of surrendering when the first American tanks swept into view. Better a live coward than a dead hero, he decided. He reflected that the Korvettenkapitan would probably chose to be a dead hero.

He seemed to be that sort of a man . . .

Vice-Admiral Hellmuth Heye, the creator and commander of the *K-Verband*, had dismissed Bergman's objection to the plan with a brusqueness that served to hide his sympathy for the young Korvettenkapitan.

"I appreciate this is your first introduction to our midget submarine flotillas, but Admiral Doenitz has specifically assigned you to the *K-Verband* and you will have to lead a special kommando whether you like it or not!"

"But it's madness, sir. You *know* it is. These men have been training together for nearly six months. They know and trust their officers. What will their reaction be when they find a total stranger in command—someone who hasn't even seen one of these new submarines let alone driven one."

"You forget you are something of a hero, Korvettenkapitan," Heye said soothingly. "You have sunk more enemy tonnage than any other living submarine commander, you have won virtually every decoration a U-boat man can obtain, and your exploits in Japan* have made you one of the best-known officers in the Kriegsmarine. With your record the men will be proud to serve under you."

Bergman ignored the flattery despite the truth of Heye's statement. But he was an ocean-going U-boat

* See *The Tokyo Torpedo*.

ace. And that was where he belonged—in the deep waters of the mid-Atlantic. Not mothering a collection of flimsy tin cans that Hitler had decided could win the war.

"I was speaking as a professional officer, sir," he explained quietly. "I have made my reputation on the high seas. I know nothing about inshore operations and even less about midget submarines."

"But you piloted a *kaiten* when you were in Japan." Heye tactfully omitted to mention that Bergman had also stolen one and brought it back to Germany. "So don't pretend you know nothing about such things. You were probably the first Kriegsmarine officer to handle a one-man submarine." The Admiral decided to bring the conference to order. Drawing himself to his full height he looked Bergman straight in the eyes. "It is a personal order from Doenitz. *That* is the end of the matter."

The Korvettenkapitan shrugged. He remained noncommittal. "Will I be permitted to select my own second-in-command?" he asked.

Heye nodded. Having won his point he could afford to be magnanimous. "Of course, my dear Bergman. Any officer serving in the *K-Verband* is at your disposal."

"Provided he has completed his training, sir, I would like to have Oberleutnant Zetterling."

The Admiral looked up sharply. He tapped his teeth thoughtfully with the ruler he'd been using as a pointer to indicate the operational areas of the three Kommandos.

"Oberleutnant Zetterling is under close arrest."

Bergman felt his stomach churn with fear. Although he knew that Zetterling was well able to look after himself he was uncomfortably aware that Rahel's brother had been skating on thin ice recently. Just one simple mistake and the Gestapo would nail him. What the hell had the young fool done now?

"On what charge, sir?" he asked.

Admiral Heye turned to his Chief of Staff. "You know more about this than I do, Heinrich. Can you give the Korvettenkapitan the details?"

Kapitan zur See Heinrich Brunheld bustled forward importantly. He was one of those men who look as if they always have a bad smell under their noses and his *pince-nez* aided the impression. It was obvious he did not like Zetterling.

"The Oberleutnant insulted a senior Gestapo officer in the Mess. He is to be court-martialled next week."

Bergman turned to the Admiral with a smile that hid his anxiety. "Hardly a capital offence surely, Herr Admiral."

"The Gruppenfuehrer seems to think so," Heye said bleakly.

"Gruppenfuehrer Görst?"

"You know him?" Brunheld queried in his high-pitched voice.

Bergman always looked his most convincing when he was lying. And the bigger the lie the more angelic he became. It was impossible not to believe him. "But of course—a very old and dear friend of mine." He turned to the Admiral with a disarming smile. "I had no idea he was up here in Lübeck. I will have a word with him immediately and see that he drops the charges. Zetterling is something of a protegé of mine. I recommended him for the K-flotillas. Görst will see the funny side of it when I tell him."

"You seem remarkably sure, Korvettenkapitan," Brunheld interjected. "My impression was rather to the contrary—that the Gruppenfuehrer would be satisfied with nothing less than a dishonourable discharge from the Kriegsmarine."

"And you obviously do not understand the Gruppenfuehrer's sense of humour, Herr Kapitan. Herr Görst is familiar with several members of Zetterling's family." Bergman had difficulty in suppressing a grin at the enormity of the half-truth. "It is his idea of a joke." He lowered his voice confidently. "The Gruppenfuehrer received a nasty head wound while serving on the Eastern Front—his sense of humour can sometimes be a little odd."

Bergman was only too aware that something had to be done—and quickly—if he was to save Zetterling from the Gestapo's clutches. He turned to Heye.

"With respect, sir. I'll take over Flotilla 271 on two conditions. Firstly that the special kommando leaves tonight. And secondly that Zetterling is immediately released from custody and appointed as second-in-command. I will stand guarantor for his behaviour. And I promise I will square matters with the Gruppenfuehrer before we leave."

In normal circumstances no Korvettenkapitan would have dared place conditions on the acceptance of an order—especially to a flag-officer. But Bergman knew the wind was running in his favour. Without undue modesty he *knew* he was Germany's top-scoring U-boat ace. And, his two personal commendations from Adolf Hitler gave him an authority that far outweighed his rank.

The Admiral glanced at Kapitan Brunheld. He was obviously unhappy about the entire affair. And, like most people in Germany, he had no wish to cross swords quite so openly with the Gestapo. On the other hand he was very conscious of his larger responsibilities. The war situation was deteriorating rapidly. The western Allies had established a firm beach-head in Fortress Europe and it was his duty as a patriotic officer to deploy his forces in defence of the Fatherland to the greatest advantage. Ignoring Brunheld's obvious disapproval he looked up at Bergman.

"I am aware of your reputation, Korvettenkapitan, and of the fact that Grossadmiral Doenitz's personal orders for you have the approval of the Fuehrer himself. In the circumstances I will agree to your *request*." The emphasis was to make Bergman aware of his insubordination in laying down conditions. "But I will hold you responsible for both the conduct of Oberleutnant Zetterling and for obtaining Gruppenfuehrer Görst's permission for his release."

Le Verdon proved exactly as Giessels had described it. A narrow concrete road, just wide enough to accommodate the Mercedes low-loaders, wound down to the deserted beach through a thickly planted pine wood. Bergman halted the convoy under cover of the trees while he and Giessels walked down to examine the wooden jetty.

"It'll be a hell of a job," Giessels observed dispassionately as they made their way back to the waiting trucks.

Bergman nodded. Short of manhandling the midget submarines down the beach and into the water on their trailers he couldn't see any solution to the problem. Without lifting gear he needed muscle power— and with less than 50 men at his disposal it seemed an impossible task.

"What's the state of the tide?" he asked.

Giessels stopped, turned towards the sea, and checked the familiar landmarks. "The sea is still covering those rocks over on the left—I'd say it's about an hour either side of high-water."

Bergman stooped down and felt the sand. "The tide's on the way out," he said brushing the wet sand from his hands. "That means we have about eleven hours until the next tide." He glanced at his watch. "That will put it around five o'clock tomorrow morning. Say an hour before sunrise."

"Couldn't be better," Giessels nodded. "But we still haven't worked out how we're going to launch them with only fifty men."

Zetterling was waiting by the leading truck as the two men trudged over the soft sand towards the trees. He was smoking a cigarette moodily. "Well?" he asked as they joined him. "What's the score?"

"High water will be just before dawn," Bergman told him. "But there's no launching equipment or cranes on the jetty—not even a slipway. And we haven't enough men to carry a 5-ton submarine down to the sea."

"Couldn't we get hold of a tank recovery vehicle from 7th Army HQ," Zetterling suggested. "They've got a lifting capacity of 50 tons."

Bergman shook his head. "We can't expect any co-operation from the Army. And they've probably got enough to worry about already."

"We could always steal one," Giessels pointed out.

"It wouldn't work," Bergman told him. As an opportunist himself he saw no reason to criticise the ex-yacht captain's morals. He was only concerned with practicalities. "The jetty wouldn't take the weight. And short of running it into the sea it would be of no value."

Zetterling rubbed his chin thoughtfully as Bergman's objections triggered an idea.

"I take it this attack will be a one-way mission," he asked.

Bergman saw no reason to minimise the hazards of the operation. The midget submarines were not suicide weapons like the Japanese *kaitens* but they had technical limitations. And above all they *were* expendable.

The concept of the *kleinekampfmittel*—the small battle weapon—had been originally prompted by the successes of the Italian human-torpedo units at Gibraltar and the Royal Navy's midget submarine attacks on the *Tirpitz*. Working day and night at their secret base in Timmendorfstrand on the fringes of Lubeck Bay the Kriegsmarine's experts quickly delighted the Fuehrer with an avalanche of design studies that culminated finally in the prototype *Pike*—a midget submarine utilising a limpet mine as its attack weapon. Then came the *Neger*.

The *Neger* itself was no more than a standard electric torpedo without a warhead and modified to carry another torpedo slung beneath its belly. A small cockpit was skilfully engineered into a nose section so that its one man crew could control and steer the weapon while an aircraft-type plexiglass canopy gave its pilot some measure of protection against the elements. The fully armed *G-7*(e) battery-powered torpedo, attached to the upper unit by electro-magnets, was the *Neger*'s sole means of attack, and it could be launched by means of a trigger in the cockpit as soon as the target came into the pilot's sights. It was primitive yet ingenious. And Hitler was convinced that with this new secret weapon, his naval forces could wipe out the Allied invasion fleet at minimum cost.

The *Neger*'s drawbacks, however, were many and various—not least being its inability to submerge.

Running awash on the surface, the dome of the plexiglass cockpit canopy was clearly visible to enemy lookouts, and close-range weapons quickly made short work of the *kleinekampfmittel* once it had been sighted. With a maximum speed of only 20 knots—slower than a destroyer—and a combat range of just 30 miles at 3 knots, the scope of its operations was severely limited.

"Yes—it's a one-way trip," Bergman confirmed. "We're about 20 miles from the attack area and once the torpedoes are launched we won't have enough battery power to return. We'll have to try and make landfall east of Le Havre. But as the enemy already occupy the coastal areas we'll be damn lucky if we can avoid being taken prisoner. *Gruppe XI* will be running E-boat patrols and our best chance of survival lies in one of them picking us up."

"If it's a one-way trip we won't be needing our trucks again," Zetterling pointed out.

"They're supposed to return to Antwerp to pick up another Kommando at the railhead. Personally I don't think they'll make it—but those are my orders. Enemy ground-attack fighters are sure to locate them on the road and they'll get cut to pieces."

"Are you prepared to write them off?" Zetterling asked.

"If it means we can get the *Negers* launched—the short answer is yes. What do you have in mind?"

"Well, it will be dark at low water," the Oberleutnant explained. "If we use the trucks to push the trailers into the sea the torpedoes should be almost fully submerged by the time the tide rises. Then we can float them off at zero-hour."

Giessels nodded. "The Oberleutnant is right, sir. I reckon there'll be a good eight feet of water over the low water mark once the tide's in. The only drawback that I can see, is trying to reverse those trailers into the sea. I doubt if a single one of our drivers is capable of doing it. I think we'll just have to drive the trucks straight into the water and leave it at that."

"They won't be much use for anything if we do," Bergman objected. "But, as you say, there seems no alternative. If we intend to make the scheme work, the trailers will *have* to be towed into position." He paused for a moment while he considered his decision. "I don't think Heye would approve," he said finally; "we had a lot of trouble getting those transporters in the first place. But if the attack is successful I doubt if anyone will count the cost. We'll try it."

The luminous hand of Bergman's wristwatch registered precisely one minute after midnight as the engine of the leading Mercedes low-loader triggered to life. Borsch trod hard on the throttle and acrid blue smoke belched from the exhausts as he warmed up the diesel units. One by one, down the length of the line, the other trucks were started by their drivers and the thunderous roar of their engines made the fir trees quiver as the blast of exhaust gases whipped the fine powdery sand into a swirling choking dust cloud.

Zetterling ran down the line to find Bergman. "No 7 won't start, sir. The rest are okay. Heinz is working on the engine."

Bergman glanced towards the sea. Heavy clouds had completely obscured the moon and the beach looked black and empty. A faint line of whispering white surf indicated the edge of the incoming tide and he was suddenly assailed by doubts. Supposing Zetterling's scheme went wrong and the trucks bogged down in the wet sand? And what the hell would Heye say when he discovered that the Korvettenkapitän intended to write off the transporter trucks which the Navy had wangled out of the Wehrmacht with such difficulty. Only one thing could retrieve the situation—success. And paradoxically success could not be achieved without the sacrifice of the trucks.

He turned to Giessels. "I'll send the transporters down to the water one at a time. Use your torch to guide them into position. I don't care how far you take them out but we *must* have sufficient depth of water for launching when the tide comes in. Do the men know what they have to do?"

"Yes, sir. Once we get the trailers into the sea they are to release the securing chains so that the *Negers* are only resting on their cradles. They will then rendezvous back here and Petty Officer Krantze will form a convoy of the remaining vehicles and head for Antwerp."

"How are they getting on with No. 7 transporter, Oberleutnant?"

"Not very well, sir," Zetterling admitted. "That *schwanz* Heinz has cocked up the ignition system. Zeidel says he can't fix it without a spare, and we don't have the correct replacement."

"To hell with the transporter! What we've got to worry about is the torpedo. The enemy is likely to be here within twenty-four hours and we don't want to give them our latest secret weapon on a plate! Can you fix demolition charges?"

"Yes, sir. Do you want a time-fuse?"

"Yes, set it for ten minutes after high water. Any sort of explosion is bound to attract the attention of enemy air patrols and I want to make sure the *Negers* are well clear before they start nosing around."

Zetterling saluted and hurried back to the command truck to prepare a suitable explosive charge. Giessels pulled on a pair of rubber thigh-boots and made his way down the beach. Bergman watched him wading into the black sea. The shaded torch moved in a circle and then flashed twice. He nodded to the driver perched behind the wheel in the high cab just behind his shoulder.

"Transporter One . . . away!"

Borsch grinned, rammed the gear shift into low, and eased the clutch pedal back slowly. The weight of the transporter and its trailer had already sunk the wheels into the sand but he inched it forward carefully and started across the empty beach towards the surf that marked the water's edge.

Giessels guided the vehicle into the sea until its front wheels were axle deep in the water and Borsch killed the engine in obedience to the Oberbootsmann's upraised hand. The Mercedes looked like some forlorn sea-monster stranded at the water's edge as it came to a stop; its headlights flickered and died. The launching crew clambered out of the cab, splashed knee-deep through the water, and hauled themselves on to the trailer to unfasten the securing chains. It was difficult work in the darkness and the rising level of the incoming tide was no help.

No. 2 transporter and its trailer trundled down the beach, swung to the left of the tyre tracks left by its predecessor, and was docked in place alongside No. 1 as the driver followed the steering directions of Giessels' shaded torch. Moments later the third truck loomed through the darkness and sent up an arch of spray as it plunged into the water to join its two companions.

Bergman had just begun congratulating himself

on achieving the impossible when the last of the transporters ground to a slithering halt in a whirl of wet sand as its wheels gouged deep into a patch of soft shingle. Unnerved by the set-back, and lacking the experience to extricate the heavy vehicle from its self-made grave, the driver tried to obtain traction by opening the throttle. It was a fatal manoeuvre. The truck lurched, tilted drunkenly to one side, and buried its wildly spinning wheels into the sand like a frightened crab digging in for safety.

"She'll have to be abandoned," Bergman told Giessels breathlessly as they ran across the beach to investigate. "It means we'll be down to only five units when we attack, but there's no alternative." He glanced around at the Oberleutnant who had joined them. "Fix a demolition charge on this bastard as well, Zetterling. She'll have to be blown up and abandoned."

"I agree we'll have to leave her where she is, sir. But we can't blow her up. We only had one time-clock in the store's truck and there's not enough wire to link her back to the other unit we abandoned in the woods."

Bergman glanced seawards at the five marooned transporters. The sea was already lapping over the upper parts of their wings and the retaining chains were trailing loose.

"What depth of water do you reckon we'll have at high tide?" he asked Giessels.

The ex-yachtman looked towards the slowly encroaching line of surf and mentally measured the distance to the high-water mark. "Difficult to say, sir. If this wind keeps up, we might have six feet if we're lucky. We must be at least two hundred yards up the beach from the others and it doesn't slope very much."

Six feet. It wasn't much—but it *might* just be sufficient to float the *Neger* clear of the trailer. And if it wasn't the midget submarine would have to be destroyed whether Zetterling had a time-clock or not. Bergman did not find the alternative attractive. Without a demolition charge there was only one way in which the *Neger* could be blown up. Someone would have to remove the whisker of the safety fan in the nose of the "live" torpedo, so that the detonator could be slid back into the explosives-filled warhead. Then the striker pin of the detonator must be struck with a hammer. And one thing was certain. *Whoever triggered the warhead to destroy the submarine would blow himself up at the same time!*

Bergman forced his thoughts back to the operation itself and glanced down at his watch. It was just under sixty minutes to zero. And ignoring the additional hazard of the stranded *Neger*, he knew that Flotilla 271 was about to embark on a suicide mission. Not one of the pilots had the remotest chance of getting back. Even if they survived the attack itself, their hopes of survival in hostile waters when the *Neger's* power supply was exhausted, were minimal.

It was at moments like this that Bergman remembered Rahel Yousoff and the sacrifice she had made to save him. The Korvettenkapitan counted his own life for little and relied only on his animal instinct for survival to bring him through. But with the memories of Rahel still etched vividly in his mind, he could not bring himself to send her brother to his death as well; even though it was probably a cleaner fate than the one Zetterling would suffer if Görst got hold of him. Bergman nodded towards the stranded *Neger*.

"*No. 8*—that's your boat isn't it, Giessels?"

The Oberbootsmann agreed unenthusiastically. Like the Korvettenkapitan he had worked out what would have to be done if the midget submarine did not float clear at high tide.

"You are to take over Zetterling's boat—*No. 2*," Bergman ordered. He turned to the young Oberleutnant. "I want you to take command of the vehicle convoy. Make for Antwerp but if things get rough, drive inland and head towards Germany. Tell Admiral Heye what was happened and follow his orders."

"But what about you?"

Bergman smiled grimly. "I'm going to take over *No. 2*. And if she won't float clear I will carry out her destruction myself."

Zetterling knew what he meant. He saluted impassively, turned on his heels, and trudged slowly up the slope of the beach to the waiting convoy . . .

CHAPTER FIVE

As the first pink fingers of dawn clawed from behind the dark rim of the eastern horizon, Bergman checked his watch. Only three more minutes remained to the crucial moment when Flotilla 271 launched off.

Under present conditions the practical value of these small battle units has still to be proved.

Admiral Heye had allowed Bergman to see a transcript of Hitler's top-secret conference with Doenitz on 29 June shortly before Flotilla 271 had left on its mission and he smiled bitterly at the Grossadmiral's customary caution. In a few more hours everyone would know whether the *Negers*—the small battle units to which Doenitz was referring—were of practical value or not. And if they weren't the men of Flotilla 271 would not survive to report their failure.

The giant Mercedes transporters were now completely submerged and the perspex hoods covering the *Neger*'s cockpits glinted red in the watery light of the early morning sun like staring bloodshot eyes piercing the grey gloom. So far as Bergman could judge, his calculations had been correct. There was ample depth of water for the flotilla to float clear at zero hour and he drew a certain consolation from the knowledge that at least the first part of his plan was working.

A flurry of white bubbles suddenly erupted from the stern of *Neger No. 5* and he saw the plexiglass canopy lurch forward as the weapon started to move. One by one the others followed and within a few minutes Giessels was steering *No. 2* to the head of the column ready to lead them steadily out of the narrow bay at a stately five knots.

The minute hand of Bergman's watch indicated the estimated time of high-water and the Korvettenkapitan peered anxiously over his shoulder at the shore line for the tell-tale signs of stranded seaweed or pieces of flotsam to show that the tide was beginning to ebb. It was difficult to judge the depth of water under the *Neger*'s keel but Bergman estimated that he needed a further rise of six inches to obtain a safe operational depth. Settling calmly inside the domed cockpit he surveyed the scene with the practised eye of an experienced seaman.

The thin mist of spray scattering from the wavelets as the wind whipped briskly across the bay, had begun to move to the east. Only slightly perhaps—and few people would have noticed the subtle change in direction—but it was sufficient to alert Bergman to the danger signal. Until the final moments before dawn the wind had been blowing directly towards the land and although he estimated its strength at little more than a Force 4 moderate breeze the impetus of the gusting 15 knot pressure had tended to pile more water into the bay, raising the level of the tide by three or more inches.

But as the depression moved up-Channel the wind direction was changing, and once the tide began to ebb the water level would drop quickly. If Bergman had read the danger signals correctly he dare not defer the moment of launching any longer. Behind him, and out of sight, the curved blades of the contra-rotating propellers should be just below the surface. It was impossible to know whether they were or not—it was a gamble that had to be taken. As he turned to check the shore line again he glimpsed the short-handled sledge-hammer cradled alongside his seat. It was an ominous reminder of what his fate would be if the launching attempt failed. He looked away sharply. It was something he preferred not to think about. Yet, subconsciously, he knew he would carry out the destruction of the *Neger* if all else failed.

The electric motor of the power unit responded instantly to Bergman's touch on the start-button and the warning needle of the ammeter jerked into the discharge quadrant to reflect the current being sucked from the batteries. Reaching down with his right hand he groped for the sliding control level of the main rheostat and pushed it forward.

The bronze tips of the half-submerged propellers tore the sea to white froth. But the lower blades bit into the water and the *Neger* lurched awkwardly like a grey seal rolling over rocks towards the sea. Bergman pulled the rheostat back as gently as a motorist easing his foot on the throttle when the wheels of a car spin in snow, and the midget submarine moved forward a few inches.

An ominous jolt followed by a screech of grinding metal rang the alarm bells in Bergman's brain and the sudden shock sent the adrenaline pumping into his bloodstream. What in hell's name was *that*? Peering through the plexiglass screen he realised that the surge of the ebbing tide had swung the axis of the *Neger* across the trailer and, although hidden out of sight beneath the surface, he guessed that the bows had tangled with the raised tailgate of the submerged transporter.

The discovery did nothing to decrease his alarm. Once the safety device had wound back up its spindle to prime the detonator the ultra-sensitive striking pin would be "live". And in that critical state the slightest touch would be sufficient to trigger the warhead.

Bergman could feel the sweat running down his face as he moved the tiller to starboard in an effort to steer clear of the obstruction. The weapon bounced against the tail-gate again and, in blind desperation, he moved the rheostat control to maximum power. He knew that each time the *Neger* lurched forward, the spinner of the safety device inched a fraction further up its spindle. It was impossible to judge how far it had progressed but every second of delay only served to increase the danger of the firing-pin being activated. And as Bergman wrestled with the controls he knew he was buying time with borrowed money . . .

The sudden surge of power thrust the *Neger* forward and the weapon tilted wildly to starboard as it grazed the raised tailgate. Then as Bergman's heart stopped beating, it ran clear of the obstruction, swung on to an even keel, and hummed purposefully in pursuit of its flotilla mates.

It was Bergman's first experience of piloting a one-man torpedo and he found it unexpectedly simple. It was like riding the back of a speeding dolphin and, forgetting the grim realities of the task that lay ahead, he abandoned himself to the exhilaration of driving his sleek grey steed through the waves.

A glance at the needle of the ammeter was sufficient to break the spell. The dial was showing a 20-amp discharge and, anxiously conserving his power reserves, he eased the rheostat control back into the cruising position. The *Neger* had already made up half the distance separating it from the rest of the Flotilla 271 and Bergman deliberately steered for the shoaling water inshore, in an effort to cut the corner and catch up without wasting too much precious battery capacity.

Giessels glimpsed the straggler as the Korvettenkapitan rounded the headland flanking the western edge of the bay, and he signalled the rest of the group to slow down so that Bergman could take up his rightful position in the van. It was not just a matter of etiquette or precedence—Giessels cared little for either—but the former U-boat commander was the only pilot in the flotilla capable of navigation, and his knowledge was essential to lead them the twenty miles or so to the Allied beachhead. The Oberbootsmann tucked his *Neger* neatly behind Bergman's tail and the remaining boats formed up in line-astern formation as the Korvettenkapitan swung on to a southwesterly course.

*Marine-Einsatz-Kommando** 271 was ready to demonstrate to Admiral Doenitz that, despite his cautious misgivings, the small battle units had a real practical value . . .

Leading Seaman Harris left his position on the No. 2 Oerlikon, climbed down to the deck on the port side,

---

* *Marine-Einsatz-Kommando*=Special Naval Commando. The official Kriegsmarine title of the midget submarine units.

leaned over the rails and spat carefully into the sea to leeward. So far as Albert Harris was concerned, the Invasion was one bloody great bore. And as he never tired of telling his companions in *HMS Dublin*'s midship's AA battery, D-day had been a picnic by comparison with the raid on Dieppe.

Dublin rolled gently in rhythm with the on-shore swell. And, as the tide of battle moved further inland, the inevitable reaction was setting in, as the threat of a counter-attack against the invasion armada, gradually receded. The destroyer formed part of the outer anti-aircraft support screen, but as the Luftwaffe was conspicuous by its absence from the Normandy skies, Commander Malcolm had allowed the gun crews to stand down from Action Stations for a quick breather. *Dublin* herself remained on the alert, with her main armament crews closed up and the watchful circling of the air-warning radar scanner ensuring an immediate alarm at the first smell of an enemy aircraft.

Leading Seaman Harris pulled the stub of a half-smoked cigarette from behind his ear and lit it. Astern, the beaches were busy with military vehicles and tanks, and even at that distance from the shore, the stentorian tones of the Beach Landing Officer were still faintly audible. To starboard, the vast armada of landing craft, infantry support ships, attack transports, and naval escorts looked like the Solent during Cowes regatta. And overhead, the squatly obscene barrage balloons glinted silver in the morning sun, while an impeccable formation of RAF fighters roared comfortingly backwards and forwards at an altitude of ten thousand feet.

Taking another pull at his dog-end Harris shrugged at the memory of the Dieppe raid. He was one of the lucky ones—he'd got out alive.

A sudden gleam on the surface of the sea some eight hundred yards out on the port quarter caught his eye. It vanished almost immediately only to reappear again as it emerged from the trough and crested the next wave. It looked very smooth and round and it reminded Harris of a turtle he had once seen swimming off the Galapagos Islands on the North American Station in 1937. But what the hell was a turtle doing in the Channel? He screwed up his eyes and peered at the round translucent object again—must be some sort of a jellyfish, he decided.

"You ain't supposed to be loafin' about on deck, Harris!"

Despite the Chief Gunners Mate's rasping reprimand, Harris kept his eyes on the strange object which had now turned and was running parallel with *Dublin*'s course. There was something odd about that bloody jellyfish but he couldn't put his finger on it.

"Control Officer told us we could stand easy for a few minutes, Chief. I thought I'd just have a quick butt," he explained without turning his head.

"What the hell are you staring at?" the Petty Officer demanded curiously. It was obvious that Harris couldn't take his eyes off the thing he was watching.

"Over there . . ." he pointed his finger. "Some sort of giant jellyfish. Never seen nothing like it before."

Jenkins followed the direction of Harris's finger. "Jellyfish, my arse! Have you ever seen a jellyfish moving against the wind?" The significance of what he had said suddenly struck him. "You get back to your gun, my lad. I'm going to report this to the bridge. Come on—look lively!"

Commander Malcolm's binoculars focused carefully on the object. The Chief was right—it was certainly no jellyfish. But what the hell *was* it? For a moment he thought it might be a drifting mine, but as he reminded himself quickly, floating mines don't move against the current either.

"There's a couple more, sir! Six hundred yards off the port bow and moving south-west. And another about one hundred yards behind."

Dublin's skipper found the other mysterious objects which Lieutenant Burgess had spotted. He lowered his binoculars.

"I think we'd better get a report off to Captain (D), Mr. Burgess. There's something about those things I don't like the look of. Resume Action Stations. And tell the depth-charge party to stand by as well."

"Signal from Flotilla, sir."

Commander Malcolm took the flimsy from his Yeoman Signaller and scanned the contents. He handed it to the First Lieutenant without comment and moved to the compass platform.

"Full ahead both! Steer zero-four-zero, Cox'n—hold the bows directly on to those things once you've made visual contact. No point in giving 'em an easy target."

"Course zero-four-zero, sir. Steering on local control."

Lieutenant Burgess passed the signal slip back to the Commander. "Do you think they're the one-man torpedoes Flotilla's talking about, sir?"

"Who knows," Malcolm shrugged. "Davidson has obviously reported a midget submarine attack on his landing-craft—and I can remember Jerry using human torpedoes during the Anzio landings. I suppose he was bound to try out something similar in Normandy."

"Do you want them tracked and reported to Flotilla, sir?"

Commander Malcolm clung to the bridge supports as *Dublin* heeled sharply in response to the helm. He ducked to escape a wall of spray spuming back from the destroyer's bows and he grinned with the enjoyment of the chase as he raised his head and shook the water from his cap.

"Not bloody likely! If they're what I think they are they won't be able to dive out of our way, Mr. Burgess, so to hell with the Asdic. And why use radar when we can see the things with our own eyes. I propose to attack with Oerlikons and machine guns—they'll be too slow to get away. And a depth-charge pattern at minimum setting will give the buggers a shaking-up they won't forget in a hurry." He grinned at the thought and leaned over the voice-pipe to the main director control perched high above the bridge. "Captain to Guns—put your lads on independent firing. I want you to select their targets so we get a good spread but let the layers fire over open sights. Even your buggers shouldn't miss at this range." The skipper was a torpedo man and he found it difficult to resist a gibe at the gunnery experts. He jammed the plug back into the voice-pipe and turned to his Doggie. (The midshipman attached to the Captain to act as his runner and general dogsbody is known as his "Doggie".) "Mr. James—get down to the quarter-deck and tell Carter to set the ash-cans for six feet with a 60 second time-delay. And tell him I'll give the firing command."

Midshipman James had only left the Naval College at Dartmouth six weeks previously and this was his first taste of action. He saluted and hurried away importantly to deliver the Skipper's orders to Chief Petty Officer Carter. The Chief, a veteran of twenty battles ranging from the North Cape to the Eastern

Mediterranean, gave a curt "aye, aye, sir" as James passed over the Captain's instructions. He didn't want to hurt the kid's feelings or to demonstrate that the ship could function quite adequately without her officers. But he had already preempted Commander Malcolm's orders a full two minutes earlier when he had first realised the nature of the impending attack. Turning away, he sucked his teeth soulfully, and watched the perspex domes coming closer.

Despite his anticipation of the skipper's orders, he was not sorry to have confirmation of his actions. If *Dublin* stopped a torpedo the shallow depth-settings on the depth-charges would mean the instant death of everyone who was in the sea when she went down. And it was a relief to pass *that* sort of responsibility on to someone else's shoulders . . .

Bergman throttled back as he saw the destroyer build up speed and turn towards the three *Negers* moving ahead of his bows. A strand of floating seaweed had snagged his propeller two miles back and the subsequent loss of power had allowed the rest of Flotilla 271 to move ahead of their leader. Not that it mattered now. He'd brought them safely to the beach-head and that had been his primary task. From then on it would be each man for himself.

He felt uncomfortably vulnerable sitting in his goldfish bowl cockpit and, as a veteran submariner, he cursed his inability to dive out of trouble. It seemed all wrong to be running exposed on the surface in broad daylight—almost suicidal, in fact. He could still remember the time when his famous *UB-44* had carried out surface attacks on the Atlantic convoys. But that had always been under cover of darkness. And those were the happy days before the enemy had perfected his radar techniques.

With its bow-wave flaring white as the stem cut through the water, the destroyer bearing down on the nearest *Neger* was obviously intent on ramming, and Bergman saw the pilot weaving and jinking his fragile craft in a vain effort to escape. Suddenly every available gun opened fire and the sea seethed and bubbled like a cauldron, as medium calibre shells, Bofors cannon-shells, and machine gun bullets ripped the surface around the three hapless human torpedoes.

The first *Neger* rolled violently as *Dublin*'s sharp steel bows sliced it in half and the two sections bounced wildly down the side of the destroyer, before vanishing into the foaming wash of the propellers astern. The second *Neger* leapt forward eagerly as its pilot released his electric torpedo but, in the wild panic of the moment, he had allowed no time for considered aim and the weapon careered harmlessly past its intended victim by a clear hundred yards.

Not that Mueller had time to reflect on the failure of his attack. A heavy shell burst less than twenty feet in front of the *Neger* and the shock of the explosion made it rear into the air like a startled horse. A line of Oerlikon shells ripped down the side of its exposed beam tearing fist-sized holes in the thin tin-can skin. Mueller's craft fell back, lurched in agony like a wounded whale, and then rolled over to disappear within seconds.

Giessels made a valiant attempt to run for it. He was farthest away from the avenging destroyer when the counter-attack started and his *Neger* leaned under full helm as he tried to steer himself out of trouble. A stream of tracer shells from Harris's midship's Oerlikon followed in his wake but the ex-yacht skipper was an old hand at ship handling and, manoeuvring violently like a cornered eel, he dodged the exploding shells time and time again.

Watching from his vantage point well astern of the battle Bergman suddenly realised that something was wrong. The nose section of Giessel's machine was gradually rising upwards while the tail was sliding slowly beneath the surface. A splinter of steel from a near miss had punctured the buoyancy chamber of the carrier-unit and the *Neger* was imperceptibly sinking. He stared in fascinated horror as Giessels clawed frantically at the smooth plexiglass canopy but the release catches had apparently jammed. He had ripped the breathing-mask from his face and his mouth was open as he screamed in terror. Then, without warning, the torpedo slipped sternfirst into the depths and the transparent bubble disappeared beneath the surface.

Bergman's hands gripped the controls a shade tighter as he tried not to think. But he knew that Giessels had still been alive when the *Neger* went down. And that meant a slow death from suffocation trapped inside the cramped cockpit. He could remember seeing an air gunner die in similar circumstances earlier in the war when *UB-44* had shot down a Sunderland flying-boat.* And the gruesome memory of the bloated corpses floating face-down in the flooded compartments of the ill-fated *UM-59* was still fresh in his mind. Poor bastard—what a way to die!

His ever-present instinct for survival jerked Bergman out of his morbid reverie. And having checked that he was in no immediate danger he sat back in his seat to watch the destroyer slow down to circle in search of survivors and wreckage. Even a

* See *Action Atlantic!*

damaged *Neger* would be a valuable prize for the Royal Navy's submarine experts and they would certainly lose no time in probing the secrets of Hitler's latest weapon. It had been the same throughout the war. German scientists produced the weapon, fate placed one into the hands of the enemy, and within a few short weeks the Royal Navy found an antidote. There was the magnetic mine which a clumsy Luftwaffe pilot had dropped over a line of Essex mudflats—and the acoustic torpedo.

Holding his course downwind he steered for the troughs and kept his low-lying craft hidden from sight behind the wave crests. After five minutes running he reduced power and allowed the *Neger* to roll up on the swell for a quick glimpse of the opposition. He breathed a sigh of relief, opened up to three-quarter power, and steered south-west for the beaches.

Dublin was lying almost stopped, moving only sufficiently to maintain seaway, and she had been joined by two flotilla mates who were slowly circling like hounds guarding a wounded fox while they waited the arrival of the huntsman. A cutter and a jolly-boat had been lowered away by the destroyer, and the two small boats quartered backwards and forwards looking for tell-tale signs of their victims. Bergman left them at it. Their chances of finding anything important was too remote to worry about . . .

Fifteen minutes later, having successfully pierced the inner defensive screen of motor launches and gunboats, the Korvettenkapitan found himself facing an embarrassment of potential targets, as landing-craft and assault boats streamed towards the beaches from the heavy transports and tank-landing-ships lying further out at their deep water anchorages. But Bergman was not interested in minnows. Doenitz wanted proof that the small battle units had a practical value. And that meant he had to find something really worthwhile!

He had seen a rough chart of the invasion beaches in Kommodore Hoyt's office the evening Flotilla 271 had set out on its long journey into Northern France, and Bergman decided to fix his position before searching out a likely target. The battery capacity of his G-7(e) motor unit was rapidly running out and he reasoned that a carefully planned course was more likely to yield success than a haphazard goose-chase amongst the scattered units of the Allied armada. Despite the risk of being spotted he turned the *Neger* inshore in search of a distinctive landmark.

Bergman knew that he was now the last survivor of Flotilla 271 but the fact did not unduly worry him. He had seen Giessels and his two companions destroyed and the others had long since disappeared. Freed from the responsibilities of shepherding the group, and operating as an independent unit, he felt as though he had been given a new lease of life. And ducking between two empty landing-craft returning to their supply ship for fresh stores, he steered the *Neger* straight for the shore.

The beach sloped gently up from the sea. The burned out hulks of wrecked tanks, and armoured vehicles half-buried in the sand, showed that the initial assault had not achieved its success without cost. Turning eastwards Bergman followed the meandering shore line from a position about 1,000 yards to seawards. It was hard to see through the plexiglass canopy and the odd wave slapping spray over the dome, sometimes blotted out visibility completely. But it was no worse than observing a convoy through the periscope of a U-boat on a rough night, and Bergman took the difficulties in his stride.

The shattered batteries of Hitler's vaunted Atlantic Wall behind Arromanches, warned him that he was further west than intended—in the landing area code-named *Gold* by the Allied planners. If Intelligence reports could be relied on, Bergman knew he had cruisers about two miles to the north, or, pushing eastwards, a mixture of battleships, monitors, and cruisers working up and down the right flank in the role of a bombardment group. Bearing in mind his fading battery the Korvettenkapitan decided to keep moving east.

He passed through the *Juno* and *Sword* beach-heads without trouble and as the estuary of the River Orne came into view to starboard he knew he was safely clear of the main traffic. At Merville he turned due North and once again headed out towards the blue rimmed horizon. The sea was beginning to get choppy and short waves banged against the fragile skin of the torpedo with the booming clang of Thor's hammers in the forges of Valhalla. But, in compensation, the clouds were swiftly building up over the French coast, minimising the tell-tale flash of reflected sun on the plexiglass dome.

Bergman felt slightly drowsy despite the tense excitement of the search. The air inside his cramped cockpit was getting stale and he reached down for the oxygen mask. The pure fresh air in his lungs again cleared the mists of lethargy from his brain, and his natural sharpness returned.

Battleships were out. And so were cruisers. Bergman knew that he stood no chance of sinking one of those battlewagons with a single torpedo. And he *had* to obtain a positive sinking. Damaging an enemy warship might be a tactical victory. But damaged ships didn't have enough propaganda value and the High Command would be satisfied with nothing less than complete destruction. This meant he would have to go after a destroyer or a frigate. And to launch an attack on a ship specifically trained and equipped for anti-submarine warfare, only served to increase the impossible risk he was taking.

As the last surviving *Neger* throbbed northwards in its avenging search for a victim, Bergman had time to reflect on the irony of the situation. His rightful place was behind the periscope of an ocean-going U-boat. Yet, here he was, riding on top of a torpedo, like a stuntman in a marine circus. His egotism would not allow him to fail in his self-imposed task—yet the success he sought would only serve to justify Hitler's faith in his bizarre secret weapons and prove that Doenitz had been wrong in his conclusions.

A wisp of smoke and the needled mast of a ship shimmered on the horizon. Moving the helm one point to starboard, he steered towards his quarry.

For the last four years Bergman had thought continually of the ultimate overthrow of the Fuehrer and his monstrous Nazi regime. Not that his personal efforts had amounted to anything in practice, it was merely a wishful dream, and after Rahel's arrest, his one tenuous link with an organised resistance group had disappeared. He was completely alone in his fight—as alone and independent as he was in his little *Neger*. And what could one solitary naval officer do to overthrow a regime that had conquered over half Europe?

The target he had selected for his attack was now well in view. Bergman shut off the motors so that the *Neger* drifted gently in the choppy sea while he sur-

110

veyed his intended victim. Luck was with him in one respect. A pair of Luftwaffe fighters were circling the horizon, and the destroyer's attention was concentrated on the threat of an impending air attack.

If only he could dive out of sight and make a submerged approach. Bergman's U-boat experience found him unprepared for a surface attack and he weighed the situation carefully before committing himself to any particular course of action.

As a U-boat skipper, with fifty fully-trained men at his command and two dozen torpedoes nestling ready in the tubes, he had controlled sufficient power to tackle the largest battleship in the world and emerge victorious. But now, alone and unsupported in his *Neger* with only a single torpedo in his armoury, he had to content himself with the lesser prize. Yet, even at this late stage of the war, the loss of a destroyer would still damage the enemy's cause and his success would encourage other "small battle units" to find larger and more important targets.

The destroyer was now only two thousand yards away and Bergman had to concentrate on the immediate task. His heartbeat was firm and slow and his hands rock-steady on the controls. And as he prepared to go into action his mask of humanity fell away to expose the professional killer beneath. Any illusions he may have had about himself had long been discarded. His duty was to kill and destroy. And he was ready to carry out that duty no matter what the cost.

Moving the rheostat control forward Bergman pushed the *Neger* to maximum speed to match the motion of the wave-crests. Then, holding a careful course that followed the swirl of the tide, he did his utmost to meld into his grey-green surroundings. The sun was now completely covered by heavy cloud and the dark grey sky dulled the sheen of the plexiglass canopy to the same shade as the sea itself. The electric motors of the G-7(e) power-unit unlike a conventional torpedo left no trail of exhaust bubbles and with no telltale track to expose his approach, Bergman moved to the attack as silently and unobtrusively as a submerged U-boat.

Whether the Luftwaffe pilots had spotted him or whether it was sheer coincidence Bergman did not know. But at the precise moment he reached his maximum firing range the two Focke-Wulf 190s peeled off and roared down on the destroyer with machine guns and cannons blazing. The enemy ship erupted in darting dragon's tongues of yellow flames as she replied with every weapon she possessed. Vivid tracers ripped the sky, Bofors light AA guns pumped a hail of shells at the screaming fighters, and the 4.5 inch dual-purpose turrets of the main armament belched and recoiled with ear-splitting rapidity.

The two Focke-Wulfs stood on their tails as they clawed for height to escape the holocaust of hot steel, but the guns followed them relentlessly. The enemy commander seemed confident that the fighters were carrying no bombs and he held a steady course to give his gunners a chance. The aircraft peeled right and left to confuse the enemy but the destroyer divided her fire with cool efficiency and chased the aircraft into cloud cover.

The sighting arrangements on the *Neger* were as primitive as the basic concept of the weapon itself. A notched "V" in the front section of the cockpit canopy served as a backsight, while a steel rod standing vertically from the nose of the torpedo acted as the foreaiming mark. For a man accustomed to the sophistication of a modern telescope attack grid, the whole contraption seemed unbelievably crude. But Bergman luckily was a keen shot and during rare spells of home leave, spent hours hunting game in the Grunnenburg mountains that formed the spectacular backdrop of his step-father's Bavarian *schloss.*

There had been no time for elaborate sighting with a shotgun. Aiming was instinctive and experience counted for everything. The gun came to the shoulder in a reflex action as the birds winged into view from behind a clump of trees, the eye squinted down the length of the Purdey barrels following the sweeping flight of the target, then a right and a left and the two birds tumbled from the sky, while the sharp report of the cartridges still echoed around the pine clad valley. The torpedo action must be the same.

One of the FW-190s broke cloud cover astern of the destroyer and swept the length of the deck with cannon fire. It banked left as it climbed away and the ship turned on opposite helm to bring the full weight of its broadside to bear on the departing fighter.

The timing of the attack could not have been bettered even if they'd rehearsed it for weeks, and Bergman offered a silent prayer of thanks to the Luftwaffe pilot as he watched the destroyer move across the centre of his rudimentary sights. He estimated its speed at 30 knots and almost instinctively he aimed ahead to allow for deflection. Reaching down he pulled the trigger, and with a gentle lurch, the G-7(e) slung beneath the *Neger's* rounded belly, fired to life and shot away.

The look-outs on the bridge were too engrossed in their struggle with the fighter aircraft, to notice the almost invisible track of the torpedo streaking towards them. Bergman didn't hang around to find out if he'd scored a hit. Swinging the *Neger* into a tight turn he steered eastward and hunched himself forward in the cockpit as if he could thus diminish the target area, if the destroyer spotted him and opened fire. He was barely three hundred yards away when the torpedo exploded directly beneath the enemy's bridge. The shock wave of the concussion rolled the *Neger* on to her beam ends. There was nothing Bergman could do to prevent his fragile craft from capsizing and he clung on grimly as the sea engulfed the cockpit canopy. But as the first shock-wave passed beyond the *Neger*, the machine came back on an even keel like a weighted cork. Unaffected by the battering force of the blast, the motors were still humming sweetly, and he glanced back at his victim.

The speed of the destroyer had sealed her fate. Thrusting through the water at 30 knots the sea had burst into the gaping hole below her waterline, tearing the thin steel plating back like a sardine can. She listed sharply to starboard and dipped her bows into the sea as she slowed. A tremendous internal explosion followed almost immediately as the cold salt water entered her high-pressure boilers; while scalding steam roared out through the fractured hull plates, Bergman could see the crew still struggling to launch the Carley floats, as she sank beneath their feet with a soft hiss of quenched hot steel.

The Korvettenkapitan's initial reaction was one of intense satisfaction at the completeness of his victory. This time the honour of the kill was his alone—there was no crew to demand their share of the credit. But the heady elation passed as quickly as it had begun and Bergman experienced a sudden sense of pity for the men now struggling in the black oil sludge which marked the grave of his victim.

114

It was a reaction he experienced every time he sank a ship. In the white heat of battle, he had no time to consider the consequences of his actions. He was a killing machine—a predator of the deep with no other thought in his mind but the destruction of his prey. He had to destroy his opponent before he himself was destroyed. It was the law of the jungle, kill or be killed, and he had learned well. But when the adrenaline of battle faded and every reserve of energy had been drained, he always suffered the same bitter pangs of regret for what he had done. For a man who had killed over a thousand innocent sailors in the course of his combat career it was a ludicrous, almost grotesque, reaction. Yet no matter how hard he steeled himself, Bergman could never escape the overwhelming sense of guilt that followed. He wondered whether there would ever come a moment in his life when he could kill and not suffer this bitter remorse.

He steered away from the scene knowing there was nothing he could do to help his struggling victims. In many ways they were lucky. The enemy had complete control of the Channel and rescue ships would be steaming into the area within minutes. When the time came for him to join them in the cold grey sea, his own chances of survival were minimal. Unless there was a miracle. And Bergman did not believe in such things.

According to his calculations, the *Neger*'s batteries ought to have been exhausted more than twenty minutes previously, and he knew he was living on borrowed time. But grasping at the chance he thrust the lever to maximum power and steered across the gaping mouth of the Seine in an effort to reach the

Flanders' coast and the protection of the Kriegsmarine.

A sudden roar made him look up. One of the FW-109 fighters came swooping across the wave tops at less than fifty feet and, as it passed ahead of the *Neger*, the pilot waggled his wings. Bergman waited while it climbed and circled and as it returned for a second run, he threw back the canopy and waved his arms.

Although he knew the odds were still weighted heavily against his survival the miracle *had* happened. The fighter pilot's report of the *Neger*'s estimated position and course would be passed on by teleprinter by the Luftwaffe ground control staff at St Pol, to the nearest naval base. And within minutes an E-boat would be speeding down the coast to pick him up. Or was he being too optimistic? Fighter pilots were notoriously bad navigators and the reported position might be miles adrift. And if the Luftwaffe ground controller was busy, any air traffic relating to purely naval matters would be given very low priority. And if it came to that, why the hell should the local Kriegsmarine commander give a damn about the fate of Korvettenkapitan Bergman?

The vibrant hum of the motors faded away as the last dregs of current drained from the batteries. The tell-tale needles on the instrument panel flickered feebly and fell back to zero, useless without the life-blood of electric power. Bergman shrugged philosophically, reached forward, and switched off the dead engine.

The *Neger* was drifting aimlessly before the rising wind, and the gathering storm clouds formed an ominous backdrop to the fiery funeral of the dying sun. In the soft blush of twilight the silence was broken

116

only by the slap of the waves against the rounded sides of the torpedo body. Bergman pushed up the cockpit canopy and surveyed the scene as the light gradually faded. So far as he could estimate, he was east of Cherbourg and well beyond the Seine estuary. With luck he had reached German controlled waters. But he was too far to seaward to be sighted by shore observers and the darkening horizon was unpromisingly empty. Lightning flickered in the eastern sky and he shivered. If a storm developed, his cockleshell craft stood no chance at all.

Like his machine the Korvettenkapitan was spent, exhausted and finished. There was nothing left now but to wait . . .

CHAPTER SIX

The strain of war had etched deep furrows in the Grossadmiral's face. His gaunt flesh had the appearance of grey parchment and the keen blue eyes were sunk deep in hollowed sockets, dark with exhaustion. The battle for control of the trade routes was going badly. And after the appalling losses of May when 42 U-boats had failed to return to their bases, Doenitz had been forced to withdraw the bulk of his forces from the Atlantic. The initiative had passed from the U-boat flotillas to the Western Allies, and for the present, all hope of victory had vanished.

Perhaps when the new super U-boats—with their *schnorkels*, streamlined hulls, and hydrogen-peroxide engines—were ready for service, Germany could once more challenge her traditional enemies for command of the seas. These new boats, capable of underwater speeds of up to 20 knots, would run circles around the Royal Navy's convoy escorts and support groups. And by their ability to recharge their batteries without surfacing they would be immune from the ubiquitous eyes of the radar scanners, and the continual threat of aircraft attack. But such dreams lay in the future. And on 22 August 1944 Doenitz could see little future left to Germany.

The stress of conducting the war at sea almost single-handed, was enough to exhaust any man. But Doenitz faced other problems as well. As a key figure in the Fuehrer's command structure, he was becoming increasingly embroiled in the day-to-day problems of the land war as well. His ships in the Baltic were already giving gun support to the German army, in its savage death struggle with the Red Army. And every day brought fresh involvement with the Generals. Hitler, too, was becoming to rely more and more on his strategic advice. And politics and military affairs were two things the Grossadmiral had spent his life avoiding.

There was a sharp knock on the door of his office and he smiled with genuine pleasure as he recognised his visitor. He stood up, brushed the papers on his desk to one side, and held out his hand.

"My dear Bergman—what a relief to see you. *Gruppe West* told me you'd got back safely. How the devil did you do it?"

The Korvettenkapitan looked almost as exhausted as his Commander-in-Chief. He shook hands with Doenitz and dropped thankfully into the armchair facing the big oak desk.

"For once in my life I have to thank the Luftwaffe," he admitted grudgingly. "One of their fighter boys spotted me in the water and radioed my position to base. Harstein managed to turn out an undamaged E-boat and they picked me up about an hour after my motors ran out of amps. There was a storm brewing. I was lucky."

The Grossadmiral liked Bergman. He could still remember the day, many years before the war, when he had first met him as an eager cadet at the Kiel Periscope School. The young man had impressed him—and Bergman had lived up to his early promise. There weren't many of the old pre-war officers left now. Prien was dead. And Schepke. Otto Kretschmer was behind the barbed wire of a POW camp in Canada and most of Bergman's contemporaries at Kiel—Ulm, Kirchen, Vargas and the others—were all dead. Gloriously killed in action in defence of the Third Reich perhaps. But dead all the same.

Bergman was almost the last of the breed and Doenitz could recall his chat with him when, as a junior Oberleutnant, he had returned from his first combat patrol. Since then he had followed his career with close attention—watching him waging war with relentless fury against the Atlantic convoys, until his tally of victims had outstripped every other U-boat captain; worrying about his mental breakdown after his famous *UB-44* had been sunk, helping him regain his health and old confidence, and witnessing his triumphant mission to the Far East from which he returned with a Japanese *kaiten*.* Not that Doenitz really approved of Bergman's piratical methods or his facility for disobeying orders. But he admired him as an honest man. And he respected the fact that his loyalty lay with Germany rather than the Fuehrer.

"I see you managed to sink a destroyer," he observed in a matter-of-fact tone. "What is your opinion of the small battle units? Are they viable?"

Bergman shook his head. "If you want my honest

* See *The Tokyo Torpedo*.

opinion, sir, they're bloody death traps. Not one man in my flotilla survived. I don't believe in fighting a war with suicide weapons even if the Fuehrer *does* consider his sailors to be expendable."

"You're being a little harsh, Korvettenkapitan," Doenitz chided him gently. "Bartel's kommando got back and there have been no disproportionately heavy losses in other units either."

"Perhaps—but did they achieve any sinkings?" Bergman retorted bitterly. "I grant you they're safe enough if you leave a margin to get back. But if you set out looking for *real* targets, their range allows no chance of a return ticket."

"I am inclined to agree with you," Doenitz nodded. "But," he smiled wryly, "I must still find adequate reasons for dissuading the Fuehrer. I'm afraid your success has only made him more enthusiastic."

Bergman was not interested in Hitler's mad ideas about the war at sea. He changed the subject abruptly. "With respect, Grossadmiral, I want another U-boat. Paddling along the coast in a tin-can canoe isn't my idea of submarine warfare. Surely there is at least one boat available."

"With your experience and seniority, Korvettenkapitan, you should be in command of a complete flotilla—not just a single U-boat. And in any case we are losing boats so fast at present that I can't risk an officer as valuable as yourself. I shall need men like you when the new Walter boats are brought into service. We can win the war with them."

Despite his anxiety to get to sea again Bergman could understand the Grossadmiral's reservations. And the thought of commanding one of the new super U-boats was certainly attractive.

"And in the meantime, sir?" he asked.

"In the meantime, Korvettenkapitan, you have been ordered to report to the Fuehrer at the *Wolfsschanze*."*
The Grossadmiral flurried through the papers on his desk and retrieved a small blue document file. "Here are your passes and credentials. A staff car will take you to the airfield. I will see you when you return."

Bergman took the bundle of official papers, glanced at them curiously, and slipped them into his breast pocket. "But why should the Fuehrer wish to see *me*?" he asked. "I'm completely out of touch with the current naval situation."

Doenitz shrugged. "Who can read the Fuehrer's mind?" he said enigmatically. "A great many things have happened recently—the situation is obscure."

Bergman realised the the Commander-in-Chief was referring to the July assassination plot, when Colonel Graf von Stauffenberg and a group of Army officers had detonated a time-bomb at Hitler's headquarters. By a miracle the Fuehrer had survived. And he had taken a swift and bloody vengeance on the conspirators. But the attack had shattered Hitler's confidence and things could never be quite the same again. Bergman stood up, put on his gold-peaked cap, and saluted.

The Grossadmiral's shrewd blue eyes searched his face for a brief moment as if seeking the answer to an unposed question. Then he returned the salute and smiled wearily. "Take care of yourself, Korvettenkapitan. I can't afford to lose any more of my top commanders. And you have my promise that I will find you a boat to command when you report back."

* *Wolfsschanze*=Wolf's lair. Hitler's field headquarters in East Prussia. He had a similar headquarters, the Eagle's Nest, in the west.

The flight to East Prussia was uneventful and Bergman had ample time to reflect on this latest turn of events as the Heinkel roared eastwards over the flat featureless fields of Pomerania and northern Poland. A Russian air raid forced the aircraft to divert to Sensburg but the Korvettenkapitan's impressive sheaf of official papers worked like a magic charm and within five minutes of his arrival at the airfield he was being driven to the railway station in a Wehrmacht staff car.

The platform was thronged with troops waiting to entrain for the Front. Bergman was appalled by the youth and rawness of the Army's latest recruits—few of whom appeared to be more than sixteen years old. An antediluvian engine wheezed asthmatically alongside, and to the shouted orders of the NCOs, the frightened recruits were herded into open trucks like cattle destined for the slaughter house. And it was an apt analogy Bergman thought grimly, as he watched.

Even his own *Krieglok* locomotive bore obvious scars of war. Withdrawn from the French railways a few months earlier its boiler was plated over in a dozen places where RAF ground-attack fighters had pumped cannon shell through the thin plating. And the tender, piled high with freshly cut wooden logs, was testimony to Germany's desperate fuel shortage. But the carriages were spotlessly clean and Bergman settled into a corner seat with a contented sigh. He was enjoying his rare experience of VIP treatment, but his personal comfort only served to increase his sympathy for those poor little bastards being transported to the battlefront from the other platform.

As the train rattled its way northwards, Bergman stared out of the window lost in his thoughts. Perhaps his invitation to the *Wolfsschanze* was an omen—a sign that the time to strike had finally come. His mind returned to the simile of the *Neger* and its possible target area, versus the great range of the U-boat. Perhaps he now had no need to content himself with a small fish after all. If, as seemed probable, he came face-to-face with the Fuehrer it would be a different matter.

He unconsciously fingered the butt of his Kriegsmarine-issue Mauser 32 automatic. And he remembered his promise to Rahel, that one day he would personally destroy the madman who was riding Germany to destruction. But it had always been no more than a wishful dream. How could a relatively unimportant U-boat captain, ever have an opportunity to kill the most powerful man the world had ever seen? And yet now, without any manipulation or intrigue on his part, the opportunity could be his for the taking.

The wheels of the train screeched noisily round the final curve, rattled over the junction points, and with the hiss of an angry iron dragon, the locomotive blew off a cloud of boiler steam, before slowing to enter Rastenburg station.

Zetterling would have seized such an opportunity. Bergman felt the tension relaxing as he remembered the young Oberleutnant. He had neither seen nor heard from him since the morning Flotilla 271 had set out on its mission. And all his enquiries since he had returned had led to the same dead end. Zetterling, the convoy of trucks, and the fifty men making up the Shore Party, had apparently vanished into thin air. The Oberleutnant had failed to report to the Group's HQ and no one knew where he was. It was a ridiculous situation but with enemy armoured columns now safely across the Seine, and with Paris once again in the hands of the French, communications had broken down completely and it was not unusual for small, unimportant units to disappear for days on end.

Even so Bergman sensed intuitively that there was something odd about Zetterling's vanishing act. What part, he wondered, had Görst and the Gestapo played in the mysterious affair. But, of course, Karl probably thought that the Korvettenkapitan was dead, too. The salvage expert was too much of a realist to rate the *Neger* pilots a chance of survival. And in Germany no one had time to go searching for dead comrades . . .

The *Wolfsschanze* had changed little since Bergman's last visit. The vast complex of buildings and underground bunkers seemed bigger than ever and there was a noticable increase in the flak defences. But as he approached the main gates he realised that something *was* different—the entire area was now guarded exclusively by members of the *Waffen-SS*. Obviously the Fuehrer no longer trusted the Army with his personal safety after the July bomb plot.

He presented his papers to an SS officer who scrutinised them carefully and then disappeared into his concrete bunker to make a discreet telephone call. When he emerged a few moments later he looked suitably respectful.

"Will you please follow me, Herr Korvettenkapitan. The Fuehrer's secretary informs me that the conference with General Guderian has just finished. He will probably see you in five minutes or so."

Bergman followed the black uniform of the officer along a labyrinth of concrete passages and narrow stone steps that took them deeper and deeper underground. They stopped finally in a small bare room with whitewashed walls. The two SS troopers standing guard eyed the visitor suspiciously.

"Will you please remove your gun, Herr Korvettenkapitan," Diesler asked politely. "It will be returned after your audience." He read the expression on Bergman's face and added quickly: "You will understand we cannot afford to take any more chances with the Fuehrer's life. Our Leader is Germany. Without the Fuehrer the Fatherland would be no more."

Bergman grunted non-committally, slipped the Mauser from its holster, and handed it to the SS officer. So much for his grandiose dreams, he thought. And then, to compound the indignity, he had to raise his arms while one of the guards searched his body for hidden weapons.

"Thank you, Herr Korvettenkapitan," Diesler said suavely. "I appreciate your co-operation." He glanced up sharply as the buzzer sounded and drew Bergman to one side while he waited for the green signal light to come on.

The huge steel door leading to the Fuehrer's private chambers, sighed softly as the electronic locks were released, and Bergman felt the welcome chill of clean refrigerated air blowing on his face as the armour-plated portal swung open. Vice-admiral Godt, one of Hitler's naval ADCs, came through into the bunker and greeted the U-boat commander with a thin tight-lipped smile.

"The Fuehrer will see you now, Korvettenkapitan." He clicked his heels and gave a curt stiff bow. "You may go through."

It was almost two years since Bergman's last meeting with Hitler and he felt a momentary shock at the man's deterioration. The strain of war, the physical ravages of disease, and a paranoic fear of the hidden assassin had each taken its fearful toll. The Fuehrer's handshake was weak as if his fingers had lost their strength and his head shook with an uncontrollable tremor. His left arm hung slackly like a paralysed limb and the palsied tremor found a fresh outlet in his hand.

Having greeted his visitor he returned to his desk with the unsteady gait of a senile old man, and every movement he made seemed to reflect utter exhaustion. Sitting forward in the chair, he rested his arms on top of the desk, and clenched his hands nervously. He seemed almost unaware of the Korvettenkapitan's presence.

"I can trust no one," he said as if speaking his thoughts out loud. "There is not a man in Germany on whom I can rely. These idiot doctors have no idea what to do. If I listened to them I'd have been dead by now." He lapsed into a moody silence which no one dared to break. Then, suddenly looking up at his guest, he said sharply, "If anything happens to me the Fatherland will be left without a leader. And who can succeed me? Hess has gone; Goering is a laughing stock; Heydrich is dead; and no one wants Himmler. Will someone tell me who is to be my successor?"

Godt cleared his throat politely. He decided it was time to bring the Leader back to the reality of the moment. "May I present Korvettenkapitan Bergman, *mein Fuehrer*. You wished to see him."

Hitler clenched his hands again as if fighting to bring his wandering thoughts under control. In the dim recesses of his mind he remembered the name. He could not associate it with any particular event but, in the sudden flash of vivid recollection, he remembered warning his Staff that Bergman was a dangerous man.* He could not recall why and the

* See *No Survivors.*

128

failure of memory irritated him. Pulling himself together he stared at his guest.

"I see you are a U-boat commander, Herr Korvettenkapitan."

Bergman realised he was in the presence of a madman, yet felt a strange sympathy for the pathetic creature sitting before him at the large desk. It was not pleasant to look at a man who had destroyed himself. He found himself momentarily at a loss for words in the pregnant silence that followed Hitler's bald statement of fact.

"Yes, *mein Fuehrer*." He hesitated. "I was the commander of *UB-44*."

Hitler was clearly uninterested. The fact that Bergman and *UB-44*, acting in obedience to his orders, had destroyed a German battleship in 1940 had long since faded from his memory. He glanced up at a large map of the world hanging on the wall of the conference room and returned his flickering stare to Bergman's face.

"Can one of your U-boats reach Argentina without refuelling?"

The question was so totally unexpected that Bergman had to pause for a few moments while he collected his thoughts. "Yes—it could be done," he ventured cautiously. "The new *Type XXI* boats could even make the entire passage without coming to the surface."

Having received the answer he apparently wanted the involuntary shaking movement that afflicted the Fuehrer's head and left hand eased slightly. His eyes softened and he actually smiled. But he said nothing and it was once again left to Godt to break the uncomfortable hiatus.

"The Korvettenkapitan has been operating a *Neger*

kommando, Fuehrer. He destroyed an enemy escort ship in the Channel last week."

Hitler's eyes gleamed triumphantly. "You see, Admiral? I was right. I told you these new weapons would win the war. Even Doenitz tried to persuade me against them but I would hear none of his pessimistic talk." The Fuehrer was warming to his customary theme and the men in the narrow room listened to the tirade with resigned patience. They had heard most of it many times before but, in Adolf Hitler's more lucid moments, it was not diplomatic to interrupt. And in any case, it was something of a relief to know that he could still enjoy moments of lucidity. "Rome has fallen. Paris is once again in the hands of the French and the enemy is across the Seine in strength. Do you know, Korvettenkapitan, that I have lost 400,000 men killed and missing in the West alone during these past three months? The 7th Army is totally destroyed!"

He stared up at Graff's portrait of Frederick the Great which he kept hanging on the wall behind his desk. "When bad news threatens to crush my spirit," he went on, "I derive fresh courage from the contemplation of this picture. Look at those strong blue eyes—that wide brow. What a head!"

Bergman made no comment. He was no connoisseur of art. To his untrained eyes, one historical portrait looked much like another. He remained silent and waited for the Fuehrer to finish his contemplation.

"Take no notice of all the defeatist talk you hear, Herr Korvettenkapitan," he resumed. "I can assure you we will still win this war. I promised the German people victory and I have never yet broken a pledge. We still have undreamed-of weapons in our armoury.

130

The flying-bombs have already shaken the British resolve to continue the war. And next month I shall order a rocket bombardment of London. Once our V-2 weapons have blasted the enemy capital to rubble Churchill and his minions will be begging for peace."

Bergman knew nothing of the rocket weapons and he was aching to ask more about them. But Hitler's tirade continued unabated like an avalanche, and he felt his head reeling under the barrage of statistics which the Fuehrer was expounding: ". . . and by September, despite our losses, the Fatherland will have 10 million men under arms—7½ million in the army and the *Waffen-SS* alone. I can still put 260 divisions in the field."

He stopped abruptly as if he had lost the thread of his argument. The tremor became more pronounced and his left hand was jerking violently as it lay on top of the desk. Godt placed his hand on Bergman's arm and whispered: "The audience is over, Herr Korvettenkapitan. The Fuehrer has an important conference with his Chief of Staff in ten minutes."

Bergman replaced his gold-peaked cap, clicked his heels, and raised his arm in salute. The Fuehrer's right hand lifted a few inches off the desk in acknowledgement and, as the Korvettenkapitan left the chamber, he turned to stare at the potrait of Frederick the Great again . . .

Although he had only been in Berlin for three hours, Bergman was already beginning to regret his impulsive decision to take a few days' leave in the capital. It had seemed a good idea at the time. He needed a tonic to raise his spirits after his demoralising visit to the Fuehrer's headquarters but, as he tramped the grim, grey streets of the city, he realised that the atmosphere at the *Wolfsschanze* had been wildly optimistic by comparison with the air of frightened defeatism that hung like an oppressive cloud over the capital.

The shops were empty of goods and Berliners queued endlessly for meagre rations that rarely measured up to the paper promises of their crudely printed meat and bread cards. Only cripples, wounded soldiers, and old men were to be seen on the streets. And piles of dusty rubble marked the ruins of famous and familiar landmarks destroyed in British air raids. Even the old, garish, Nazi propaganda posters had gone from the walls, and in their place hung haunting appeals for the 1944 Winter Relief Fund—or visually disturbing placards featuring wounded servicemen and demands to *Help the Fatherland!*

Bergman turned left off the *Unter den Linden* and threaded his way through the once prosperous streets in search of amusement. But the theaters were shut and the few cinemas remaining open were showing only war propaganda films. Emerging into *Friedrich-strasse* he crossed the street to look for *Bon-bonnière*—the cabaret where he had spent many a happy evening before the war. But all that remained was a fire-gutted shell and a smoke blackened facade on which a gaudy painted notice still proclaimed *TAUSEND NAKTE FRAUEN!* He moved on. *Alkazar* in *Bernstrasse*, another favourite nightspot with German naval officers on leave in the capital, had been hit by a British block-buster bomb, and a vast flattened site on which fire-weed was growing in abundance, marked the area of gay cafés in the *Potsdamerplatz.*

The women loitering expectantly in the *Tiergarten* bore little resemblance to the attractive girls of pre-war days, and Bergman hurried past ignoring their false smiles and luring invitations. The women swore harshly at his lack of interest but he took no notice and, turning left he found a small café in one of the side streets still open for business.

The place was deserted except for a middle-aged woman behind the bar and a despondent looking man sitting at one of the tables reading a newspaper. Bergman sat down and read the small black-edged card standing upright like a paper tombstone in a menu-holder in the centre of the table.

> *Given for the Glory of the Fatherland*
> *Hans Groener*
> *Wilhelm Groener*
> *Georg Groener*

Frau Groener bustled across to take his order and Bergman could see the dark circles under her eyes and the furrowed lines of strain around her mouth. He ordered beer and waited. He could feel the man at the other table staring at him, but taking no notice, he kept his eyes towards the window.

The *stein* was filled with an anaemic brown brew on the surface of which floated a few dispirited bubbles masquerading as froth. Bergman sipped it cautiously. It tasted flat and warm.

"Drink up, sailor," the man at the next table chuckled. "You'll be drinking sea water soon—that's if the Russkies don't get you with their bayonets first."

"Take no notice of my husband, sir," the woman said quietly as Bergman paid for his drink. "Lost both his legs at Stalingrad—it's turned his mind. That and our three sons. It's a terrible thing this war. God help all of us is what I say."

133

Bergman finished his beer and fled. If he stayed in Berlin much longer he felt he'd end up as mad as Herr Groener and the rest of them. His meeting with the Fuehrer had already unnerved him and the depressive atmosphere of the dead capital was gnawing at his mental stamina like an insidious cancer. All he wanted to do was to escape to the open sea again. He knew that the odds against survival were minimal but he welcomed the prospect of a clean death to the alternative slow decay that would be his inevitable fate, if he remained inside embattled Germany. But there was still one final task left, and stopping on the corner of *Wilhelmstrasse* to get his bearings, he started to walk towards the old Admiralty building.

Zetterling's strange disappearance continued to worry him. And one of the main reasons for his sudden visit to Berlin was the hope of discovering where the remains of Flotilla 271 had gone after leaving Le Verdon. The armed sentries guarding the sandbagged entrance to Kriegsmarine Headquarters saluted smartly, as he hurried inside in pursuit of his quest.

The Oberleutnant summoned to deal with Bergman's enquiry was respectful but unhelpful. Communications with *Gruppe West* were, he explained, chaotic. Some units had not been heard from for more than a month.

"You know how it is, sir," he said apologetically. "You saw what it was like yourself when you were in France. And, believe me, it's even worse now."

Bergman was tempted to tell him that the Fuehrer's headquarters were in an even more chaotic state. But he decided against it—morale must be maintained at all costs. Once the Navy, or for that matter any of the fighting services, discovered the truth about the higher direction of the war, the Third Reich would dissolve into anarchy. He could just remember the Naval Mutiny of 1918, and the fear of a similar collapse haunted him continuously. Whatever happened this time the Navy must stand firm.

By virtue of being difficult Bergman succeeded in getting his request referred to Kapitanleutnant Zeiter, the Duty Officer of Department G-9. From there he progressed to Department N after a brief excursion into the esoteric world of Section 14. The bureaucratic ant-hill of the Oberkommando der Kriegsmarine was proving even larger and more ponderous than he had anticipated but with the dogged perseverance he exhibited in combat he persisted with his enquiries and was finally ushered in to see Kommodore Gratz—the Staff Officer responsible for all transfers and appointments of junior ranks serving with the Unterseebootflotilles.

Bergman remembered Gratz from the Flensburg naval academy where they had both trained as cadets. And although the Kommodore had been two terms the senior he recognised Bergman immediately he entered the room.

"Konrad—good to see you. I thought all the old faces had gone. It's like living with ghosts in this bloody place. Sit down and make yourself comfortable."

The Kommodore pushed a pile of dusty files from the only other chair in the room and shifted it awkwardly with one hand. Bergman noticed the empty sleeve. He glanced up at Gratz's face and saw the shrapnel scars across his forehead and left cheek. The Kommodore read the concern in his visitor's expression and laughed easily. His solitary good eye sparkled.

"Nothing to worry about, Konrad. I'm okay now.

135

The Royal Navy thought they'd use me to get their revenge for what the French did to Nelson."

"Where the hell did you catch that packet?" Bergman asked.

"With our destroyers at Narvik. It's so long ago now that I've almost forgotten about it." He grinned at his visitor enviously. "Perhaps I should have volunteered for the U-boats like you."

"I've been one of the lucky ones," Bergman shrugged. "You don't get wounded in U-boats. You either live or you die. So far I've lived . . ." He left the sentence unfinished. "How's Greta and the family?"

The lively sparkle in Gratz's good eye suddenly went out. He looked away and stared down at the top of his desk. "Greta's parents lived in Munster. She took the children to see them in March just when the Yanks were bombing our railway communications in Westphalia. They hit the locomotive of her train and the whole lot ended up in the Ems. Those who weren't killed by the bombs were drowned. They tell me no one survived."

"I'm sorry. There's not much one can say, is there?"

"At least they've been spared the horror of seeing Germany destroyed. Let's hope Eisenhower's troops get here before the Russians. If they don't, then God help us!" He paused for a moment as if lingering over a memory. When he looked up again the sparkle in his solitary eye had reawakened. "Now, tell me, what's all this nonsense about you searching for this damned Oberleutnant fella? What's he to you, eh?"

"He was my second-in-command in Flotilla 271," Bergman explained. "I knew his family as well. He was supposed to bring the Transport Section back to Antwerp after we'd launched the *Negers* but, so far as

136

I can gather, he never reported to HQ and nobody's seen or heard of him since."

"The name's Zetterling, I believe."

"That's right." Bergman frowned. "But how the hell did *you* know?"

Gratz grinned. "Oberleutnant Bocke telephoned me when you started making your enquiries. That's why I told them to bring you up here. I was curious."

"Why?"

"Well, a couple of days ago I had two Gestapo officers in this room asking exactly the same thing. It seems that Zetterling had been under arrest but that some U-boat commander had wangled his release right from under their noses. It wouldn't have been a certain Korvettenkapitan Bergman would it?"

Bergman ignored the question. "Did you tell them where he was?" he asked anxiously.

"Of course not—not that I'm sure myself. But I make a point of being as unhelpful as I can be in these matters. In any case, as I told them, the Gestapo has no authority over a serving officer of the Kriegsmarine and if they wanted to find him they should take the matter up through the appropriate channels—Department Z-1."

"Were they satisfied?"

"No—but they went away."

"Do you *know* where Zetterling is?" Bergman asked.

Gratz shook his head. "Not precisely. But I *do* know that up to a week ago he was still alive. Apparently those trucks were needed in the Baltic and Admiral Brückner had put in an urgent request for a salvage expert to clear the harbour at Riga in readiness for a seaborne evacuation if our northern Army Groups got themselves cut off by the Russians. Zetterling was to take his convoy to Konigsberg, hand it over to the Kriegsmarine commander there, and then go on to Riga to supervise the harbour clearance."

"But surely Riga is almost in the front line."

"It's quite likely to be *behind* the front line soon, old boy. *And* on the wrong side. The Russians are massing at both ends of Lake Peipus and if we can believe the latest intelligence reports they're likely to break through as soon as their new offensive is launched. Riga, and the whole bloody Baltic coast will probably be in their hands by the end of the month—and we'll have to fight like hell if we want to, hold on to Konisberg."

Bergman suddenly wondered if that was the reason why Zetterling had chosen to volunteer for service in the Baltic. He dismissed his doubts. The very idea was preposterous. More probably Karl had gone eastwards, in the knowledge that the Russian front was the one place Görst was unlikely to follow him. If so it was a smart move. He picked up his cap and grasped Gratz's solitary hand warmly.

"Many thanks for the information, Kommodore. At least you've put my mind at rest on one score. Would you like me to put a word in for you when I see Doenitz—sitting behind a chair all day obviously doesn't suit you."

"Thanks all the same, Konrad—but it has to be no. I'm going to stay here with the rest of the cripples. A one-eyed, one-armed sailor isn't much use at sea. Don't worry about me, I'll still see plenty of fighting. We have started laying our plans already. Berlin will never surrender."

Bergman walked to the door, opened it, and hesitated.

"I'm sure it will never come to that," he told Gratz.

"The new U-boats should be in service by the end of the year. And once the V-2 rocket weapons are launched against London it won't take the enemy long to come begging for peace."

"Perhaps, Konrad. But that won't stop the Russians. They're the ones we *ought* to be worrying about."

Bergman shrugged. "You may well be right—I've given up worrying. We seem to have the whole damned world against us now. Look after yourself. And good luck in those trenches."

Gratz made a rude gesture with his arm. Despite the broad grin spreading across his scarred face he felt slightly envious.

"And good luck with your bloody U-boat, you ugly old bastard!"

CHAPTER SEVEN

Bergman's stomach had acquired an almost total immunity from the rigors of sea-sickness over the years, and he prided himself on an ability to face even the fiercest hurricane without a qualm. But the vicious corkscrew motion of *UB-702* was something he had never experienced before. Clinging grimly to the conning-tower rails, he stared out over the gale-swept ocean wishing he was dead.

The green seas, running fast before the wind, heaved with relentless monotony from horizon to horizon and white spray flecked the driving rain as the gale whipped angry foam from the wave crests. The heaving movement of the ocean reminded him of a large Manta ray swimming beneath the surface and the recollection of the powerful undulatory motion of the great fish only served to stir the contents of his stomach more violently.

"Keep her bows into wind, Cox'n!"

Oberbootsmann Schlieger's black oilskins made him look like a monstrous bat as he crouched over the wheel. He wondered why the skipper didn't dive down into the sheltered safety of the depths, in this sort of weather. Bergman was the first U-boat captain he'd ever encountered who seemed to prefer running on the surface in the teeth of a North Atlantic gale. Leaning his full weight on the helm, he obediently turned the shark bows of the submarine into wind.

UB-702 crested the first wave and bottomed into the following trough with a thunderous crash that echoed through the hull and made the off-watch crewmen sit up in their bunks and exchange nervous glances. The bows rose slightly then fell again as the stem sliced into the next rising wall of water, and the sea swirled down the foredeck to smash against the stout steel plating of the lower conning-tower, with an angry roar. Water streamed down the curved sides of the hull as the U-boat lifted clear of the tumult and the foaming sea gurgled noisily into the deck scuppers.

The violent corkscrew motion was reiterated as the stern swung wildly and Bergman tasted his breakfast again. *UB-702* bucked and pitched—then rolled drunkenly to leeward before digging her bows into the next towering wave. Ripping the plug from the engine-room voicepipe he held his lips close against the funnelled mouth.

"Can you give me a couple more knots, Chief?"

He ducked instinctively as the sea broke over the conning-tower and hurled cascade of cold white water over the exposed bridge.

"Not a chance, sir. We're blowing so much oil out of No. 2 she'll likely blow up if we don't shut down soon."

Bergman swore, thrust the plug back into the mouthpiece, and wiped the water from his face. *UB-702* corkscrewed again and unable to resist any longer, he emptied his churning stomach over the deck.

What the hell was he doing on a bloody pig-boat like *UB-702* anyway? Why did they need a full Korvettenkapitan in command of a boat that leaked like a sieve, dived like an inebriated whale, and behaved with the unpredictability of a scorned woman. And, worst of all, the boat that carried the stink of death in every plate of its cranky hull. Bergman cast his mind back to November 1944, in an effort to forget the immediate pangs of nausea that assailed his stomach with every lurching roll . . .

There had been something uncomfortably familiar about *UB-702* from the moment he first set eyes on her in the refitting basin at Kiel. The fact that she was an old obsolete boat with a new number puzzled him initially, but the task of commissioning her and her crew for combat patrol had quickly pushed the problem out of his mind. It was only during the forenoon watch of the third day that he discovered the uncomfortably facts of her true history. And by then, 300 miles out into the North Sea and skirting the Scottish coast on his way to the U-boat's Atlantic patrol area, it was too late to turn back.

Only an experienced skipper could successfully run the gauntlet of the surface and air patrols, that had now tightened their strangle-hold around the throat of Germany's remaining submarine bases. Bergman remained on Watch for forty-eight hours—only turning over to the Second Officer, Bornheim, when he was satisfied that they were clear and into safe waters. Then, having snatched a few hours of precious sleep, he had called up Oberleutnant Schaft,

UB-702's Executive Officer, to take him around the boat on a tour of inspection.

It was, as he had expected, a dispiriting task. Even to a casual glance it was obvious that *UB-702* should have been sent to the scrapyard many months before; but the tremendous losses suffered by the U-boats during the summer and early autumn of 1944 had made it impossible. She was worn out and weary. And shortages of vital materials had prevented the Kiel experts from refitting her to the old demanding standards of the Unterseebootflotille.

Her diesel engines had been repaired with spares taken from a Berlin omnibus and her electrical system was a nightmare wonderland of hastily taped circuits and non-standard wiring. In fact, Chief Engineer Meitzer confessed when they stood grouped around the smoking diesel units in the main engine-room, that one of his mechanics had stolen a length of heavy-duty cable from the refrigerator in the Flotilla base's canteen, to link the main switchboard to the control-room telegraph. Even the hull plates had been patched with cement after the last shipment of steel had gone into the Elbe when saboteurs blew up the supply train. And the beads of water weeping through the fresh white paint in the control room, provided unnerving evidence that the U-boat was leaking like a sieve.

It was as they were turning away that Bergman first noticed the strange mildewed line running around the control room about eighteen inches below the curved span of the overhead bulkhead. Moving away from the Oberleutnant he ducked through the circular hatch connecting the control room to the forward crew space. The dark line, now lower down the white painted side plating, continued steadily through

144

the compartment until it reached the watertight bulkhead leading to the bow torpedo flat.

For some inexplicable reason it irritated him. With far more important things to worry about he should have ignored it. But his eyes kept returning to the mildewed mark until it completely dominated his thoughts. He ducked through the hatch into the control room.

"Do we have any paint aboard, Number One?"

"I think so, sir. Shall I check?"

Bergman nodded. "Yes—straight away if you please. And get some of the off-duty Watch to go round and paint out that bloody line."

Oberleutnant Schaft looked upwards. "You won't get rid of it by painting, sir," he said cheerfully. "We gave it three coats before we left Kiel but it just reappears as soon as the paint dries. I wouldn't worry about it, sir. There's bound to be some sort of tidemark left when a submarine has spent nearly two years lying on the bottom."

Bergman looked up sharply. A cold finger traced slowly down the length of his spine and he felt the muscles of his stomach knot with fear. "What the hell are you talking about, Oberleutnant?"

"Didn't you know, sir. This is the old *UB-59*. They salvaged her from the bottom of Jade Bay about six months ago. After she'd been cleaned out and refitted . . ." he grinned at Bergman's snort of disgust, ". . . they gave her a new number. The British did the same sort of thing when they raised the *Thetis* at the beginning of the war—she was recommissioned as the *Thunderbolt*. Not that it did her any good, mind. The Italians got her off Cape San Vito, early last year."

So that was the significance of the discoloured rim of flaking paint, Bergman thought. His mind went back to that bleak February morning when he and Zetterling had entered the sunken U-boat for the first time. He shivered at the memory of the bloated corpses floating aimlessly inside the flooded control room in which they now stood. Doenitz had certainly kept his promise and given him a boat. But did it have to be *this* one!

"Do the men know she's the old *UB-59*, Number One?"

"Yes, sir. You can't keep that sort of thing quiet. So far as I can see they don't seem to mind. These days anything is better than a posting to the Eastern Front."

Bergman was inclined to agree with the crew's sentiments, but he wasn't too sure for himself. Commanding a ghost ship that had once been the tomb of 37 men was not an appetising prospect. And for once in his life the Korvettenkapitan felt physically afraid of the submarine he now commanded . . .

But despite his forebodings *UB-702* had proved a tough little craft. And by the conclusion of her third patrol, Bergman's tally of ships destroyed had increased by eleven vessels, totalling a further 87,600 tons. Not that he derived any satisfaction from his latest successes. After five years of war killing came easy. Other and more vital matters now preyed upon his mind. The end of each patrol brought fresh news of Germany's growing plight. And as the wall maps in the Operation's Room reflected the daily advances of the Allied armies from East and West, he knew that despite the Fuehrer's promises, the Third Reich was doomed to extinction.

Only the demand for unconditional surrender held the Fatherland's dwindling military resources together and prevented total collapse. A negotiated armistice

146

would have had the support of all but the diehard Nazis. And it would have saved Germany from the final holocaust of utter defeat. But to professional fighting men like Bergman, unconditional surrender meant an abject abdication of honour that could not be considered under any circumstances. They would fight to the death. And although each man no longer believed that death was the ultimate glory of war, it became a worthy sacrifice if it served to maintain the honour of the Fatherland . . .

UB-702 slithered sideways as the wind whipped her stern. The U-boat's bows rose high to expose her rust-red belly and she rolled violently like a harpooned whale. Bergman's morbid train of thought came to an abrupt end as a sickening lurch threw him bodily across the bridge. A wall of roaring white water crashed down on the exposed conning-tower, and he grabbed for a handhold as the sea sucked him greedily towards the rails. Half-blinded by salt spray he clung grimly to a stanchion until the U-boat came back on to an even keel. Then forcing himself to his feet, he waded through the swirling knee-deep water.

Oberbootsmann Schlieger was crumpled forward and hanging limply from the safety harness with his voluminous oilskins billowing and cracking in the wind like great black sails. His body was twisted awkwardly and the helm spun wildly out of control as *UB-702* danced and shuddered at the mercy of the storm.

Bergman swore as the whirling spokes of the helm battered his hands, but ignoring the bruising pain, he grabbed the wheel, steadied the U-boat, and brought her head into the wind again. The corkscrew motion subsided as *UB-702* came back under control and Bergman reached towards the voicepipe.

"Bridge to control room! Schlieger's been hurt. Get him below. And stand by to dive."

The Oberleutnant put the order into execution and turned to Bornheim with a wry grin as two seamen shinned up the ladder to bring the coxswain down. "Must be bloody rough if the Old Man wants to dive."

Bornheim nodded. He, too, had noted Bergman's predeliction for remaining on the surface until the last possible moment. It was almost as if the skipper was frightened to submerge. And that was plain bloody daft for a U-boat commander with his reputation. He made no comment on the Oberleutnant's observation, but waited at the bottom of the ladder as Schmidt and Eisen bundled the unconscious Oberbootsmann into the crowded control room.

"Upper hatch shut!"

Taking his cue from the skipper's shouted report the Executive Officer began the diving routine. "Clutches out—switches on—planes to dive—stand by to open main vents!"

Baderhoff shut down the diesels and closed the exhaust valve. "Clutches disconnected, sir."

In the motor room abaft the diesel unit, Chief Electrician Inquart heard Baderhoff's acknowledgement and pulled the switch to the main motors. The electric units hummed to instant life and the flickering needles of the Bosch ammeters measured the amperage being sucked from the batteries under the deck plating.

Bergman threw off his oilskins and joined Schaft at the periscope. His feet squelched wetly inside his sea boots and he hung on to one of the steel support beams as Jessel pulled them off.

"Take her to fifty feet and trim level. Steer Course 1-7-5."

"Speed, sir?"

Bergman glanced at *UB-702's* senior engineer, Meitzer. "Are we fully charged, Chief?"

"Aye, sir. But I don't think the power cables can stand up to full amps for long. It's the diesels I'm more worried about."

Bergman slid his feet into the slippers Jessel had placed ready for him. He looked around the control room and felt his eyes inexorably drawn to the discoloured rim of paint that marked the water level inside *UB-59* during her two year sojourn on the bottom. He shivered and turned away.

"What's wrong with the diesels, Chief?"

"Number 2 has been running hot for the last couple of hours. And we seem to be leaking oil from Starboard-8 bunker."

"Serious?"

Meitzer rubbed his chin. Like the other two officers he had noted the skipper's apparent reluctance to run submerged. He shrugged. "We've got enough fuel if that's what you mean, sir. But it won't be sufficient to get us back if we run on the surface."

UB-702 levelled at fifty feet and a sharp hiss of compressed air and the gurgle of water echoed inside the hull as Bornheim shifted ballast to correct the U-boat's trim. Bergman walked to the chart table and stared down at the map. The Executive Officer had traced their course in pencil and he followed the Oberleutnant's line—projecting it forward in his mind as he visualised the next step. He suddenly realised that his hands were sweating and he surreptitiously wiped them dry on his trousers. Normally he was only happy when he was safely submerged beneath

149

the surface. But the haunting memory of the drowned men in *UB-59*'s flooded interior stirred every time the ill-fated U-boat sank below the waves and the black rim of death marring the fresh white paintwork was a constant reminder that, like a mad dog, a submarine that had killed once was certain to kill again.

Exhausted by his vigil on the bridge and seeking an escape from his fears in the oblivion of sleep Bergman handed the Watch over to Schaft and ducked his head through the narrow hatchway leading to his minuscule cabin abaft the control room. He pulled the curtains aside and paused to look at the photograph of the Grunnenberg Mountains hanging beside the repeater depth-gauge over the head of his bunk. The picture represented his last link with sanity. The constant reminder of what he was really fighting for. Not the Fuehrer nor his monstrous creation of the Third Reich. Not even his family or the woman he had loved. But Germany—the *real* Germany. The Fatherland.

He pulled off the slippers and slipped the heavy sweater over his head. He made no attempt to remove the rest of his clothing. A U-boat captain, even when asleep, was always in command and on call. In an emergency, there was no time to dress.

Bergman swung his legs on to the narrow bunk. He hadn't washed for three days but the stale smell of sweat no longer offended his senses. Blended subtly with the pungent odour of diesel oil, the sour scent of cabbage water, and the tang of salt-damp steel, it was the familiar aroma of U-boat warfare. And to the Korvettenkapitan it was the sweetest smell on earth. Resting his head on the pillow he stared up at the haunting rim of mildewed paint over his bunk. But he was too tired to worry over omens any longer. His hand found the light switch and his eyes closed gently . . .

"Captain to the control room!"

Bergman was awake in an instant. Swinging his legs off the bunk he slid his feet into the waiting slippers and pushed the curtain to one side. The alarm buzzer was still emitting its steady double bleep and he had to push his way through the crowded passage against the tide of the Duty Watch hurrying to their diving stations.

"I'll take over, Number One," he told Schaft as he entered the control room. "What's the score?"

The Oberleutnant stood away from the periscope to make way for the skipper. "Target bearing 290 degrees, sir. Range about three miles. We're at thirty feet and speed is three knots. Crew closed up to battle stations."

Bergman jerked his thumb to Weisner and waited for the periscope to glide upwards from its well in the centre of the deck. He glanced up at the chronometer set in the bulkhead over the diving table. He'd had only two hours sleep since he'd gone off Watch.

Pushing his face into the soft rubber cups protecting the eye-piece of the 'scope he swung the lens on to 290. His thumb flicked the high-magnification attack lens into position. Schaft was right—target bearing 290 at a range of three miles. A nice fat looking freighter.

"Slow ahead both. Bring me five degrees to port, helmsman. Bow tubes to stand by."

"Bow tubes ready, sir. Caps open. Depth setting ten metres."

Bergman examined his quarry carefully. The ship was down by the stern and the mainmast, splintered at its base, was lying across the poop like a fallen pine. The storm had spent its fury but the sea was still running high and the freighter was rolling—wallowing was a more apt description—in the heavy pounding swell. And, he noted, she was flying a white flag with a red diamond in its centre from the jury-rigged gaff of her foremast.

"What torpedoes are we shipping this trip, Number One?"

"We loaded a mixture, sir. But they're Type 5 models in the bow tubes at the moment. I kept the *G-7(e)s* in reserve as reloads."

Of all the bloody luck!

Bergman slammed the handles of the periscope upwards and stepped back. "Down 'scope! Steer southwest for one mile and then circle the target. Reduce speed to two knots." He snatched the telephone to the bow torpedo room. "Jacobssen! Get those Type-5 fish out of the tubes and reload with the reserves."

The Type-5, or GNAT,* was not Bergman's favourite weapon at the best of times. With a success rate of only 6% it was one of the worst torpedoes ever produced by the Kriegsmarine and the majority of experienced U-boat skippers preferred the tried and trusted battery-powered *G-7(e)*. The GNAT was also driven by electric motors but at 25 knots it was too slow as an attack weapon and its maximum range of 6,000 yards was restrictive. Its main defect, however, lay in the acoustic receiver unit—a complex of four magneto-striction hydrophones wired in alternating pairs. And the sensitivity of the homing unit was limited to ships travelling at between 12 and 19 knots.

It was, as Bergman had quickly realised, utterly useless against a target lying disabled in the water

---

* The Allied code-name for German Naval Acoustic Torpedo. The German name was *Zaunkonig*=Wren.

with dead engines. And the distress flag flying from the freighter's foremast showed that such, indeed, was her plight.

In his younger days, before war had hardened him, the Korvettenkapitan would have allowed his prey to escape. The old chivalry that had inspired his earlier career would have tempered instinct with mercy. It was no part of a German officer's creed to destroy a vessel already in distress.

But those days had gone and while the crew sweated in the cramped confines of the bow compartment as they struggled with the awkward ungainly weapons, Bergman fretted impatiently lest he should miss the opportunity to attack. Each torpedo weighed 3,300 lbs and the reloading routine was usually carried out at leisure between attacks—not against the clock with the target within range. The men cursed and swore as they manhandled the heavy weapons out of the tubes, ran them back to the reserve storage space suspended from the rails of the overhead track, and pushed the standard electric torpedoes into the vacated tubes.

"Bow compartment reporting, sir. Tubes reloaded. Standing by."

"Good work, Jacobssen," Bergman acknowledged. "Set all weapons for ten feet."

There was a brief pause as the hydrostatic valve settings were altered, and a few moments later Jacobssen reported the bow tubes ready.

"Flood tubes!" The Korvettenkapitan stared up at the attack display panel, as the warning lights went from red to green. "Up periscope!"

The bronze column hissed from its well and Bergman seized the handles to survey his victim again. *UB-702's* obsolete design provided no separate attack centre from which the Commander could con his vessel into its firing position. Bergman's station was in the centre of the control room shoulder to shoulder with the other two Watch officers, the coxwain at the hydroplane controls, the helmsman, and three other members of the Duty Watch. It was like travelling on the Berlin subway in the rush-hour—and as conducive to bad temper.

"Steer one point to port!"

"Port one, sir."

"Hold her level—we're bobbing up and down like a bloody cork!"

Bornheim leaned across the Second Coxswain sitting at the fore hydroplane controls and twisted the valve wheels to shift the water ballast and improve the U-boat's trim. Bergman shook his head impatiently and gestured him away.

"For Christ's sake, leave it alone—you're only making it a bloody sight worse!" He turned to Brecht. "Starboard one point, helmsman!"

"One point to starboard, sir."

Bornheim exchanged a rueful grin with Oberleutnant Schaft as he stepped back from the diving table. *UB-702* was tricky enough to trim at the best of times and Bergman knew it. The Old Man's irritability seemed to get worse every bloody day. He shrugged—that's what comes of living on your nerves, he told himself. Be a good thing for everybody when he was transferred to one of these new Walter boats he was always talking about.

The freighter was squarely in the sighting graticules of the periscope and Bergman examined her carefully from stem to stern coldly observing her total helplessness. At one time in his career he would have surfaced and done his best to help the marooned men

154

on the crippled ship. But not any more. These were the men who were slowly and systematically tearing his beloved Germany apart—why should he show them mercy?

The drum and ball strung from the halyards of the foremast—the international visual signal for a ship in distress—was a last cry for help. The sea anchor, which the crew had carefully paid astern in an effort to hold their disabled boat into the wind, had been torn away by the heavy seas; and the ugly wallowing motion of the groaning hull showed that the end was near. The storm had splintered the lifeboats to matchwood and the survivors were huddled miserably in the bows waiting their fate.

Bergman circled his crippled prey like the merciless hunter he had become. As the captain of the U-boat the ultimate decision to fire was his—and his alone. Even now, as he prowled cautiously around his wounded victim, there was still time to call off the attack and leave the disabled vessel to the mercy of the sea. But five years of unceasing combat had drained the last dregs of compassion from his heart.

"Bow one—*fire!*"

His thumb pressed the firing teat—the verbal command intended only as an executive warning to the men in the bow compartment if the trigger failed to operate. But there was no necessity for other hands to consummate the task. The torpedo hissed from its tube and streaked remorselessly towards its helpless target. It was impossible to miss at such short range and a single torpedo would be more than sufficient to send the freighter to the bottom.

"Bow two—*fire!*"

Bergman seemed unaware of what he had done. It

was like emptying the chambers of a revolver into the body of a man after killing him with the first bullet.

UB-702 shuddered with the concussion of the explosion. But the crew showed no sign of jubilation or elation as the first torpedo struck home. Killing was just one additional element in an unexciting routine. It meant nothing any more—only that the sooner all their torpedoes were fired the sooner the skipper would turn for home. And even had they known that Bergman had wantonly destroyed a crippled ship flying distress signals, not a single man aboard the U-boat would have criticised his decision.

"Secure from battle stations. Half speed ahead. Steer 1-9-0 Hands to fall out to Watch diving stations."

Bergman drew his face away from the rubber pads of the binocular eyepiece of the periscope. There was no point in watching his victim sink. He'd seen the same thing a hundred times before. He stepped back like a gunfighter blowing the smoke from the barrel of his six-shooter.

"Down periscope!"

Bornheim waited while the Korvettenkapitan entered the attack in the U-boat's War Diary. The entry was brief and to the point.

02.57 *19 Apr 1945. Attacked unidentified cargo vessel ten miles south of Fastnet Rock. Approx 8,000 BRT. Two torpedoes fired. Target destroyed. Gale moving to NW and abating to Force 3. Sea moderate. Course changed to 190 mag. Bergman. K/K.*

"Pity we didn't get her name, sir."

Bergman looked at the leutnant's eager face and

recognised his own youthful enthusiasm in 1939. It seemed like a lifetime but it was barely six years ago.

"Who the hell cares," he said shortly.

He could still remember the name of the very first ship he had sunk when he commanded the old *UB-44*—Haven Court! It was a name he would never forget. Bergman still carried a vivid picture of the survivors in their lifeboat—the English captain smiling gratefully as the young U-boat skipper gave him a bottle of brandy. And his wife, shivering in her thin nightdress, huddled in the stern. If he had not known the name of his victim he could have persuaded himself that they had survived the long 80-mile haul to the Norwegian coast. Now he preferred his targets to remain anonymous. That way he could sleep better at nights.

"Can I have a word, sir?"

He turned to find the Chief Engineer half way through the hatchway that led back to the engine-room. The expression on Meitzer's face indicated bad news. "Certainly, Chief. Wait for me in the wardroom." He nodded to the Executive Officer. "You'd better come along too, Hans. Bornheim—take over the Watch. Surface in fifteen minutes and maintain speed and course."

The wardroom occupied the starboard side of the U-boat immediately abaft the control room. It was barely six feet in width and a fraction short of ten feet long. Only a heavy curtain separated it from the busy communication passage running down the central axis of the submarine. Meitzer was already sitting on the leather settee wiping the oil from his hands with a wad of cotton waste as Bergman and Schaft entered. The Korvettenkapitan lifted the coffee pot from its ring, put three tin mugs on the table, and poured the *ersatz* brew of powdered acorn that was now standard Kriegsmarine issue. The days of fresh coffee had long since passed.

"I can see you're dying to tell me the worst, Chief."

"All the starboard fuel bunkers are empty, sir," Meitzer said simply and undramatically. "The storm probably opened the leaks I told you about. And," he added with masochistic satisfaction, "two of the port side bunkers are contaminated with sea water."

"You're sure it's *sea* water, Chief?" Schaft gibed. "If you ask me it's more likely some of your stokers are too bloody idle to walk to the heads."*

"Well, nobody *did* ask you!" Meitzer bit back sharply.

"That's enough, gentlemen," Bergman intervened. He was not in the mood for bickering. "How much fuel do we have left, Chief?"

"Difficult to say, sir." The gauges on this old tub gave up accurate readings weeks ago. I usually check fuel levels with a dip-stick when we're on the surface." He shrugged. "I'd say we've got to go up through the Channel if we want to get home before the bunkers run dry."

"Couldn't we make it to one of the Norwegian bases?" Schaft asked.

"No—it's the Channel or nothing."

Bergman swallowed his coffee quickly to avoid tasting it. He put his mug down on the table. "Very well, Chief. It's the shortest way home."

"And the quickest way to the bottom," Schaft added.

Bergman looked at the Executive Officer coldly. "Do you have an alternative, Oberleutnant?"

"No, sir."

* "Heads" is the naval euphemism for lavatories.

"Then I suggest you go to the control room and prepare a suitable course for my approval. I have a number of things to discuss with the Chief."

Schaft looked suitably abashed. Perhaps that was how the Korvettenkapitan had acquired his reputation. By doing the impossible. He pushed through the curtain and went back into the control room to work on the charts.

Bergman poured himself another cup of *ersatz* coffee, more from habit than any enthusiasm for the revolting brew. "I intend to keep running on the surface as long as I dare," he told Meitzer. "But we'll need maximum amperage all the same. We'll *have* to dive in the end. Can the batteries stand it?"

"Perhaps—who can say? I'll put a good charge in them tonight. But if that No. 2 diesel keeps playing up you'll have to double the normal charging time. I daren't overload it."

Bergman nodded and glanced at his watch. "I'll put the charge on as soon as we're up. I shall stay on the surface until the enemy realise they've got a U-boat coming up the Channel." He paused. "You know we might even get away with it—no one but a fool would expect to find a submarine in these waters. And I doubt if the enemy is as alert as he used to be now that the war's nearly over."

"Do you think we *can* make it, sir?"

"Frankly—no. But as I told young Schaft we've no alternative. And if the enemy *do* pick us up they're going to throw everything they've got at us."

Meitzer seemed unconcerned. "You've got out of difficult situations before, sir," he pointed out quietly. "My money says you'll do it again this time—given luck."

Bergman put his empty mug on the table and

159

stared blankly at the curved steel bulkhead that vaulted above their heads. He was recalling all the times in the past when he'd done the impossible and extricated his boat from certain destruction. But he did not share the Chief Engineer's optimism . . .

"It isn't going to be pleasant, Chief. Our engines are likely to fail at any time. The motors are practically burnt out. We daren't dive below 150 feet in case the hull plates give way. And we're likely to run out of fuel before we're halfway home. I should put your money away. You won't find many takers when I tell the crew what I intend to do."

Meitzer grinned and pulled a roll of banknotes from his pocket. He threw them down on the scrubbed wooden table-top.

"Let's leave it right there, sir. If you're right neither of us will need it where *we're* going!"

CHAPTER EIGHT

The green light of the internal telephone glowed brightly and Bornheim lifted the receiver. According to the control room chronometer it was 21.55 precisely.

"Officer of the Watch!"

"This is the captain. Stand by to surface in five minutes."

Bornheim acknowledged Bergman's laconic warning and quietly passed the word to the men of the Duty Watch. Baderhoff hefted himself out of his bunk grumbling, slipped an overall on over his singlet and underpants, and settled into his control position beside the silent diesel engines. Further aft, in the Motor Room, Inquart checked the acid levels of the U-boat's batteries for the third time in less than an hour and noted the figures in his log. Kantor and Veitch, the port and starboard Duty look-outs, pulled on heavy woollen sweaters and sea boots, tied their

161

cork life-jackets in place, and then made their way unhurriedly into the control room, ready to climb the ladder behind the skipper the moment UB-702 broke surface.

The tension building up inside the boat was heightened by the dim red lighting. Night vision was of paramount importance and the safety of the entire crew depended on instant reaction to the faintest shadow on the blackness of the horizon. And it was standard U-boat routine to light the control room with softly glowing red lamps, so that the eyes of the lookouts did not have to adjust to the darkness on the surface.

In common with most small ships, UB-702's crew had discovered and discussed the news of their projected Channel dash many minutes before Bergman informed them officially over the boat's loudspeaker system, and his announcement came as no surprise. But while most of the men had implicit trust in their veteran skipper, few could discern any prospect of success. It was a gamble that *had* to end in disaster. The Channel defences, especially now that the enemy again occupied both sides of the narrow strip of water, were completely impregnable. And any attempt to break through the Straits was tantamount to suicide.

Yet despite their personal misgivings not a man protested and even the chronic grumblers remained silent. Like Bergman they were veterans of the U-boat war and none had expected to survive even this long. And with the fatalism of men who knew they should have died many months before, and for whom the present reprieve could only be temporary, they accepted the captain's decision with stoic courage. Better to die fighting their enemy than to be shot down like helpless animals by the Russians, when they got ashore.

Bergman appeared in the red cavern of the control room at exactly 21.59. His eyes missed nothing as they checked quickly around the crowded vault and he nodded approvingly at finding everyone at his appointed station. The depth-gauges showed *UB-702* trimmed at thirty feet, and walking to the low-powered steering periscope, he gestured Weiner to raise it. Gripping the guide-handles he swept the lens through 360° to check that the surface was clear.

There was a slight lop on the sea and although the moon was in its second quarter the heavy cloud cover obscured it most of the time. With his customary caution, however, Bergman ordered a slight course change to reduce the U-boat's silhouette when it finally emerged from the depths.

"No HE, sir."

Bergman nodded as Klaus, the hydroplane operator, turned in his seat to report that nothing was audible on his sensitive listening apparatus.

"Sky search radar?"

Langstrom lifted his face from the coned baffle shrouding the luminous screen of the radar scanner.

"All clear, sir."

"Stand by to surface!"

Bergman gripped the conning-tower ladder, wedged himself securely on the steel rungs, and unclipped the lower hatch.

"Down periscope! Surface!"

Throwing back the heavy hatch-cover, and followed by Kantor and Veitch climbing the ladder at his heels, he clambered up into the salt-damp darkness of the conning-tower compartment while Schaft executed the standard surfacing routine.

"Shut main vents. Group up—slow ahead together. Blow all main tanks!"

A series of muffled thuds echoed through the hull as the vents slammed shut and compressed air roared into the tanks to blow them clear of water. Terse orders and obedient acknowledgements filtered up the narrow shaft from the control room and Bergman waited patiently with his hands on the clips of the upper hatch as *UB-702* angled upwards.

"Twenty feet . . . fifteen feet . . . ten feet, sir!"

Bergman's arm jerked the lid of the top hatch open and a sickly stench of oil, sweat, and stale food funnelled past him as the air pressure in the U-boat forced the foul odours out through the narrow hatchway. Water streamed down the side plating of the submarine as she emerged from the depths and the sea, trickling over the lip of the hatchway, splashed his face. Wiping it away with his sleeve Bergman hoisted himself up on to the bridge and quickly surveyed the night horizon through his binoculars. Kantor and Veitch joined him and, as they took up their look-out positions to port and starboard, he thrust his head back into the mouth of the conning-tower shaft.

"Stop blowing!"

The deafening roar of high-pressure air cut off abruptly. And as the Kingston valves closed in instant obedience, the cauldron of foam created by the water ballast slowly subsided. Floating gently astern the angry froth fragmented and dissolved to leave a moving tracery of tiny white air bubbles on the surface of the grey-green sea. Far below in the crimson warmth of the control room he heard Schaft passing the order to start the fans.

Through a break in the overcast sky Bergman could see the stars swaying slowly backwards and forwards as *UB-702* rolled in the sluggish swell. It all looked peaceful enough. But for how long, he wondered. He pulled the rubber plug from the voicepipe and called up the Oberleutnant.

"Shut down the motors and engage the clutches."

Schaft acknowledged the command and turned away from the voicepipe. "Switches off! Clutches in! Stand by engines!" His mouth found the funnel of the voicepipe. "Motors are off, sir. Diesels standing by."

"Transfer control to the bridge, Number One." Bergman ripped the cock from the engine-room pipe. "Bridge here, Chief. Obey telegraphs."

"Standing by, sir."

Bergman waited for the helmsman and the Duty signaller to climb up on to the bridge.

"Start main engines—half speed ahead. Secure for patrol routine."

A shrill whistle brought Bergman to the voicepipe from the engine-room.

"Yes, Chief?"

"Can we start putting on the charge yet, sir?"

The Korvettenkapitan swept the horizon with his binoculars and paused to search the stern quarter—the direction from which the danger of attack was most likely to come. But the black darkness revealed nothing.

"Carry on, Chief. Let me know when you've finished."

He peered up at the dark clouds scurrying swiftly above his head. What they needed now was a bloody good storm. But the glass was rising and his hopes were no more than wishful thinking. Leaning his arms on the conning-tower coaming he stared ahead into the night as *UB-702*'s sharp bows cut a hissing phosphorescent path through the sea . . .

Bergman's plan was both simple and cautious. The U-boat would make maximum speed on the surface during the hours of darkness and would rest on the bottom throughout the day. They could have run submerged during the day but the Korvettenkapitan did not trust the submarine's unreliable electrical system. Better, he reasoned, to keep the motors for emergencies. And, in any case, as UB-702 would have to pass through the neck of the Straits submerged he wanted to keep plenty of power reserve in the battery cells.

UB-702 passed between Land's End and the Scilly Isles shortly after midnight and, after steering south for twenty miles, Bergman ordered a change of course to the east at 01.00. Then, handing over the remainder of the Watch to Bornheim, he slid down the ladder and went through to the wardroom for a quick meal. Cooking was only possible when the U-boat was surfaced and the main meal of the day was normally served at night. The crew ate an hour or so before midnight but the skipper and the officers had to grab their food when Watch duties permitted.

Apparently undisturbed by the mounting tension, Bergman ate a large meal even though the food itself was canned, synthetic, and unappetising. Then, having poured himself a mug of *ersatz* coffee, he settled back on the settee and lit a cigarette. Drawing the smoke deep into his lungs he reviewed the sequence of events and found them far from discouraging. Perhaps his gamble would pay off after all. Now that the fighting had moved deep into Germany he felt certain that the enemy sea defences were not at their old peak of instant readiness. And having reached the threshold of victory who could blame them for taking it easy. Stubbing the cigarette out in an old tin lid he stood up, stretched, and made his way back to the control room.

It was almost three o'clock. Bornheim had had long enough on the bridge. Grasping the steel ladder the Korvettenkapitan hauled himself up into the clean night air.

"Nothing to report, sir."

"Very good, Bornheim. Get below and grab some sleep. We shall be diving in two hours."

The clouds had cleared as the depression passed to the south and the sea had settled into a smooth black quilt. Bergman could hear the soft hiss of tumbling water under the bows, while below decks and muted by the stout steel plates of the hull, the men in the bow torpedo flat were singing quietly. Suddenly another sound intruded and he stiffened.

His binoculars searched the sky for the source of the noise but everything seemed quiet and peaceful. And yet he was certain he had caught the faint but unmistakable drone of a distant aircraft. He shrugged. Probably an enemy communications plane on its way home from France with some VIPs. Acting on a hunch he moved to the voicepipe.

"Any signs of bandits on the radar, Schaft?"

There was a pause while the Oberleutnant checked with Langstorm. He thought he could detect someone cursing. Then Schaft reported back.

"Sorry, sir. Radar's on the blink again. Langstrom is replacing a valve."

"How long has the bloody set been dead?"

"About fifteen minutes, sir."

Bergman swore. "Why the hell wasn't it reported immediately," he demanded angrily. "There's an aircraft prowling around somewhere and we're helpless without a radar plot."

As if to confirm his fears a beam of blinding white light stabbed down from the empty sky without warning, flooding the exposed bridge in its brilliant glare. Almost simultaneously the roar of aero-engines deafened the ears of the men standing Watch on deck.

Bergman knew all about the enemy's latest anti-submarine techniques but this was his first encounter with the fearsome new weapon.* The dazzling glare of the searchlight and the crash of engines caught him unprepared. And deafened by the noise, his eyes blinded by the fierceness of the concentrated beam of light, he stood gripping the guard rails unable to think.

The initial shock passed quickly and he recovered in time to check his instinctive movement towards the button of the diving alarm. A half-remembered warning flashed across his brain. These Leigh-light aircraft were armed with depth-charges which made them only fully effective against a submerged U-boat. Any attempt to dive would invite an immediate, and almost certainly fatal attack.

The Wellington fired a stream of coloured tracer bullets from its nose turret by way of encouragement but Bergman stood his ground. Heavy calibre machine gun bullets tore the U-boat's outer skin and he saw Kantor spin to the deck—his fingers clawing at the gratings in the final agony of death.

Zooming low over the periscope standards, the Wellington climbed away on full throttle and circled ready for a second attack. The blinding glare of the searchlight swept astern and the men on *UB-702*'s

---

* The Leigh light was a radar controlled searchlight. It was fitted to Costal Command A/S patrol aircraft to locate surfaced U-boats.

exposed bridge experienced a strange comfort from the sudden darkness. Bergman was tempted to man the flak guns but he realised the area was probably saturated with patrol aircraft, and that any attempt to fight back would merely attract the attention of more enemy predators. He turned to check the bridge.

Kantor's body was crumpled awkwardly in one corner and Korch, the helmsman, had blood trickling down his left arm. Veitch seemed all right and, seemingly unaffected by the shambles behind his back, he was following the Wellington up into the sky with his binoculars. Herman Klemper, the Duty Signaller, was standing a few feet away from the lookout with a portable signalling lamp clutched tightly to his chest. He was only nineteen years old and this was his first U-boat patrol. He looked scared but he had made no effort to run for cover. The lamp gave Bergman an idea.

"Klemper! Fire two green flares and then start flashing the aircraft as it circles for the next run."

The signaller slipped two cartridges into his flare pistol. Raising his arm straight he pulled the triggers and two green balls of light arched up into the black sky and then drifted to leeward with white smoke trailing behind them. Klemper stuck the pistol back into his belt and swung up the lamp.

"What do I signal, sir?"

Bergman shrugged. "How the hell do I know—send anything you like. But keep it to short repeated groups."

Klemper balanced the portable signalling lamp on his crooked arm, squared the shadowed fuselage of the Wellington in the "v" sight on top of the mirror and began operating the shutter, Bergman leaned over the voicepipe.

"Schaft!—switch on the navigation lights. Then get someone to find a White Ensign in the flag locker and bring it topsides."

The Oberleutnant wasted no time on questions. The discipline of U-boat warfare demanded instant obedience no matter how strange the command. He had heard the sound of the engines followed by the sharp clatter of bullets striking the hull and he knew they were under attack. He obeyed without hesitation. Shouting for someone to bring a White Ensign he reached for the switches of the running lights and, as the tumblers clicked under his fingers, the red and green navigation lights sparkled bright pin-points of colour on either side of the conning-tower.

Bergman held his breath as the Wellington rumbled past on a parallel course. Suddenly the engines of the bomber throttled back and the Aldis lamp winked from a small window just behind the pilot's cockpit. Bergman stared up at the flashes and read them off:

I-D-E-N-T-I-F-Y . . . I-D-E-N-T-I-FY . . .

Well, at least he'd given them pause for thought. It was a sad fact of life that signals often became garbled in transmission and recognition codes became changed without the knowledge of everyone involved. And that was the filmsy basis of his bluff. The pilot of the Wellington, equally aware of such human frailties was obviously holding his hand until he was certain. Bergman thanked his lucky stars that *UB-702* bore more than a superficial resemblance to one of the Royal Navy's U-class coastal submarines.

Raising his cap he waved it enthusiastically as the aircraft crossed overhead. The British submarine ace Martin Nasmith had used a similar ruse to spoof a zeppelin in 1914. And while Bergman did not subscribe to the theory that history repeated itself it was always worth a try. Klemper, acting on his own initiative without waiting for the skipper's order, raised his lamp and flashed an immediate, and apparently incomprehensible reply to the interrogative signal.

The Wellington banked sharply to starboard and swept past the U-boat at wave-top level. The wing-tip lights flicked on and off in friendly greeting and Bergman saw an anonymous arm waving in the dim blue glow of the cockpit. Then the enemy climbed away towards the clouds, extinguished his lights, and vanished into the darkness of the western horizon.

The Korvettenkapitan let out a heart-felt sigh of relief and bent his mouth to the voicepipe. "All clear. Number one. Kill the lights." He paused for a moment. "Kantor's bought it—send up a couple of hands to clear the bridge. And I'll need a relief lookout at the double."

Pushing the plug back into the voicepipe Bergman turned to Klemper. "Good work, lad," he said quietly. "I'm glad you kept your head. It obviously did the trick—but what the hell did you send in that last message?"

The young Duty signaller had the grace to look slightly abashed. "I just sent—*fuck off you bastards!*" he told the skipper with a grin.

"Did you, by God," Bergman chuckled. It appealed to his sense of humour. "In English?"

"As a matter of fact, sir, yes—in English."

Bergman chuckled again. No wonder the Wellington pilot had taken *UB-702* to be a friendly vessel. It was just the sort of blistering retort a British submarine captain would have made in similar circumstances . . .

Despite Bergman's forebodings they reached the approaches to the Dover Straits without further incident and, having spent the whole of the following day lying doggo on the bottom, *UB-702* rose to periscope depth at sunset in readiness for the final and most dangerous part of her desperate dash for home.

The sea in the Narrows was calm and, with the moon just rising in the east, visibility was excellent. In fact, from Bergman's viewpoint, conditions could not have been worse. Peering carefully through the periscope he could see the screened head-lamps of cars moving slowly down the Kentish coast roads, while an occasional flash of bright light showed that someone ashore, forgetting the black-out regulations, had incautiously opened an unscreened door. Over on the port bow, and hugging close inshore to skirt the minefields, a coastal convoy chugged slowly towards the South Foreland—the shaded signal lamps of the escorts flashing instructions as they shepherded their flock into position. The treacherous Goodwin Sands, now darkly menacing with all navigational warning lights removed, lay less than 10 miles ahead, and the convoy commodore was anxious to have his charges firmly under control before moving into the danger area of mudbanks, shoals, and quicksands.

Swinging the periscope to starboard Bergman could just make out the dim outline of the French coast. It looked very quiet and peaceful. The scourge of war had moved on since those bloody days of June and July 1944 when he had taken Flotilla 271 searching for targets off the invasion beaches. The Allied armies were now deep inside Germany itself as East and West joined in the harsh race for the heart of the Fatherland. Bergman centered the periscope and forced himself to concentrate on the task in hand.

The black shape of a Hunt-class destroyer passing from Dieppe to Dover shifted quickly across their bows at a safe distance and *UB-702* maintained course and speed. The existence of a swept channel through the middle of Straits had been known to German Naval Intelligence for several months and although the precise limits of the swept area were not charted Bergman could hazard a reasonably accurate guess where they lay. Checking the gyro-compass and chart at regular intervals he held the U-boat closely to the course he had calculated the previous evening.

At least, he thought thankfully, he did not have to contend with the nets and destroyer patrols of the old Dover Barrage, like the U-boat skippers of the 1914-18 war. Air patrols, radar defences, and minefields sealed the Straits equally effectively but, somehow, they did not hold the same psychological terrors as the heavy steel-meshed nets that snared their victims twenty fathoms down leaving them helplessly tangled in wire, to die a slow and agonising death as their air supply gradually ran out. There had, in fact, been one instance where a U-boat captain had shot his entire crew rather than see them suffering such a fate.

"HE to starboard—three miles and moving fast."

Bergman turned the periscope to starboard and peered into the darkness. His eyes found a black shape moving against the horizon with the white froth of a bow-wave curling from her stem.

"Group down. Slow ahead both."

Baderhoff pulled down the double-pole rheostats of the port and starboard motors and cut the power. Turning the page of his magazine he resumed reading where he had been interrupted and waited for the next order. *UB-702* slowed to a crawling two knots and Bergman felt the bows slew sideways as the surge of the tide-race swung them to starboard.

"Increase to 200 revolutions! Hold her steady, *steuermann!*"

The extra power was just sufficient to counteract the thrust of the tide and *UB-702* came obediently back on course as Cap Gris-Nez slipped astern. The intruder, a Vosper motor gunboat moving at nearly forty knots, passed ahead on her bustling unimportant mission, and no one noticed the questing cyclop's stare of the one-eyed periscope feathering the water some 4,000 yards on their beam.

Bergman increased speed as soon as the danger had passed. He glanced at his watch. They had been running for two hours already and, making due allowance for the current and the speed variations occasioned by the odd alarms, they were now through the ten mile mark of this final hurdle. It was heartening to know that 75% of the obstacle course had been completed without incident.

The Korvettenkapitan's primary object was to remain at periscope depth as long as possible. The British had already begun sweeping the surface mines—those laid at shallow depths to trap surface vessels—and the anti-submarine fields were normally layered at eight fathoms and deeper to catch submerged U-boats at their most vulnerable. And while he could hold *UB-702* at between twenty and thirty feet, he had an even chance of passing over the deep-laid mines unscathed. Contact mines were her main danger—his de-gaussing cable ensured immunity from the magnetic variety. And, fortunately, the British had so far failed to perfect an acoustic weapon.

"HE dead ahead—three miles and approaching, sir."

Bergman cursed as he stared into the darkness. If

the enemy ship was on their reciprocal track a course change was unavoidable. And *that* would mean leaving the safety of the swept channel.

"Down periscope!"

He held course and speed while he waited anxiously for the next report.

"Radar plot—two bandits approaching from northeast, sir. Speed two hundred."

Obviously not fighters. The low speed suggested Coastal Command patrol aircraft on anti-submarine duties. And that raised another question—had the U-boat been spotted?

Bergman found himself facing a dilemma. Before turning away and leaving the swept channel it was vital to fix his position accurately. Yet even the briefest use of the periscope at this critical juncture increased the danger of being seen tenfold. And according to the rumours he'd heard, the enemy's new radar sets were so sensitive they could locate and track a U-boat periscope at a distance of two miles. Having reviewed the alternatives he decided to take the gamble.

A whisper of spray fanned the surface as the thin bronze attack 'scope emerged from the sea. Bergman had already lined the lens in the direction of the latest hydrophone report and he picked up the speeding shape of the frigate almost immediately. There was no time to take a positional fix. The enemy patrol ship was barely two miles ahead and he could just discern two more submarine hunters astern, mere shadows in the darkness.

The Bofors bow-chaser of the leading frigate was manned and he could see the barrel being depressed in readiness for instant action, the moment the U-boat broke surface. He cursed and lowered the periscope.

The enemy was closing in for the kill. There could be no doubt about it.

"Hard a'dive! Full ahead both—steer eight points to starboard!"

UB-702 tilted sharply in response to the hydroplanes and the vibrant hum of the motors rose to a shrill whine as Meitzger turned on full power. Water gurgled and roared into the ballast tanks and the U-boat plunged towards the bottom.

"Stop motors!"

The vibrations faded away and, in tomb-like silence, *UB-702* dropped down to the sea-bed in a state of negative buoyancy. Bergman halted their descent at 30 fathoms and waited while Schaft caught the trim and brought the U-boat on to an even keel.

"Rig for silent running! Secure for depth-charge attack!"

The warning was not issued a moment too soon. And as *UB-702* came level, the crack of the first explosion kicked her to starboard. Clinging tightly to one of the steel roof pillars Bergman wondered how much of a pounding his cranky unseaworthy command could take. He *could* just lie doggo and sweat it out. But those frigates carried up to 300 depth-charges apiece and he did not relish the prospect. Two more detonations shook every seam in the submarine, and as she swung back on to an even keel, Bergman could hear the trickle of water where the sea had found a weakness in the rusty hull plating. Moving quietly in his slippered feet, he ducked through the bulkhead hatch and found Chief Engineer Meitzger.

"Do we still have that contaminated fuel oil in the port bow bunker?" he whispered. Meitzger nodded. "Good—When I give you the signal I want you to open the feeder valves and release it. Then give me the maximum revolutions on the motors."

"It'll never work," Meitzger pointed out. "It's the oldest trick in the book—not even the greenest U-boat hunter would get taken in by it. And they'll track us on their Asdic which ever way we go."

Bergman grinned. "I know—that's what I *want* them to do. I intend to use the oil slick to show 'em *exactly* where we're going."

Meitzger wondered whether the Old Man had gone mad as Bergman squeezed through the circular hatchway and returned to the control room. He shrugged. And then, like a good U-boatman, he did as he was told—even though he knew it could mean utter and total annihilation. Sending two of his men to stand by the bunker valves he warned the rest of the motor room to be ready.

Bergman stood in the centre of the control room and waited. He had to select exactly the right moment or the plan would fail—the last twenty or so depth-charge explosions had been too far away. He *had* to make it look natural.

CRUM-M-P!

That was close! Close enough, in fact, for his purpose. Cork insulation was scattering down from the overhead seams like fine brown snow, and several light bulbs shattered in the reverberating concussion of the explosion.

"Full ahead both, Chief! Open the bunker valves!" He turned to Necker. "Port the helm one point and hold her steady."

"One point to port, sir," Necker intoned stolidly. "Steady as she goes."

UB-702 rolled violently in the shadow of two further explosions and the men in the control room clung

177

on grimly waiting for death. No one spoke a word. And no one held the skipper to blame for their terrifying predicament. Better to make a run for it even though they knew escape was impossible—at least it gave them something else to think about.

"HE spreading, sir. They seem to be circling."

Bergman nodded absently. His mind was concentrating on his mental picture of the Channel chart he had examined at Flotilla HQ. Everything now depended on the sureness of his memory and the accuracy of the Intelligence reports on the width of the swept channel.

Ping . . . ping . . . ping . . . ping . . .

The Asdic search gear of the hunters on the surface had found them and the steady metallic pulses echoed through the stuffy interior of the frightened U-boat like a clock ticking away the final minutes in the cell of a condemned prisoner. A pattern of three depth-charges flung the bows to the left and Bergman ordered a quick alteration of the helm to correct the course. Another vicious crash rolled *UB-702* on to her beam ends throwing everyone on to the deck; the unnerving hiss of fractured air lines and the insidious drip of water from the leaking hull increased tension to breaking point. But the next series of explosions were at least a hundred yards astern. And the following batch faded even further into the distance.

"HE falling astern, sir."

The hydrophone operator sounded more puzzled than relieved, by the unexpected reprieve. He listened carefully. "They seem to be turning away."

Bergman nodded. His gamble had apparently paid off. But could he expect his luck to hold much longer? Schaft broke the tension.

"They seem to have broken off the hunt, sir. How

the hell did you do it? They had us stone cold a few minutes ago."

"I merely turned their own weapons against them." Bergman smiled wearily. "It was a calculated risk but worth a try."

"But how?"

"If you remember, we were running up the centre of the swept channel when we had to dive. I changed direction in an attempt to fox them and then lay doggo while they thrashed around trying to find us. Well, they *did* find us, so I had to think of something else. I decided to leave a trail of oil to show them where we were going and then I steered straight out of the swept channel into the minefields."

"I follow you so far, sir," Schaft nodded. "But why did you wait before making a bolt for it?"

"I wanted to start moving after a near miss so that they'd think I was making a run for it with damaged bunkers. I had to play it that way or they might have figured what was up to and tried to cut me off before we were clear of the swept channel. I just made them over-confident."

"So that's why they stopped following us. They were scared of running on to their old mines." Schaft whistled softly. "You certainly think cool, sir."

"Don't get too carried away, Number One," Bergman said sourly. "You've overlooked one small detail."

"What's that, sir?"

"*We're in the middle of the bloody minefield ourselves now!*"

The grin on Schaft's face vanished. He swallowed hard.

"Christ almighty," he said fervently.

Bergman stood up and clapped his hand on the

179

Oberleutnant's shoulder. He'd enjoyed his humourless joke for long enough. "You can stop wetting your pants, Number One. It's not as bad as that. We should be in an area of surface mines, so provided we stay deep, we ought to make it. In fact I'd say we stand more chance of grounding in these waters, than we do of hitting a mine." He moved across to the chart and stared down at it thoughtfully. It was impossible to judge *UB-702*'s exact location but by deliberately maintaining a steady course and constant speed during the depth-charge hunt, he had a tolerably accurate idea where they were.

Despite his nonchalant explanation to the Oberleutnant, Bergman had laid his plans with customary care. This attention to detail was one of the reasons why he had survived six long years of war. He made a pencil mark on the chart and ringed it.

"Reduce to half speed—we've got to conserve battery power until we reach the Goodwins. Steer 0-4-0 and bring her up to 50 feet—we're standing towards shoaling water and I don't intend to get stuck in a sandbank."

Making a bare two knots against the strength of the flood tide *UB-702* glided north-eastwards on almost silent motors. Bergman brought the U-boat up to periscope depth at fifteen minute intervals, and having satisfied himself that there were no search patrols in the vicinity, returned to the depths again. The moon was now riding high in the night sky and he was able to use the reflected light to fix his position by silvered landmarks along the French coast. It was a rough-and-ready method of navigation but there was no time to take accurate bearings. And it was sufficient for his purposes.

By dawn UB-702 was safely east of the treacherous

Goodwins. Confident that the worst dangers were now behind them, the Korvettenkapitan handed the Forenoon Watch over to Schaft as eight bells tinkled. Then, heavy-eyed with exhaustion he disappeared into his tiny cabin to snatch his first sleep for forty-eight hours.

The strident clash of cymbals sent the blood tingling through Bergman's veins as the orchestra soared to an ecstatic climax. The teutonic majesty of Wagner never failed to excite his emotions and *Tännhauser* was the composer's greatest masterpiece. With Rahel's hand grasped tightly on his own he relaxed and surrendered himself to the music. The fact that the Opera House was completely empty except for the orchestra did not worry him. Stranger things could happen in dreams.

But some damned fool fiddle player was spoiling it. The inharmonious scrape of his bow on the strings of the violin sounded like a taut steel cable sliding reluctantly across a hollow metal cylinder. The muted screech drowned the titanic might of the Berlin State Symphony Orchestra, and the grating noise snapped the Korvettenkapitan angrily upright in his seat . . .

Bergman rubbed his eyes as he sat up in the narrow bunk. The Opera House had disappeared. So had Rahel. And the entire orchestra. But the nerve-grating rasp of the lone fiddler remained.

He was awake in an instant and he swung his legs off the bunk with a curse. Pulling on a heavy sweater, he hurried to the control room. The ghostly screech of the tortured violin followed mockingly at his heels.

The drawn grey faces of the men in the control room reflected the cold fingers of terror clutching their hearts. Even Schaft looked worried and

Bergman could see beads of sweat trickling down his forehead. He strode to the chart table, glanced at his watch to check the elapsed time, and stared down at the map.

"Stop engines!"

"Sounds like some sort of A/S sweep or grappling tackle," Schaft volunteered as the throb of the electric motors faded away.

Bergman had seen all he needed in his swift examination of the chart. He turned on the Oberleutnant. "Don't be a fool, man," he snapped. "They stopped using explosive sweeps against submarines in 1918— and grappling gear is only employed for locating sunken wrecks. Why the hell didn't you check the chart and use your intelligence?"

Bergman was understandably angry. And he had every right to be. As the Officer of the Watch, Schaff had had a chance, a small one admittedly but a chance nevertheless, to save *UB-702*. The tidal flow was virtually due west and the scraping noise was located on the port side of the hull. With the U-boat's bows pointing north-east a quick touch of the helm to starboard would have swung them clear and the flood tide would have swept the danger away. But it was now probably too late. The Korvettenkapitan swallowed his anger.

"That noise is being made by the mooring cable of a mine scraping down the side of the hull," he explained. "It's passed the midships section and is now running towards the stern. If we're lucky I may manage to get clear. And if I don't . . ." he left the rest of the sentence unfinished.

But the wind and tide, Bergman's trusted allies on so many previous occasions, had turned traitor. And as *UB-702* drifted on dead engines the tidal current forced the U-boat more tightly against the taut steel mooring cable until it curved round the ballast tanks like a trapped fly straining to escape from the strands of a spider's web.

It seemed ironical, that having been saved from destruction by the presence of the enemy minefields in the Dover Straits, they should now fall victim to one of Germany's own minefields protecting the coast of Flanders. And Bergman's only consolation lay in the fact that he at least knew the type of weapon he had tangled with. Having spent several months at the mine warfare school on Heligoland he could strip most types of Kriegsmarine mines blindfolded—and the *Mk 17* was no mystery.

"We still have a chance, Oberleutnant. Von Krantz put this field down to protect our inshore convoys from attack by enemy coastal forces. He used conventional contact weapons designed for use against shallow draught surface ships—motor gunboats and things. They're moored to sinkers on the sea bottom and the detonator horns are all set in the upper part of the sphere. So, even if we bump upwards against the canister, we're unlikely to trigger off the explosive charge."

No one inside the control room seemed very convinced by Bergman's explanation. Too many U-boats had fallen victim to mines in both world wars and, after the depth-charge it was probably the most lethal anti-submarine weapon yet devised. And, right now, the mooring cable attached to one of these deadly explosive-filled canisters, was slithering and sliding along the plating of *UB-702*'s hull with only the fickle jade of the wind and tide between them and eternity.

"Slow ahead starboard motor."

Bergman whispered the instruction as if the sound of his voice would be sufficient to trigger the sensitive detonators. Raw fear could be contagious in the confined and crowded space of a submarine's control room.

The answering tinkle of the telegraph filtered back from the motor room and *UB-702* quivered softly as Inquart opened the current from the batteries. The U-boat groped to starboard and not a man dared to breathe as Bergman eased the vessel away from the clinging vine of the mine cable. Then, suddenly, they heard the scraping rasp of the fiddler's ghostly bow again. And this time Bergman knew beyond doubt that *UB-702* was the instrument upon which he was playing his terrifying tune.

"The propeller guards on the fan-tail will push it clear," he whispered as much to boost his own confidence as to encourage the others.

"There's no guard on the port quarter, sir," Schaft whispered back. "That was one of the refitting jobs they didn't complete before we left Wilhelmshaven."

"Stop engines!"

But it was too late. With no protective steel guard to push the cable aside it slithered along the inner side of the hydroplane's horizontal fin and jammed against the pivot gearing like a fishing line snagged by a hidden rock. The U-boat shuddered to a lurching stop as the cable pulled taut and Bergman felt his mouth go dry. Although he knew nothing beyond the tell-tale succession of sinister noises on the outside of the hull he did not need a diagram to work out what had happened.

UB-702 hung motionless in the water like a fly trapped on sticky paper, as the mine cable anchored the submarine to the heavy sinker, buried in the mud on the bottom of the sea, ten fathoms below. The tide was due to turn in a matter of minutes and, when the direction of the prevailing current altered, the mine would be dragged down on to its helpless victim. Bergman weighed the possibilities with the probing clarity of a surgeon at the critical point of a dangerous operation. If he did not act immediately his patient would die—yet one slip of the knife would be equally fatal. He seemed destined to lose in either event. But it was not in his nature to sit back and allow the inevitable to happen without some action on his part.

"Blow the stern tanks!"

As the valve wheels were spun down and the sharp whine of high-pressure air hissed through the U-boat, Bergman felt the stern lift. The ebbing tide was still pushing the mine away from the U-boat's cigar-shaped hull, and he could picture the cable tightening into a sharp angle as the stern began to rise.

"Stop blowing! Blow bow tanks 3 and 4!"

The cable straightened out as the bows lifted and after twenty seconds Bergman gave the order to stop blowing. According to the depth-gauges the U-boat was trimmed at 25 feet—which meant, after allowing for the vertical width of the hull, that the explosive canister was now poised no more than six feet above the level of the deck plating. It was as far as he dared.

"Up periscope!"

Pushing his face into the hooded eye-pieces he turned the bronze column towards the stern and tilted the viewing lens until it was pointing down towards the fan-tail. The water was fairly clear and he could just make out the vague shape of the deadly *KM*

Mk-17 mine swaying gently above the shadowed darkness of the hull like a cobra poised to strike.

"Slow ahead both . . . *stop!*"

The mine was drawn downwards towards the stern as the cable shortened around the hydroplane, and Bergman halted its descent barely twelve inches from the unyielding steel of the deck plates.

"Slow astern both . . . *stop!*"

The cable slid a few inches along the hull and then jammed against a protruding rivet head. Bergman wiped the wetness from his face and tried again.

"Slow ahead both . . . steady . . . *stop!*"

The metallic clatter of the mine casing striking the hull sounded like a death-knell and for an instant every heart stopped beating. But Bergman had been right. The sensitive detonator horns were on the upper section of the sphere and the unnerving bump proved to be as harmless as he had predicted. Taking a deep breath, and watching every movement of the mine through the lens of *UB-702's* periscope, he made another attempt to throw off their unwelcome passenger.

"Slow astern both . . ." The cable scraped ominously along the side of the U-boat, hesitated for a moment as it snagged the rivet ahead, strained free of the obstruction, and started to move forward again.

"Stop port motor!" The telegraph tinkled its vital message to the motor room. "Full ahead starboard!"

UB-702 pivoted on her tail with the grace of a ballerina as the mooring cable slipped clear of the hydroplane. Her stern swung to the right and her bows circled left. Bergman watched the evil canister bobbing gently astern as the wash from the starboard propeller swept it safely away from the hull.

"Hard a'starboard, *steuermann!*" Pretz spun the

helm and *UB-702* came up straight as the rudder counteracted the drag of the idling propeller. "Full ahead both—steer 0-7-0. Hands to stand down to cruising routine."

Utterly drained by the physical and mental demands of the last thirty minutes the men in the control room slumped into sitting positions on the deck. No one spoke a word. They were like pale shadows of men who had shaken hands with Death and walked away again to tell the tale. And as the inevitable reaction set in, even the Oberleutnant had to grip the edge of the chart table to hide the trembling of his hands.

There was no jubilation in the drawn grey faces of the exhausted U-boatmen. Not even satisfaction at still being alive. And no word of thanks to the man who had brought them back from the very threshold of eternity.

Bergman felt no resentment at their apparent lack of gratitude. He did not expect their thanks either.

He was a U-boat commander.

That was satisfaction enough.

CHAPTER NINE

Bergman's mind was haunted by memories as *UB-702* rounded the black and white chequered buoy marking the starboard entrance to the dredged channel and glided slowly towards the main jetty of the U-boat basin. He could still recall the happy days when submarines leaving on war patrol were garlanded with laurel leaves. And when a military band and a bevy of eager girls loaded with flowers and bottles of wine waited on the quayside to welcome them back.

But not any more. The only sounds to greet *UB-702* on her return to Wilhelmshaven were the dying cadences of the warning sirens heralding the start of another air attack. The main jetty was deserted as the dockyard workers scurried for cover in the bomb shelters. And the only flowers were the purple fire-weeds blossoming profusely in the ruins of burned and blasted buildings. Green wreck markers fringed the graveyard of the deep channel leads and, at low water, the masts and funnels of sunken ships thrust forlornly above the surface like skeletons.

All remaining operational U-boats had been withdrawn to Gruppe West's new base at Bergen the previous month and the majority of the surviving ships still moored in the outer roadstead were battle-scarred and unfit for service. Only the 6,650 ton light cruiser *Koln*, tied up to Pier 12, gave any impression of fighting value and Bergman stiffened to attention and saluted the ensign fluttering at her stern as *UB-702* slid past.*

Leaving Schaft to supervise the final stages of the mooring routine Bergman jumped on to the quay the moment the U-boat came alongside and hurried up the stone steps leading to the top of the jetty. Circling the piles of rubble and picking his way carefully across the bomb craters he found the sandbagged entrance to 94 Flotilla Headquarters, showed his pass to the sentry, and went down the narrow wooden stairs to the underground operations room, burrowed deep under the earth beneath a solid concrete roof. As he reached the bottom of the steps he heard the flak batteries open up defiantly as the first wave of bombers approached.

Kommodore Keitler was half-dozing in his chair and he awoke with a start as Bergman entered. His face was lined with exhaustion and he had obviously not slept properly for days—possibly weeks. A spluttering oil lamp swung a few inches above his head while another, standing on the side of his desk, illuminated the papers on which he was working. Allied

* *Koln*, almost the last of Hitler's major warships, was sunk by Allied bombers in Wilhelmshaven on 30 April 1945.

bombing had destroyed the main electricity power-station several weeks earlier, and Germany's dwindling reserves of fuel oil could not be spared to operate the emergency generators.

"You were told to report to Bergen," Keitler snapped impatiently as he recognised Bergman in the dim light. "Why the hell can't you ever obey your orders?"

"I received your orders three days ago, sir. But there was only sufficient oil in our bunkers to get this far." The Kommodore's attitude needled him. "How the hell did you expect me to get to Norway—paddle?"

"For all the good you'll do here, you might just as well have done so," Keitler said sourly. "As soon as the enemy discovers there's a serviceable U-boat tied up to the pier he'll throw everything he's got at us until it's been destroyed."

"But why Bergen?"

Keitler put his elbows on the desk. He rubbed his hands wearily across his face. "How long have you been on patrol, Korvettenkapitan?"

"Twenty-three days, sir."

The Kommodore looked up at the calendar on the wall. Someone had added nipples to the smooth-breasted Nordic beauty surmounting the catalogue of days. Bergman decided that green didn't suit her. But perhaps they were short of red ink as well.

"When you sailed with *UB-702* the enemy had just crossed the Rhine at Ossenburg," Keitler explained in a flatly expressionless monotone. "By the beginning of this month they were spearheading towards the Ems—the British 2nd Army pushing up through Holland, and the Americans advancing beyond Frankfurt. Since then, the entire German defence system has collapsed. Units are fighting where they can and with what they can. There is no cohesion, no centralised command, and no master defence plan. Just complete and total chaos. Russian tanks are already in the outskirts of Berlin itself and the Red Army has occupied Vienna. Does that explain why the U-boat flotillas have been pulled out and sent to Norway?"

Bergman nodded. The war situation was even worse than his most pessimistic expectations. Surely the end could now be only days away. He said nothing.

"We thought at one time the Yanks would try to race the Russians for Berlin," Keitler continued. "I even heard talk of a scheme to link our military forces with them to prevent the Red Army penetrating any further west." He shrugged. "But it never came to anything. The British moved northwards towards Hamburg and the Yanks piddled about and lost their chance. It smelled of a political deal if you ask me. I can't imagine Eisenhower or the other enemy top brass letting Stalin get to Berlin first—unless they received orders to do so."

Bergman nodded impatiently as Keitler droned on. It was obvious that the Kommodore had already resigned himself to the prospects of defeat and surrender. He seemed to be showing a marked preference for the role of armchair strategist, rather than giving constructive thought as to how the fight could be continued.

"We can leave those sort of problems to OKW," he told Keitler. "Right now I want to know what I'm to do with *UB-702*."

"Nothing," the Kommodore snapped curtly. "Oberleutnant Schaft has been appointed to take over command." He fumbled with the papers on his desk, pulled out a pink coloured signal flimsy, and moved the oil lamp across the desk so that he could read it. "You're to go to Berlin—direct orders from the *Fuhrerbunker*. There's no transport available so you'll have to take my staff car."

"But why send me to Berlin? Didn't anyone tell OKW that it's over a hundred miles from the sea. What am I supposed to do when I get there—torpedo the bloody rowing boats on the *Poltzen See*?"

Keitler ignored the outburst. "Certain selected personnel from the *Kleine-kampfmittel-Verband* are being recalled to the capital. Apparently the Fuehrer has dismissed his bodyguard and will trust no one with his personal protection other than the K-flotilla men." He smiled cynically. "I suppose you could regard it as an honour."

"But I've been out of the *K-Verband* for more than six months," Bergman protested. "Why pick on *me*?"

"I really cannot imagine," Keitler said with heavy sarcasm. "But those are your orders. I have briefed my driver on the route to take. And you are to report to Admiral Lüben when you get there."

Bergman knew it was useless to argue. He bowed stiffly. It seemed utterly pointless to recall him to the capital. But, then, the whole bloody war was pointless now. He consoled himself with the thought that he'd probably never get to Berlin anyway. Most of the bridges had been blown up, and any vehicle trying to move along the remaining roads, was immediately shot up by enemy ground-attack fighters the moment it was spotted.

Keitler stood up wearily and held out his hand. "I don't envy you your prospects, Korvettenkapitan. Berlin is certainly the last place I'd want to be at this particular moment—you've no doubt heard what the

Russians do with any officers they capture." He released Bergman's hand and turned away. "I shall be lucky. Wilhelmshaven will undoubtedly fall to the British in a matter of days. And the Royal Navy is certain to treat senior officers with its customary politeness and consideration. You know I'm looking forward to a hot meal, and a bath, and a nice clean bed to sleep in. In fact I can hardly wait for them to get here."

"And sod you too," thought Bergman.

Berlin, the ancient capital of Prussia, the cornerstone of the Thousand Year Reich, and the nerve centre of Nazi Germany's war effort, was little more than a smouldering heap of rubble by the time Bergman reached the beleaguered city on the evening of 28 April.

The night sky glowed an angry red as uncontrollable fires raged in the streets of the eastern suburbs and the thunder of the Russian artillery barrage rumbled incessantly. Every now and again a searing yellow flame marked the death of a Soviet tank as *Volksturm* units hit back from the ruins–their success more than counter-balanced by the crashing roar of buildings tumbling to the ground, as Russian shells tore out the heart of the defiant capital.

Bergman had completed his gruelling journey from Wilhelmshaven on the back of an army motorcycle–Keitler's staff car had run out of petrol at Brandenburg–and he arrived in Berlin tired, mud-spattered, and bad-tempered. The soldiers guarding the entrance to the Chancellery were unsympathetic, and despite his protests they refused to allow him through the barrier until his papers had been inspected and verified by the security office. The area around the Chancellery was already under sporadic fire by Russian artillery, and he was forced to crouch inside a narrow sandbagged slit trench while he waited for permission to enter. A high-explosive shell, bursting less than 20 yards from his makeshift shelter, slammed him against the damp earth at the back of the trench. The experience did little to improve his appearance or his state of mind.

A guard—the grey dust which grimed his uniform making it impossible to determine to which branch of the services he belonged—appeared out of the darkness, saluted smartly, and told the Korvettenkapitan to follow him. They ducked behind a wall of sandbags, slithered into a half-dug trench, crossed an open stretch of grass that had once been an immaculate lawn, and stopped at a barbed wire fence. Bergman could feel the earth shaking beneath his feet as more shells exploded around the massive grey stone building, and in the midst of the din, he heard the faint tak-tak-tak of distant machine gun fire, as Soviet tanks and infantry advanced deeper into the city.

A Wehrmacht officer opened a gate in the wire fence and escorted him down the steps to the vast complex of bunkers beneath the Chancellery. Strings of naked electric bulbs hanging down from temporary power cables lit the maze of concrete tunnels, and the throb of diesel generators echoed through the narrow passages. Bergman was conscious of an appalling smell.

"You'll soon get used to it," his escort shrugged. "I don't suppose it's any worse than the stink inside your bloody U-boats. A Russian shell fractured the main sewer pipe last night, and it's leaking into the bunkers," he explained. "There's no air conditioning and the ventilators have been sealed as a precaution against a possible enemy gas attack. There's nothing much we can do about it."

Bergman looked at the brown sludge oozing down the walls and shuddered. He wondered whether the Fuehrer's bunker had a similar decoration on its walls.

Admiral Lüben occupied a small concrete hole somewhere on the western side of the complex. A young *Leutnant-zur-see* was crouched over a portable wireless transmitter in the corner rapidly scribbling down the signal crackling into his headphones. Two signal ratings sat on the floor alongside him each with a telephone—one painted red, the other black. Bergman noted that both men had a revolver holstered to their belt webbing, and that even the Admiral kept a Walther P-38 at hand on top of his desk.

Lüben, a tight-faced man with greying hair, wasted no time on pleasantries. "We have had to change our plans since you were recalled from Wilhelmshaven, Korvettenkapitan. It is now possible that you may be sent to Kiel."

"What the hell's going on?" Bergman demanded. Admiral or no admiral he was angry. And he made no effort to disguise it. "First of all they take my boat away from me. Then they tell me to report to Berlin on the personal orders of the Fuehrer. And when I get here *you* tell me I'm to go to Kiel. Can't any one make their bloody mind up in Germany these days?"

"I can sympathize with your feelings, Korvettenkapitan," Lüben said suavely. "But you must appreciate that we are labouring under some difficulty. It was intended originally that you would be given command of the K-flotilla unit when it arrived. That is why the

196

Fuehrer personally asked for *you*. But, unfortunately, this is no longer possible."

"Why? What happened?"

"Everything went wrong. We managed to get 30 K-men assembled at Rerick yesterday—and we even got hold of three Ju-52 transports to fly them in. As you probably know, *Tempelhof* and all the other airfields are in enemy hands, so we planned to land the aircraft on the east-west axial road between the Victory Column and the *Brandenburger Tor*. Unfortunately, the operation had to be postponed after a Luftwaffe scouting machine reported that our proposed landing-strip was within range of Russian flak. And this morning, we've heard that the road is now pitted with shell craters and completely unusable.*

"But surely we still have *Waffen-SS* units in Berlin. Why do we have to use Navy personnel to fight the Russian army?"

Lüben shook his head. "There is no time to explain, Korvettenkapitan. A great many things have happened in the last few days. I understand the Fuehrer has dismissed Himmler and he can therefore no longer trust the SS. Even Goering has been arrested for trying to negotiate peace terms."

"So what do *I* do? Sit on my arse and wait for a Russian bayonet?"

"No, until the situation has clarified, you are to take over the north-west perimeter covering the defence line along the *Berliner Spree*. You will be replacing your friend Kommodore Gratz—his command post in the *Sportsplatz* was over-run by Soviet tanks last night. Your task will be one of co-ordination. And pay particular attention to traitors. The Fuehrer has given

---

* This account is quite true.

personal orders that all traitors—and that includes any man who retreats in the face of the enemy or who endeavours to surrender—are to be shot on sight."

Bergman knew it was useless to argue. The struggle could not go on much longer and no matter what else might happen, he was determined to survive these final days. He had not endured six years of savage war at sea just to die in the gutter of a Berlin street. He saluted truculently, turned on his heel, and left the bunker . . .

Command Post 19 was situated in a ruined house on the *Kurfürst Platz*. The upper windows at the rear overlooked the river and the Wehrmacht leutnant in charge of the sector obviously resented taking orders from a Kriegsmarine officer, even though the Korvettenkapitan was his superior by four ranks. He was brusque, unhelpful, and generally bloody-minded. Bergman wondered idly whether the young army leutnant could possibly be categorised as a traitor and decided, a trifle reluctantly, that he would be stretching the rules too far.

"Have you checked along the river bank? The Russians might try using inflatable rafts to ferry an assault group across."

"I have no men to spare," Fürstt retorted. "My platoon—or what's left of it—is well sited and we've got good cover. All the bridges in this sector have been blown up and I don't intend to send any of my men along the river bank to be picked off by Russian snipers. As a member of the Kriegsmarine," he added sarcastically, "I would have thought a river patrol more *your* mark."

Bergman was too tired to engage in a wordy argument. And, as a realist, he could understand the army officer's reluctance to send his men out into the open. But the river worried him. It was the last natural obstacle guarding the centre of the city and once the enemy had bridged the water nothing could prevent their final victory. Looking out of the top windows at the front of the house he could see the roof of the Chancellery barely a thousand yards away behind the trees of the *Tiergarten.* He shrugged and went down the back stairs into the garden.

The gate opened directly on to the river but everything seemed quiet and deserted and there was no sign of life on the opposite bank. Bergman turned left towards the remains of the Luther bridge. He walked slowly, his keen eyes searching for some indication of enemy activity, and his body tensed like a tautened bow string. It was an ideal spot to make a landing, and glancing back over his shoulder, he realised that a clump of tall poplar trees screened the river bank from Fürstt's observation post on the roof of the house.

With his feet scrunching on the gravel path Bergman knew that stealth was impossible, and as he began searching the area in detail, he took the precaution of unholstering his pistol. It was an obvious weak point in the perimeter defences, and whether Fürstt liked it or not, he would have to send a couple of men down to the bank with a field telephone, so that the waiting troops received some sort of advance warning if the Russians attempted to land.

"Halt! Raise your hands and don't move!"

The order was given in German, and assuming he had encountered a Wehrmacht patrol moving east from the Charlottenberg sector, Bergman stopped and raised his hands obediently. A powerful flash-light suddenly cut through the darkness and he blinked in the blinding dazzle. The bushes edging the tow-path rustled and two figures emerged. They were wearing Russian uniforms and were carrying *Degtyarew* submachine guns.

The third man switched off his lamp and joined the others. He, too, was wearing a Soviet army uniform and two metal stars glinted on the high-button collar of his tunic. Bergman could not see the officer's face and he stood like a frozen statue, his eyes looking straight ahead, as the third figure walked around behind his body and examined him from all angles. Then, to his surprise, he heard the officer chuckle. And even more surprisingly, there was something very familiar about the sound.

"Good God! Of *all* people—what the hell are you doing in Berlin, Konrad?"

Zetterling!

What was a Kriegsmarine oberleutnant doing in an enemy officer's uniform? Was he on some sort of special mission that took him behind the Russian lines—or had he defected. Bergman kept his arms raised. He decided to play it carefully.

"Well, I'm danned. I wondered where you'd disappeared to." He took a chance and lowered his hands. "What's going on?"

Zetterling said something to the soldiers and they moved discreetly out of earshot. The Oberleutnant waited until they were far enough away and then, taking the Korvettenkapitan's arm, guided him into the shadow of the bushes.

"This is great," he told Bergman. "You were the last person I ever expected to see in Berlin. In fact it couldn't be better. But I thought you'd be in Kiel by now."

"Kiel—why the hell should I be in Kiel? Gruppe West's flotillas are operating from Bergen now."

Zetterling nodded. "I *know* that—I meant I thought you'd be getting your boat ready for your Argentine mission."

"*What* Argentine mission?" Bergman sounded slightly exasperated. The whole situation seemed strangely unreal and he half-expected to find himself being woken by the familiar shout of *Captain to the control room.* Here was Zetterling, appearing like a shadow from the past, wearing the uniform of Germany's enemy. And himself trapped in the blazing ruins of Berlin within earshot of Russian guns. Had the entire world gone mad—or was it only himself?

Zetterling took a crumpled cigarette from his pocket, lit it carefully so that the flame of his match did not reveal their position, and blew a stream of smoke towards the river. "Don't you know why you were recalled to Berlin?" he asked.

Bergman shook his head. "No, I damn well don't. And if *you* do I'd be interested to find out. But first of all, why the Russian uniform? Are you on special duties?"

Zetterling grinned, took a final puff at his cigarette, and threw the stub into the river. The glowing ash hissed as it struck the water. He decided it was time to tell Bergman the truth.

"I've been working for the Russians since 1939. Who do you think found the cash to operate Group Anton?" He stared at Bergman's face to see his reaction but the Korvettenkapitan's expression did not even flicker. "I fed them all the information I could until Görst and the Gestapo got on my tail. I wound up the Group and tried to get across Poland. And when that didn't work I joined the Navy—it was the

201

only way I could keep out of the Gestapo's clutches, you see," he added by way of explanation, "the Kriegsmarine were only too happy to enlist the services of a top salvage expert so nobody asked too many questions."

"I see," Bergman said slowly. "So that business with UB-59 was just a pack of lies."

"Only to a point. Georg Holst was certainly carrying a list when the U-boat sank. But it was a list of *British* agents the Russians wanted to liquidate so that they could infiltrate their own people. My job was to retrieve the list and get it back to Moscow."

"And did you?"

Zetterling nodded. "Thanks to your help—yes. All the British and pro-Western agents in Poland and eastern Germany were removed. That's why the Russian army was able to move so fast once they were across the Oder river. Everything was organised and ready for them. If you hadn't helped me get that list the Red Army would still be two hundred miles east of Berlin. And those guns you can hear banging away out there would have been British or American."

Bergman said nothing as he digested Zetterling's bombshell. It was incredible and yet it made sense. Why the hell hadn't he realised what Rahel's brother had been up to? To think that he, of all people, had allowed himself to be manipulated by the Communists. And now he was seeing the bitter fruits of the harvest he had helped to sow. He shrugged. It was too late in the day for regrets.

"Perhaps I knew what I was doing," he lied hopefully. Survival was all that mattered now. And perhaps something could be salvaged from the wreck even at this eleventh hour. "But what's all this nonsense about Kiel?"

Zetterling smiled. He could afford to. Bergman had already unwittingly helped him once and this unexpected meeting was a gift from the gods that could not be ignored. Zetterling's reputation with his MVD* masters was already high. And here was a chance that only a fool would pass up. The Oberleutnant had other old scores to settle too. He had always considered Bergman directly responsible for Rahel's torture and death at the hands of the Gestapo. If the fool had played his cards correctly, Görst would never have got her into his clutches. Well, Zetterling thought, let's save the Korvettenkapitan a little while longer. He still has his uses.

"Ah, yes . . . Kiel," he said slowly as if he had been considering his reply to the question Bergman had asked. "You obviously haven't been told yet but you've been appointed to command one of those *Type XXI* boats you were always talking about—*U-2555*. She's lying under camouflage nets at Friedrichsort to keep her well clear of the bombing."

Bergman knew the town from his pre-war service at Kiel. It was situated a few miles down the fiord north of the main dockyard and it was on the seaward side of the Baltic entrance to the canal. It marked the end of the nine fathom channel and he could remember watching for the small jetty as a landmark each time he passed up or down Kiel Fiord.

"How do *you* know all this?" he asked. "Admiral Lüben mentioned Kiel but he said nothing about a U-boat."

Zetterling grinned and tapped his nose with his finger. "I imagine we know more about German plans that even OKW does itself. Soviet technicians have

* Russian secret police.

got direct taps on all landlines from Berlin and we've broken both your military and diplomatic codes. In addition to that we have reliable agents working in nearly every key communications centre. Even Hitler couldn't blow his nose without us knowing." He paused, lit himself another cigarette, and drew the smoke into his lungs. "And speaking of the Fuehrer—he'll be one of your VIP passengers."

"Rubbish! The Fuehrer is still in his bunker at the Chancellery." Bergman had been prepared to listen and believe most of Zetterling's story, but he was not *that* gullible.

"That's what *you* think." Zetterling was enjoying himself. "You've met him on several occasions so you'd recognise him. Did they take you in to see him when you arrived."

Bergman hesitated. "No—but there's nothing unusual about that, surely? Why should the Fuehrer want to see me as soon as I arrive in Berlin?"

"Not even when you'd been personally selected to command his bodyguard?" Zetterling retorted. "I'd say that was very odd. Unless, of course, someone was afraid you wouldn't recognise him."

"All right," Bergman snapped impatiently. "Stop talking in riddles. Why not let me into the secret."

"A few months ago there was a Polish tailor living in Cracow. He bore a remarkable physical resemblance to the Fuehrer. In fact the local kids used to call him Adolf when he walked down the street. Then one day, out of the blue, the SS arrived and drove him off in a large Mercedes. No one took any notice at first. But then the MVD discovered that Grodowski—that was his name, by the way—was receiving treatment in the private wing of Berlin's most important dental hospital."

He paused to smoke his cigarette. "Fortunately we had someone on the staff of the hospital and we found that the surgeons were duplicating the Fuehrer's dental work in Grodowski's mouth," he went on. "Odd, you may think, but not very significant. Well, to cut a long story short, he was moved into the Potsdamer General Hospital a few weeks later for surgery—a left testectomy to be precise."

"What the hell does that mean?" Bergman asked.

"It means they cut one of his balls off," Zetterling grinned. "Now do you see what they were doing? They were giving Grodowski the exact physical characteristics that properly belonged to Adolf Hitler. The very characteristics that forensic experts would use to identify a burned or mutilated corpse. They were setting Grodowski up to impersonate Hitler's corpse!"

"So you're trying to tell me that the man in the Chancellery is not the Fuehrer but some Polish tailor? And that's why I wasn't allowed to meet him. I don't believe a single word of it. And supposing this phantasy is true—where is the Fuehrer now?"

"I can tell you that too," Zetterling said easily. "He's hiding in a small farm at Scharnhagen about five miles from Kiel. Eva Braun is with him and so is Martin Bormann. And as soon as you arrive they'll all embark on U-2555. Incidentally you'll probably be interested to know that the U-boat is carrying over 20 million marks' worth of gold bars in sealed containers."

"I've never heard so much preposterous rubbish in my life," Bergman snapped angrily.

Zetterling shrugged. "I don't care whether you believe it or not. That's the way it's going to happen. You'll find it's true enough when you get on board U-

2555. And that's why I'm going to let you go. I *want* you to take over command."

Although the whole story sounded totally incredible Bergman was curious to know what his former Oberleutnant planned to do. "All right," he said grudgingly. "Let's suppose your story is correct. Why do you want me to command U-2555? And, equally important, what do *I* stand to get out of it?"

"Your task will be simple enough. As soon as you're clear of Kiel Fiord you will steer eastwards into the Baltic and make for Gdynia. Soviet patrol ships and aircraft will escort you so you'll come to no harm. And then you'll hand your passengers over to the proper authorities."

"But why do you want Hitler? If you know where he is why not kill him and have done with it. He's no threat to the world any more."

Zetterling smiled at Bergman's lack of politcal instinct. Like most professional naval officers he was unable to see further than the nose on his face.

"The Soviet Government will try him as a war criminal," he explained. "We intend to prove that the Nazi war machine was controlled and financed by the western capitalists and that the attack on Russia was a carefully planned assault on Communism and the world proletariat. We already possess documents proving that the Western Allies intend to fight side-by-side with the German army, to prevent any further advance into Europe by the forces of the workers' democracy."

Bergman ignored Zetterling's flights of fancy. Standing with both feet firmly on the ground he was concerned with the realities of the situation.

"All right," he said. "So I hand the Fuehrer over at

Gdynia. But then what happens to me and the rest of the crew of *U-2555*?"

"The men will be repatriated if they wish—you have my word on that. As for yourself . . ." Zetterling paused. He was deadly serious. "Your services would be invaluable to the Soviet Navy. I can personally guarantee you an excellent appointment—probably flag rank—if you carry out your part of the bargain. We intend to develop our submarine flotillas on a large scale. By 1960, in fifteen years time, we plan to have 400 submarines in service—as many as Doenitz had at the peak of the U-boat war.* Just imagine the opportunities."

Bergman made no comment. He nodded. "I still don't believe a word you've said, Karl. But if I get orders to go to Kiel and *if* I am posted at *U-2555* I may consider taking up your offer—I'd like to be able to look forward to some security in my old age. I must insist on one condition however."

"And what's that?"

"I must have twenty-four hours free of all interference, after I leave Friedrichsort. I will need to put the boat through her paces in case of emergencies." He shrugged. "Just a routine precaution, you understand. But if Russian aircraft start buzzing me it's bound to attract attention from other quarters and it won't take long for the Yanks or the RAF to poke their noses in. And I don't give your plan much chance of success if they do."

Zetterling could see Bergman's point. He nodded his agreement. "Very well—twenty-four hours."

* The greatest strength of the U-boat flotillas was reached in January 1945 when Germany had 433 submarines in service. In 1970 the Soviet Navy was estimated to possess 65 nuclear-powered and 320 conventional submarines.

"I wonder what would have happened if the long arm of coincidence hadn't led us to meet like this?" Bergman mused.

"I would have contacted you by radio as soon as *U-2555* sailed," Zetterling said. "I felt so certain where your sympathies lay that I *knew* you would agree to carry out the plan. It might have been more difficult if some other captain had been appointed." He paused and stared reflectively into the water. Then he looked up. "Let's hope our luck continues. I must get back to our side of the lines. There's going to be a lot to do before you get to Kiel." He held out his hand but Bergman ignored it. He recovered quickly and hid his embarrassment with a grin. "Cheerio, Konrad. Give me five minutes to get across the river and then you get back to the Chancellery and see if they've prepared your new orders. See you in Gdynia."

Bergman stood on the bank and watched as one of the soldiers slid the inflatable rubber assault raft into the river and helped Zetterling climb into it. The paddles dipped into the water and the raft started towards the opposite bank.

So that's what a traitor looks like, he thought to himself. He fingered the butt of his Mauser but despite his orders and the urges of his own patriotic instincts he could not bring himself to do it. Zetterling might be a traitor but who could blame him in the circumstances? And when Bergman remembered the fate of the Jews at the merciless hands of their Nazi oppressors he felt a certain sympathy for the young political idealist. Yet, as he turned away and started walking back to Command Post 19, Bergman knew that he was merely finding excuses for his own weakness. There was only one reason why he had not shot Zetterling. And that reason was Rahel Yousoff.

There was a strange irony in the way events unfolded, Bergman reflected. Rahel had sacrificed herself to prevent him from falling into the clutches of Görst and the Gestapo. And by doing so she had unwittingly saved her brother from a bullet in the back.

Bergman threw himself flat on the ground as a shell burst in the centre of the *Volksturm* machine gun post barely twenty yards away, on the corner of *Dorotheenstrasse* and the narrow lane leading into the *Platz der Republik*. A group of *T-34* tanks had penetrated to the eastern end of the *Tiergarten* and the sharp *tak-tak-tak* of their machine guns, forced him to detour through the ruins of the Reich Ministry of the Interior building to reach the *Unter den Linden*. He was covered with a fine grey dust and his hands were bleeding where he had crawled across piles of sharp rubble on his belly.

As he paused for breath behind the shelter of a half-demolished wall he wondered whether Command Post 19 was still holding out. After his meeting with Zetterling he had decided that his initial impression of Fürstt had been a little harsh. The young army leutnant was no traitor. In fact like most officers trapped in the blazing inferno of the beleaguered capital he was probably as bewildered as everyone else by the turn of events that had brought the Russians to the gates of Berlin. Bergman knew that Command Post 19 would resist to the last man and the last cartridge. And so would every other pill-box, strongpoint, and bunker in the city.

Stepping up on to the pavement to avoid the flames roaring from a fractured gas main in the middle of the road, his attention was attracted by a noisy commotion at the sandbagged barrier sealing the street off from the approaches to the Chancellery. The troops manning the road-block appeared to be arguing with someone and, on an impulse, Bergman walked across to investigate.

Korporal Albracht snapped to attention at the arrival of a senior officer. He was obviously getting the worst of a verbal dispute and seemed glad to have someone on whom he could off-load the responsibility.

"What's going on?" Bergman demanded.

The Korporal clicked his heels with parade-ground precision, as if the shells bursting a few hundred yards away had no connection with reality. A stolid and rather unimaginative peasant from Saxony he could rarely cope with more than one problem at a time, and so far as he was concerned, the shells were not his primary concern at that particular moment.

"My men found someone trying to get through the barrier," he explained. "He has various passes in his possession and he insists he has full authority." There was something in the Korporal's tone of voice, that suggested he was more than a little scared of his unwilling prisoner.

"What authority, Korporal?"

"*Gerheimestaatspolizei*, sir. And a pass signed personally by Reichsfuehrer Himmler, sir."

"The Reichsfuehrer has been dismissed," Bergman told the Korporal. "He has no authority now." A sudden thought crossed his mind but he dismissed it as quickly as it had appeared. It seemed to be a night of coincidences and strangely unexpected meetings—but surely it was impossible. Curiosity finally got the better of him. "Let me see the passes, Korporal."

Albracht produced two leather-covered wallets and handed them over to the Korvettenkapitan. There were no street lights but the roaring flame from the fractured gas pipe gave sufficient illumination to read by and Bergman opened one of the folders.

Görst! For Christ's sake—*everyone* must be in Berlin tonight.

He snapped the folder shut. "I am familiar with Gruppenfuehrer Görst, Korporal," he told Albracht. "Bring this man over so that I can identify him."

The Korporal shouted an order to the soldiers manning the barrier and they dragged their prisoner across to where Bergman was standing.

Görst's face was covered in dirt where he had fallen over a pile of rubble and his cheek was smeared with blood. He had discarded his black Gestapo uniform and was wearing a nondescript raincoat over a threadbare suit. He peered up at the officer but the darkness obscured Bergman's face and he did not recognise him.

"Thank goodness these dolts have found someone with authority," he whispered hoarsely. Despite his fear he had lost none of his old arrogance. "Order them to release me at once—the *Reichsfuehrer* will hear of this. I am engaged on an important mission. I demand the return of my papers and my immediate release."

"You'll demand nothing," Bergman snapped.

Görst's mouth opened and his jaw dropped as he recognised the voice. He peered myopically at the face confronting him in the flame reddened darkness.

"*Gott in Himmel*! Bergman!"

Bergman said nothing. He held the two passes tantalisingly just out of Görst's reach. Clutching eagerly for the dangling prizes the Gestapo officer stepped

211

towards him but Albracht caught him by the collar and hauled him back unceremoniously. He shook himself free from the Korporal's ungentle grip.

"Herr Korvettenkapitan," he wheedled hoarsely. "You remember me. Tell them who I am, please."

Bergman savoured his moment of triumph as he stared into Görst's frightened face. He had never forgotten the horror of that fateful day when they had met in the Gestapo office at Lorient after Rahel's arrest. And the memory of what Görst had done to her was still burned indelibly into his soul—the glazed deadness of her eyes, the bruises on her face, the blouse ripped open to the waist, and the angry marks of the electrodes on her nipples.

"This man is not Gruppenfuehrer Görst, Korporal. He has obviously stolen these papers."

"My God, Bergman!" Görst screamed. "Look at me—you *must* remember me." He tore off a glove and thrust the maimed remnants of his right hand in front of the Korvettenkapitan's face. "Look at this—this is what frostbite did to me at Stalingrad. How could I have these scars if I wasn't Görst." His eyes were glistening with frustrated tears. "You *know* who I am—tell them!"

Bergman shook his head. "A complete impostor, Korporal. Probably a Soviet spy trying to get back through the lines with information. Take him away and shoot him."

The Gruppenfuehrer threw himself at their feet blubbering like a terrified child. And as the soldiers dragged him upright Bergman could see the tears streaming down his cheeks. He was still screaming for mercy as they pushed him up against the remains of a brick wall and raised their machine guns.

Bergman turned away as they fired. He walked

slowly towards the burning Chancellery building. And as he walked he carefully tore Görst's identification papers into shreds and dropped them into the gutter.

CHAPTER TEN

"Our Fuehrer, Adolf Hitler, fighting to his last breath, fell for Germany in his headquarters in the Reich Chancellery. On 30 April the Fuehrer appointed Grossadmiral Doenitz to take his place. The Grossadmiral and successor to the Fuehrer now speaks to the German people."

Bergman reached forward and switched off the radio as the sombre voice of the announcer was replaced by the measured strains of a Wagnerian lament. Even in the moment of final defeat the lies of the propaganda machine continued in full spate and he felt sickened by the whole sham.

So much had happened in the past seven days that the stolid bedrock of reality no longer existed. Every event that Zetterling had prophesied had come true. And even now, sitting quietly in the steel-walled security of the Kriegsmarine's last operational U-boat

Bergman could still not wholly grasp the enormity of the tragedy that had overwhelmed his beloved Fatherland. A week ago! It seemed like a lifetime. And he had to search deep into his memory to recall the frantic confusion of events that had overtaken him since the night he had talked to Zetterling on the banks of the *Berliner Spree* . . .

Having disposed of Görst he had returned to the Chancellery to find Admiral Lüben anxiously waiting for him at the entrance to the bunker. The orders to report to Kiel were handed over and before he had time to protest an *Sd Krz-232* rattled out of the darkness to take him on the first stage of his journey. The nightmare escape through the narrow corridor that still linked Berlin with the remains of embattled Germany brought terrors that would haunt him for the rest of his life. And even now, in the calm solitude of his cabin, he could feel his hands trembling at the memory.

Russian artillery surrounded all sides of the escape route and, peering out through the armoured observation slits cut into the steel sides of the eight-wheeled monster in which he was travelling, Bergman could see the continuous flashes of enemy guns lighting the night sky with the awful magnificence of a magnetic storm venting its fury on the empty wastes of the North Atlantic. Twice he heard the unmistakable thud of machine gun bullets raking the sides of the *Sd Kfz* and once, when the armoured car detonated a land-mine on the verge, he thought the whole contraption would turn over.

But somehow they made it. And in the misty half-light of dawn he was decamped into a small field some 20 miles west of Berlin where a Luftwaffe officer hurried him into a Fiesler Storch communications aircraft, waiting in the shadow of a friendly hedge—its Argus engine already ticking over ready for take-off as he scrambled inside.

And, six hours later, dirty, dishevelled, and still breathless, he had found himself sitting in the Port Admiral's bunker in Kiel Dockyard being briefed about his forthcoming mission in *U-2555*.

Not that Vice Admiral von Hertz had any idea of the *real* purpose of Bergman's top-secret journey. So far as von Hertz was concerned *U-2555* had been slated to ship the Reichbank's gold reserves to South America. Twenty-four million marks in neat yellow bullion bars. And as a meticulous bureaucrat of the old school—the Admiral had reached flag rank without ever serving outside the Supply Branch—he was intent only on Bergman signing a full and sufficient receipt for the treasure now loaded in his U-boat. Paperwork struck the Korvettenkapitan as a somewhat academic exercise in the circumstances but, at von Hertz's insistence, he put his signature on the necessary documents. And twenty minutes later he was being driven to Friedrichsort . . .

Having listened to the news announcement of the Fuehrer's death over *U-2555*'s radio system, Bergman suddenly realised that Zetterling's crazy story about the Polish tailor, seemingly so incredible at the time of telling, now made sense. When the Russians began searching the smouldering ruins of the Chancellery, they would undoubtedly find a body—a body with a dental chart that exactly matched that of the Fuehrer's in every respect. And, in confirmation, a semi-emasculated scrotum containing only one testicle. In the face of such evidence a positive identification would be inevitable. And the world would be complacently content that Adolf Hitler was, indeed, dead.

He looked up as Kreitzler knocked on the cabin door. Taking the signal slip from the radio operator's hand, Bergman pulled down the flexible desk-lamp, and read the message.

Immediate. All U-boats. Attention all U-boats. Cease fire at once. Repeat. Cease fire at once. Stop all action against Allied shipping.

Doenitz

Bergman digested the signal without emotion. He placed it carefully with the other routine papers lying on his desk as if it was of no great importance. Then remembering that the message had been transmitted *en clair* he looked up at the radio operator.

"You are not to repeat this signal to any member of the crew, Kreitzler. I will make an announcement when I am ready. It may not be genuine and I need to check its authenticity first. Understand?"

Coming on top of the radio announcement of the Fuehrer's death, Kreitzler thought Bergman's caution a little academic. But the Old Man had come to U-2555 with a reputation for taut discipline and he didn't intend to buck him on his first day. He saluted and closed the thin partition door quietly behind him.

Bergman stared up at the photograph of the Grunnenberg hanging in its customary place just above his desk. He wondered when, if ever, he would see the glistening white slopes of the mountain again. Then, slumping forward in the chair, he put his elbows on the desk-top, and buried his face in his hands. He was tired—desperately and unbelievably tired. Yet the final mission still lay ahead. And closing his eyes he prayed for the strength to carry out the duty which Fate had thrust upon him.

The intercom speaker set high on the bulkhead dividing his cabin from the wardroom emitted a sharp metallic click and he could hear a faint buzz of static.

"High Water in five minutes, sir. Control room standing by."

He acknowledged the report and heard the intercom go dead. Rubbing the exhaustion from his eyes he stood up and opened the partition door. Biergratz—a stout and balding ex-SA officer who had been one of Hitler's closest aides since the days of the 1923 Munich *putsch*—was standing outside.

"The Fuehrer wishes to know if it is safe to depart, Herr Kapitan," he told Bergman. "He has certain reservations about the immediate naval situation and suggests you defer departure pending clarification from Grossadmiral Doenitz."

In other words, thought Bergman, he's shit scared. Obviously no one had dared to tell the Fuehrer that the war was over. Or if they had he had ignored it. In his frenzied imagination the war was still being fought. And that meant that a U-boat was in constant danger of counter-attack by aircraft and surface ships. Hitler had never had any stomach for the sea. And the very thought of being trapped inside a submerged submarine at the mercy of enemy depth-charges was sufficient to unhinge his already unbalanced mind beyond all hopes of recovery.

In fact Siegmann, *U-2555*'s surgeon, had already told the Korvettenkapitan that he'd been pumping tranquilliser tablets into the Fuehrer ever since he and his companions had boarded the U-boat two days previously. "He eats them like sweets," Siegmann had complained. "And for all the good they've done him that's what they just as well might be."

Bergman looked at Biergratz coldly. "My respects to the Fuehrer but as captain of this submarine *I* make the decisions. You may tell him, with my compliments, that the war is over and that enemy forces have been instructed not to attack any U-boats providing they are flying a white or blue flag. As we shall be running submerged," he added gleefully knowing what effect his words would have on his frightened passenger, "he has nothing to fear."

Biergratz was clearly unhappy about the message he was to deliver but he was given no opportunity to argue. Bergman pushed him to one side, ducked through the narrow circular hatch to the control room, and made his way up on to the bridge. The camouflage netting had been rolled back and the Executive Officer, Kapitanleutnant von Schoon, an experienced U-boat skipper in his own right, greeted his arrival with a crisp salute.

"All hands on board, sir," he reported. "Fore hatch and engine room hatch secured. Main engines ready, hydroplanes tested, steering tested, telegraphs tested. Singled up fore and aft. Standing by to cast off."

Bergman listened attentively to the routine reports and nodded. "What is the latest Met situation, Kapitanleutnant?"

"The glass is steady, sir. We picked up an RAF weather report an hour ago. Forecast Force 3 breeze in the North Sea and 10 miles surface visibility. There's a depression deepening over the Shetlands and the outlook's none too good for the next twenty-four hours west of Norway."

"And the Baltic?"

Von Schoon's eyebrows lifted. Why worry about

the Baltic, he wondered. It was hardly on the route to Argentina.

"No information I'm afraid, sir. We can pick up the Russian weather stations but no one can translate their reports."

Bergman stepped up on to the compass platform. He could see the fore and aft deck parties lined up on the casing ready to cast off. Then having stared up at the sky as if making his own private forecast he nodded to von Schoon.

"Carry on, Number One. You can take her out."

The Executive Officer walked to the port side of the bridge, leaned over the edge of the coaming, and shouted to the dock workers standing on the quay.

"Let go fore-spring! Let go after-spring!"

The men on the quay released the securing wires from their bollards and the heavy cables splashed into the water as *U-2555's* deck parties hauled them inboard.

"Let go after breast . . . let go for'ard!"

The two remaining lines were slipped and von Schoon waited for them to be dragged clear of the water so that they could not snag the propellers.

"All gone aft. All gone for'ard," Koenig reported from his vantage position on the periscope standards.

"Obey telegraphs," Von Schoon instructed the motor room through the voicepipe.

"Main motors ready and grouped down, sir."

"Half astern both."

The telegraph tinkled as Molitor pulled the lever over and, far below in the distant recesses of the motor room, Bergman heard the repeater tinkle its acknowledgement. *U-2555* glided slowly backwards on reversed motors to clear the curving arm of the jetty and, as the bows came level with the crane at the end of the quay, von Schoon turned to *Obersteuermann* Siegel.

"Starboard twenty, Cox'n."

"Starboard twenty, sir."

"Stop port motor—half ahead starboard."

The bows began swinging, the water astern frothed whitely as the propellers reversed their thrust, and *U-2555* started to glide gently forward. Bergman watched appreciatively. He always admired good ship handling and von Schoon certainly knew his job. Getting an unfamiliar boat out of a strange berth could be a tricky business especially in tidal waters. But the Executive Officer handled his new charge as if he'd been steering her out of harbour for months.

"Port fifteen, Cox'n. Stop motors. Clutches in. Start main engines. Half ahead both."

It was a superb demonstration of the pilot's art. Kiel Fiord was relatively narrow and, with all navigational marks removed, it was a nightmare of shoals and fierce cross currents. But von Schoon had gone over to the main diesel engines at the earliest opportunity to save his batteries, picked up the deep channel like a hawk diving on its prey, and was taking the U-boat out to sea at a crisp ten knots. Bergman decided he couldn't have done better himself.

Zetterling's prophecy had only been wrong in one small detail. *U-2555* was not one of the new *Type XXI* boats. The handful that had been completed before Allied bombing attacks had stopped production, were on shake-down exercises when hostilities ceased and the only ocean-range submarine available for the mission was a *Type VII c/41*—an old and trusted design but fitted with all the latest modifications.

Her prime advantage lay in her *schnorchel*—a Dutch invention taken over and perfected by German

U-boat scientists in 1942. The *schnorchel*, or snort, was a hollow mast similar to a large diameter periscope without lenses through which air could be drawn into the diesels while the submarine was running under-water. Snorting reduced submerged speed to six knots but it gave the U-boat the invaluable ability to remain at periscope depth for days on end. And by using the diesel power units for submerged running there was no drain on the precious batteries. It was noisy in operation and the sharp variations of the internal air pressure made snorting an uncomfortable exercise for the crews. But as it granted the U-boat almost total immunity from radar detection the discomfort was accepted with stoic resignation.

U-2555 had other refinements which Bergman had been denied in his previous commands. She was equipped with the very latest navigational and air/service search radar, in addition to a *Bug* radar detector—a development of the old *Metox*—which could pick up the enemy's new short wavelength radar beams. For defence she relied on a single *M-42u* 37mm anti-aircraft gun at the rear of the conning-tower platform backed up by two *M-38u* 20mm close-range flak cannons. And the reassuring protection of a fully armoured bridge gave her an even chance of survival if she was surprised on the surface by aircraft.

But an air attack was now unlikely unless he did anything suspicious and Bergman knew that the guns would probably never speak in anger. *U-2555* was a warship without a war. And with her torpedoes removed to make space for the cargo of bullion bars nestling like squat golden eggs in the iron womb of her inner hull, she was also a ship without weapons.

U-2555 was a member of the German Navy's last

flotilla. She was also the Kriegsmarine's last operational U-boat. And as the rust streaked remnants of Doenitz's once proud underwater fleet, cruised slowly to the surrender ports selected by the victorious Allies, U-2555 was setting out on a mission which promised to be as dangerous as any previous U-boat patrol of the war.

Bergman remained on the bridge until the submarine ran clear of the fiord and entered Kiel Bay. The stark choice of routes was still undecided in his mind and he told von Schoon to hold course north-eastwards while he considered his options.

Zetterling's plan offered a secure future and the promise of a continuing career in his first love—submarines. But did he *really* want to throw in his lot with the Russians. And what guarantee did he have that he would not be conveniently liquidated when he had served his immediate purpose of building up the strength of the Soviet Navy's underwater flotillas. Over the past ten years Bergman had seen too much of totalitarian regimes and police states to accept any promise without cynicism.

Argentina, though, promised that most precious of gifts—freedom. But what use could he make of it? And would Hitler allow anyone connected with his escape plan to survive to be a risk to his security. Bergman felt his own personal survival was safe enough. Hitler obviously thought highly of him—the fact that he had been picked to command U-2555 was proof enough of the Fuehrer's trust—but the rest of the crew would be expendable. Like the crew of a pirate ship burying treasure on a lonely island they would be a threat to their chief as soon as their task was completed. And Bergman's loyalty to the men who served under his command had been proved beyond question on many occasions in the past.

Could there be a *third* alternative? The Korvettenkapitan was still pondering the problem as Landau thrust his head through the opened hatch.

"We've picked up a radar probe, sir."

Bergman dismissed his personal thoughts. Moving quickly across the bridge he picked up the telephone to Rawicz, *U-2555*'s radar operator.

"Bridge to RS-1. Anything on the plot?"

"RS-1, sir. We've just picked up a blip on the A/W screen. Bearing three-zero-zero. Range five miles. Large bandit."

Bergman instinctively glanced up at the periscope standard to check that the regulation blue flag of surrender was flying. It was.

"I've got it, sir." Von Schoon was searching the north-west sky with his glasses. "A Liberator by the look of it—about 3,000 feet."

Raising his binoculars Bergman checked the Executive Officer's report and, satisfied, he returned to the telephone. "Bridge to control room."

"Control room, sir."

"Send Hartzig to the bridge with his lamp." He paused for a moment—the heavy drone of the Liberator's four Pratt & Whitney Twin Wasps now clearly audible above the throb of the diesel engines. "Pass the word to stand by for diving. Don't sound the alarm except in an emergency—it might disturb our guests."

"Diving stations standing by, sir."

Hartzig clambered up through the hatch as the Korvettenkapitan replaced the telephone. He hoisted himself on to the deck and reported for duty.

Bergman nodded to him to wait while he stared up at the sky again.

It was a tense moment and the fact that hostilities had ended did nothing to relieve the strain of responsibility that lay on the Korvettenkapitan's shoulders. Radio reports from the 13th Flotilla at Bergen indicated that no fewer than five U-boats had been sunk by British aircraft since Doenitz had signed the cease-fire. Most of them had been sent to the bottom off the Danish coast in the very area *U-2555* was now approaching. If all of the reports were to be believed, a total of 16 boats had been lost since the war officially ended.

The Liberator turned, lost height, and swung towards the surfaced U-boat. Much as instinct and experience demanded, Bergman made no effort to man the flak defences. With a trigger-happy enemy poised overhead, any such move would have invited instant annihilation. And, spotting Kreiz, the Chief Gunner's Mate, sidling cautiously towards the guns, he waved him away impatiently.

Bergman could see the large white recognition stars of the USAF painted on the slab-sided fuselage as the Liberator came closer. A signal lamp flashed from the cockpit and Hartzig read off the message letter by letter while the Korvettenkapitan translated it into German for the benefit of the others.

D-O Y-O-U H-A-V-E R-A-D-I-O T-E-L-P-H-O-N-E?

Bergman nodded his head at Hartzig. "Tell him— yes."

The U-boat's lamp flashed back an affirmative and a few moments later, having received details of the frequency and tuned *U-2555*'s radio into the waveband, Bergman found himself in conversation with the Liberator pilot.

"What ship and who is commanding?" An American voice drawled.

Bergman hesitated. Had there been a security leak? Was it just a routine check on U-boats which had not yet reported in to the surrender bases or did the enemy authorities know the secret of *U-2555*? Perhaps they knew he had been selected to command the mission but they were unaware in which U-boat Hitler was trying to escape. He decided it wasn't worth bluffing. If the aircraft called up a surface patrol to investigate, his dangerous game would be well and truly up. He needed to buy time and shake off the Liberator as soon as possible. The entrance to the Fehmarn Belt was already on the starboard beam and the dim shape of Laland Island was faintly visible off the starboard bow quarter.

"*U-2555*," he replied curtly. "Korvettenkapitan Bergman in command. Will you please also identify?"

It was one way of ensuring immunity from attack. Countless ears would be eavesdropping on the dialogue and if anything happened to *U-2555* there would be no difficulty in identifying the culprit.

"Walt Maynard—Major, 23rd Bombardment Squadron, USAF." The mid-West accent had a softly pleasant burr. "Say, captain, where are you heading?"

"Wilhelmshaven."

"Why not Kiel—it's a helluva lot closer."

"Just left there, Major. Your boys have knocked out all our facilities. Wilhelmshaven is our flotilla base. And besides," Bergman lied easily, "my family's there and I'd like to see them."

"Received and understood, *U-2555*." There was a brief pause while the Major consulted his fuel tank readings. "I'll stay with you up as far as the Skagens

Horn.* Just as a friendly gesture, you understand. We've had reports of several U-boats being attacked in the Kattegat. No names—no pack-drill. But I guess you'd feel safer with us escorting you."

Bergman could think of several far more desirable events that would make him feel safer but he tactfully kept them to himself. "Thank you, Major. I appreciate your consideration. I intend to proceed through the Great Belt and enter the Kattegat at Reef Ness. I shall follow the regular Gothenborg shipping lane until I cross the line of the Malo and North Rynner lights when I propose to steer north-east. Standard crusing speed 20 knots."

"All received—understood. I'll keep you in sight. *Bon voyage*."

"Acknowledged. *U-2555* out."

So that was the end of Zetterling's scheme Bergman thought as he put the radio-telephone back on its cradle. With the watchful eyes of the Liberator following every move he made there was now absolutely no chance of *U-2555* doubling back through the Fehmarn Belt into the Baltic. Zetterling and his Russian comrades would be waiting at Gdynia in vain. And with the unexpected appearance of Major Walt Maynard USAF on the scene Bergman knew that the die was irrevocably cast.

The impossible dream that had pursued him for the past six years was about to be realised. Fate had delivered the Fuehrer into *his* hands. And he alone could undertake the grim task that would restore German honour to its former proud position . . .

Two inquisitive Tempest fighter-bombers vectored in on the surfaced U-boat as she passed north of Laso

* The northernmost tip of Denmark—also known as the Skaw.

Island but the presence of the rumbling Liberator discouraged them from close inspection and, disappointed, they swung south towards Kiel. An hour later a Mosquito wearing Dutch markings came out of the sun from astern but, as her pilot saw the large blue flag fluttering from the conning-tower, he banked sharply to the left and waggled his wing-tips in salute. There were no further incidents and U-2555 remained unmolested as she continued passage around the tip of Denmark.

The Liberator parted company at 18.00 hours as the U-boat was steering westwards into the Skagerrak. And as the big bomber pulled ahead of U-2555's plunging bows and set course for her base in Norfolk a friendly lamp flashed a last farewell signal from the pilot's cockpit. Bergman returned the compliment and stood grasping the bridge rails as the aircraft vanished into the gathering evening mist building up over the North Sea. He waited a full five minutes after the Liberator's final disappearance, while Rawicz's radar scanner carried out a careful check to ensure that they were completely alone.

There was only one little touch left to complete the deception. Bergman felt sure that the American major had reported the U-boat's position and he needed to maintain the pretence if he was to avoid the attentions of another shadower. He lifted the telephone link to the *Telefunken* operator in the radio cabin.

"Nils—I want you to transmit the following *en clair* to Wilhelmshaven. Repeat until acknowledged and let me know when you have completed transmission."

"Understood, sir. Go ahead."

"Message reads: From CO U-2555 to Base Commander Wilhelmshaven. Diesels giving trouble. Propose to dive and proceed on motors. ETA 18.30

Tuesday at Hohe Weg light. Position now 57° 10′ N . . . 7° 58′ E. Steering direct to Vyl lightship and then to Roter Sand LV. Repeat proposed course to AMG patrols. Bergman. K/K."

Nils read the message back, acknowledged Bergman's confirmation, and began transmitting.

"Clear the bridge for diving, Number One. Stand by diving routine." Bergman leaned on the bridge rails staring towards the bows at the lookouts and von Schoon squeezed down through the hatch. There were two options left, he decided. Through the Channel or north about Scotland and then out into the Atlantic. Or . . .? The alternative plan had not yet finally clarified itself in his mind. But the more he considered it the more attractive it became. The buzzer of the bridge telephone broke into his thoughts. He lifted it from its cradle.

"*Telefunken raum,* sir. Message transmitted and acknowledged by SNO Wilhelmshaven and AMG repeater station No. 14, Hamburg."

Bergman put the telephone down and walked slowly to the open hatch. Lowering his legs into the oval void he grabbed the handle of the counter-weighted hatch lid and drew it shut.

"Dive!"

The main vents swung open and there was a rushing roar of water as the sea flooded eagerly into the empty ballast tanks. *U-2555's* bows dipped below the surface in response to the sharp downward angle of the forward hydroplanes, and the submarine was swallowed by the grey sea.

"We're running on *snort,*" Von Schoon reported as Bergman came down the ladder into the brightly lit cosiness of the control room. The noise of the air being drawn down the hollow pipe and the steady thud of the engines made his statement slightly super-fluous. "Is that okay sir?"

The Korvettenkapitan shook his head. "No—the *schnorkel* throws up too much spray. We'd be spotted immediately. Switch to motors."

"Stop engines! Clutches out—switches on. Down *snort!*"

"Full ahead both, Kapitanleutnant."

"Ay, aye, sir. Grouper up! Full ahead both!" Von Schoon turned to Bergman having passed the order back to the Motor Room. "How long do you intend to maintain maximum speed, sir?"

"Until I tell you to reduce it," Bergman said unhelpfully. He knew what the Kapitanleutnant was getting at. A U-boat's battery power was strictly limited and running the motors on full amperage would cut the life of the batteries to a few short hours. But that was all he needed. And he had no intention of telling von Schoon about his plan. "Steer 2-7-0," he told Siegel.

"Two-seven-zero, sir."

So Bergman intended to take the northerly route into the Atlantic via the Pentland Firth von Schoon thought as he heard the course change. Probably a sensible decision in the circumstances. He'd have taken a similar route himself.

"Herr Korvettenkapitan!"

Bergman turned to find Biergratz in the control room. The former SA-man was sweating and he blinked nervously as he saw the flickering needles of the instrument gauges and the glowing colours of the warning lights over the diving table.

"Yes?"

Bergman was characteristically curt. He had almost forgotten the presence of his distinguished guests even though they were the vital core of his plan. It was difficult to accept that the Fuehrer, Adolf Hitler—the man whose death had already been announced to the world—was sitting in the snug security of his special compartment little more than ten feet away. And not only Hitler but also Bormann and that slut Eva Braun.

They were already aboard U-2555 by the time Bergman had arrived from Kiel yet, despite his position as commander of the U-boat, he had received no invitation to meet his guests. In fact the Korvettenkapitan had not set eyes on the Fuehrer and his ill-assorted entourage for even the briefest moment. Siegmann, U-2555's surgeon, had reported Hitler as suffering from sea-sickness—and that was even before they'd left the shelter of Kiel Fiord. And not another soul on board the U-boat had been permitted to pass the locked and guarded door of the compartment.

Was it really Hitler in there? Or was it yet another impostor like the unfortunate Polish tailor whose burned and blackened corpse was, at that very moment, being probed and dissected by Russian forensic experts. It was a question to which Bergman knew he would never find an answer. In the demi-world of vengeance, double-dealing, and treachery he could rely only on his instinct.

"The Fuehrer orders you to return to the surface, Herr Korvettenkapitan," Biergratz told him aggressively. "He refuses to travel underwater."

"You may inform the Fuehrer I have no alternative. And if he doesn't like it he knows what he can do!" Bergman took a savage delight at the terror in Biergratz's eyes. It was, he felt, but the merest shadow of the fear which the Fuehrer was enduring as he sat shivering on his quilted bunk. " Now get back to your kennel and stay there. The rest of us have work to do!"

Biergratz scuttled back through the hatchway with his tail between his legs. Bergman heard him open the door to the Fuehrer's compartment and, despite the deadening baffles of the steel bulkheads, Hitler's scream of anguished rage was clearly audible in the control room. Yet not even this final insult was sufficient to bring him out of the cloistered security of his compartment, to confront the man who dared to challenge his authority.

U-2555's surgeon vanished through the circular hatchway with his mysterious box of medical talismans and the terrified sobs slowly subsided as the drugs took effect.

"How long will your damned pills be effective?" Bergman asked Siegmann when he returned to the control room ten minutes later.

"About six hours or so, sir."

Bergman glanced at his watch—the timing was perfect. He needed the Fuehrer fully conscious and aware of what was going on when his plan came to fruition. It would be a pity if he missed the fun . . .

Lieutenant Commander Faversham pulled up the hood of his duffle-coat to shield his neck from the chill breeze sweeping across the Pentland Firth. *HMS Galston*, leader of the 164th Minesweeping Flotilla, buried her bows into the swell and threw a cascade of ice-cold spray over the bridge as she came round on to her new course. The other five boats of the flotilla followed in succession and the towing lines of the paravanes strained taut as they turned.

The war might be over but for the men of the

minesweepers it had scarcely begun. Night and day, with unceasing vigil and facing instant death if things went wrong, the little ships of the minesweeping service now faced the gargantuan task of clearing the seas of their deadly harvest. Sown by friend and foe alike—parachuted from aircraft, dropped by surface ships, and laid from submarines, the lethal canisters posed a threat to any vessel that chanced to cross their path.

Britain's own defensive minefields had to be cleared first. Then, when accurate information could be culled from German records, the enemy's extensive fields would be tackled. And finally, when all the charted mined areas had been swept clean, mine-hunters would search out and locate the secret fields and the stray floating mines that would continue to threaten the shipping lanes of the world for the next twenty-five years.

At the moment Faversham's flotilla was operating on the Royal Navy's own minefields covering the approaches to Scapa Flow. With each mine carefully charted it was a relatively simple task and the Lieutenant Commander felt justified in taking it easy as his six small ships streamed their paravanes and got on with their unenviable job.

"Submarine surfacing—starboard bowl"

The lookout's warning roused Faversham from his doze. Snatching up his binoculars as he searched the sea area to the right of *Galston's* blunted bows. There she was—a bloody U-boat! What the hell was she doing up here in the approaches to the Flow? He turned to his Yeoman of Signals.

"Tell the flotilla to disregard my movements, Yeoman. And then signal that damn fool U-boat to steer hard a'starboard. Tell him he's heading straight for the Ronaldsay No. 2 field."

Galston rolled violently as the swirling current from the Pentland Firth struck her beam and, burying her bows into the rising sea, she swung out of formation and turned towards the U-boat. Having passed the SO's orders to the rest of the flotilla, the Chief Yeoman of Signals aimed his Aldis lamp at the conningtower of the submarine.

Heave to. Danger. Minefield ahead. Stop engines.

Faversham's binoculars could detect no sign of life on the bridge of the surfaced U-boat. The submarine seemed as deserted as a ghost ship being steered by supernatural hands. A white bow-wave flourished from her sharply raked stem and she was steaming at all of 20 knots.

"Fire a warning shot over her bows, Gunner! We've got to stop the stupid bastard before he runs headlong into those bloody mines."

A brass cartridge case clattered into the gaping breech of the bow 12-pounder and Jenks thrust down the locking lever. The long barrel fingered half a length ahead of the U-boat's bows, and there was a sharp crack of cordite as the gun barked its imperious warning.

Bergman watched the minesweepers through the steering periscope. He could still remember the approximate location of the enemy minefields from the days when he and Gunther Prien had searched the area for targets in the winter of 1939* and the warning signal flashing from the bridge of the leader

* See *No Survivors.*

minesweeper merely confirmed what he needed to know.

The muffled report of *Galston*'s warning shot was barely audible inside the control room but it was sufficient for von Schoon to twist round sharply and frown at the skipper.

"Hard left rudder! Full ahead both!"

To the Executive Officer, a veteran of a dozen desperate convoy battles, the sound of the shot and Bergman's sudden change of speed and course was an indication of immediate danger. The Korvettenkapitan sensed the unspoken question.

"Some damn fool British patrol boat exercising her guns," he said calmly. "I'm altering course to clear the range."

It sounded plausible and von Schoon accepted the explanation. Like every other man aboard *U-2555* he was totally dependent on the man at the periscope. And whether he wanted to or not he *had* to trust the skipper.

Locked inside the steel walls of his special compartment the Fuehrer glanced anxiously at Biergratz. His body trembled convulsively and his hands clenched and unclenched with nervous tension. With the sixth sense of a hunted animal he knew something was wrong but he was too terrified to send Biergratz into the control room to find out what had happened. Bormann, too, could feel the sweat running down his face but he managed to conceal the fear gnawing at his heart. Only Eva Braun seemed oblivious to the growing tension. Sprawled naked along the lower bunk, she manicured her nails patiently and thought about the sunshine in Argentina . . .

Bergman knew the minefield lay directly ahead of the 164th Flotilla's diagonal sweeping formation. He could not see the black horned canisters swaying gently from their mooring cables like a nest of hooded cobras poised to strike, but there was no possible doubt in his mind that they were there. The shark-like bows of the U-boat nosed impetuously into the venomous underwater nest and *Galston* blasted her siren in a last attempt to save the submarine. The sleek grey hull seemed to gather speed as if some supernatural hand was thrusting her inexorably towards her destiny. And as he stepped back from the periscope Bergman knew he had done everything he could.

U-2555's bows ripped and crumpled as the mine detonated immediately below the forward torpedo room. The thin steel plating bulging inwards for one brief horrific moment and then vanished as a wall of black water roared in through the gaping hole.

"Close all watertight doors!"

Von Schoon's immediate reaction snapped Bergman back to reality with a sharp jerk.

"Order countermanded!" he shouted into the intercom.

The heavy counterweighted doors swinging shut in obedience to the Executive Officer's command were checked, and then hauled back as Bergman's voice crackled through the loudspeakers.

U-2555 was already sinking by the bows and a torrent of oil-stained water burst over the lip of the bulkhead into the crewspace abaft the torpedo compartment. Two of the torpedo-men who had survived the initial explosion ran towards the control room with the sea hard at their heels. The submarine lurched into a steeper angle, their bare feet scrambled for a grip on the slippery deck plating, and with a despairing shriek they fell back into the bubbling fury of white water as it surged upwards to devour them.

"Hard right rudder!"

The stern responded sluggishly as if reluctant to obey the Korvettenkapitan's harsh command and the U-boat swung broadside into the second row of mines. The explosion hurled U-2555 sideways and the fuses of the main switchboard blew with a blinding flash of vivid blue flame. The lights went out and the screams of the trapped men rose high above the crashing roar of water flooding into the submarine's interior from fore and aft.

The deadly fumes of chlorine gas began seeping up through the deck gratings as the encroaching sea water contaminated the acid in the batteries. Struggling wildly in the pitch black darkness the men coughed and choked as the cold sea swirled around their waists. The rising air pressure brought an agonising pain in their ears and they began beating at the unyielding sides of their steel coffin in demented fury. Nothing could save the U-boat now. Torn open at stem and stern, and sinking steadily under the growing weight of water rushing into her hull, she heeled to starboard as she settled deeper into the sea.

And above the noise of roaring water, the screaming hiss of ruptured high-pressure air lines, and the dying shouts of drowning men, rose a shriek of terror that dominated and devoured every other sound.

Bergman knew it came from the locked and guarded compartment immediately behind the control room. The unearthly scream told him that the impossible plan had blossomed to fruition. And the task he had sought to accomplish for six long and weary years was finally complete. Struggling against the surging flood of water the Korvettenkapitan raised his hand in salute as the sea closed over *U-2555*.

He had saved the honour of the Fatherland. But history would never know the grim secret of his last command.

EPILOGUE

My U-boat men!

Six years of war lie behind you. You have fought like lions. An overwhelming material superiority has driven us into a narrow corner from which continuation of the fight is no longer possible. Unbeaten and unblemished, you lay down your weapons after an heroic fight without equal. Solemnly we remember our fallen comrades who sealed their loyalty to Fuehrer and Fatherland with their death.

Comrades! Preserve that spirit in which you fought so gallantly for long years for the Fatherland. Long Live Germany!

Your Grossadmiral

(The text of Grossadmiral Karl Doenitz's last signal to the officers and men of Germany's U-boat service.)

Edwyn Gray enjoys an international reputation as both a crisply exciting storyteller and a serious naval historian. Born in London "sufficiently long ago" he was educated at the Cooper's Company School and the Royal Grammar School, High Wycombe, and now lives in the Buckinghamshire village of Penn with his family "and an ever increasing number of dogs."

His first short story was published in 1952 and he has been a contributor to leading British, American and Australian magazines for over 20 years. His first full-length book appeared in 1969 and his time is now equally divided between standard works on modern naval history and novels based on the war at sea—both above and below the surface.

Starting with four great American historical novels by Bruce Lancaster, one of America's most distinguished historians.

_____TRUMPET TO ARMS An exceptionally crafted romance spun beautifully amidst the fury of the American Revolution. (PB-887, 1.75)
"Explosive in style . . . *Trumpet to Arms* is always easy to read and strikes a note as stirring as a call to battle."
—*The Boston Globe*

_____THE SECRET ROAD A fascinating, yet little known account of the exploits of Washington's Secret Service. A gripping story of America's first espionage unit. (PB-889, 1.75)
"A veteran craftsman at the top of his form."
—*The New York Times*

_____PHANTOM FORTRESS A masterful treatment of the career of General Francis Marion, known to history as "The Swamp Fox." (PB-905, 1.75)
"History that is good and galloping, for competent scholarship underlies the romantic story."
—*New York Herald Tribune*

_____BLIND JOURNEY An absorbing tale of romance and adventure that moves from 18th-century France and its grandeur to the carnage of revolutionary America. A story no one should miss. (PB-915, 1.75)
"Romance, adventure . . . full pulsing life. Bruce Lancaster's best."

—*The Boston Herald*

Two rich blooded, romantic historical novels by "America's favorite storyteller*"

(*The New York Times)

———**I, BARBARIAN** The days of Genghis Khan, the fiercest and most terrifying days of man since the birth of civilization. Against this forceful and dramatic scene weaves a love story as bold and as powerful as the mighty Khan himself. It is a tale of a brave young warrior from Frankistan and his love for a beautiful Oriental princess, a concubine of the Mongol king. A spellbinding novel of romance, intrigue, and adventure, storytelling at its very best. **P971 $1.50**

———**VEILS OF SALOME** The story of Salome, the beautiful Judean princess, duty-bound to the service of her father, Herod Antipas, and victimized by her mother's selfish ambitions. It is also the timeless and moving love story of the princess's lost and hopeless love for one man, Marcus Catullus, physician of Rome's Fifth Imperial Legion. Set in a time of the greatest decadence, at the same time the world's single most influential period, it is a magnificent saga of human love and inhuman agony—a woman who had to lay her pride aside to win the man whose love she desperately wanted. **P972 $1.50**

Both by **JOHN JAKES,** author of the American Bicentennial Series, the only writer ever to have three books on the national paperback best-seller lists at the same time!
